"Kathy Herman's books should come with a warning label: Once started, you won't be able to stop! *A Fine Line* leads us down a path rich with intrigue to expose that which is most deceitful—the human heart. If the Baxter series has to end, this book is the perfect finale."

LOIS RICHER, author of *Blessings in Disguise*

"*A Fine Line* is fast-paced entertainment that also enlightens. Kathy Herman tackles important issues such as sin's consequences and the need to keep those we love in prayer."

SYLVIA BAMBOLA, author of *Refiner's Fire* and *Tears in a Bottle*

"May we never discount the threat of wreckage caused by our white lies and our 'little' sins. *A Fine Line* promises well-crafted intrigue intertwined with strong biblical discourse. This book is a fitting farewell to the Baxter series—but, oh, how we will miss Baxter!"

DEIDRE POOL, author of *Loving Jesus Anyway*

"An outstanding message, skillfully portrayed. *A Fine Line* leads to suspense, revelation, and finally justice."

LYN COTE, author of *Summer's End*

"What a wonderful love story—fast-moving and full of intrigue."

LOIS GLADYS LEPPARD, author

"*A Fine Line* is not only an engrossing story, but a wonderful portrayal of marriage relationships at their worst and best. Baxter fans will be delighted with this next installment—and those encountering Baxter for the first time will quickly discover what we all love about Kathy's characters and storylines. This book is a feast for both the heart and the spirit."

JANELLE BURNHAM SCHNEIDER, author

Other books in the Baxter series:

A Fine Line

THE BAXTER SERIES BOOK FIVE

KATHY HERMAN

Multnomah®Publishers *Sisters, Oregon*

A FINE LINE
published by Multnomah Publishers, Inc.
© 2003 by Kathy Herman

International Standard Book Number: 1-59052-209-5

Cover design by Chris Gilbert–UDG/DesignWorks
Cover images by Photonica/Toshi Ishida

Multnomah is a trademark of Multnomah Publishers, Inc.,
and is registered in the U.S. Patent and Trademark Office.
The colophon is a trademark of Multnomah Publishers, Inc.

Printed in the United States of America

For information:
MULTNOMAH PUBLISHERS, INC.
POST OFFICE BOX 1720
SISTERS, OREGON 97759

Library of Congress Cataloging-in-Publication Data
Herman, Kathy.
   A fine line / by Kathy Herman.
      p. cm. -- (The baxter series ; bk. 5)
   ISBN 1-59052-209-5 (Paperback)
   I. Title.
   PS3608.E59F56 2003
   813'.6--dc21

                                                    2003010039

03 04 05 06 07 08—10 9 8 7 6 5 4 3 2 1 0

To Him Who is both the Giver and the Gift.

ACKNOWLEDGMENTS

I would like to express my heartfelt gratitude to my pastor, Terry Cadwell, the elders of Bethel Bible Church, and my entire church family for their amazing support during my bout with breast cancer and my husband's emergency bypass surgery, which occurred simultaneously during the writing of this book. When Paul and I were in separate hospital rooms, unable to be there for each other, you were the Father's arms around us and a living reminder that He never leaves us or forsakes us.

I would also like to thank my mother, who dropped everything and traveled here to care for us; our amazing kids who held us together; all those who brought us meals, ran errands, or took time to encourage us; and especially those, both near and far, who held us up in prayer. I will *never* forget.

I want to acknowledge two special women: Donna Skorheim and Deidre Pool, whose words of encouragement stoked the fires of creativity as I raced to meet the deadline on this book. Thanks for touching me in ways you'll never know.

I'd like to offer a warm thank you to Will Ray, professional investigator, state of Oregon, for taking his valuable time to explain the ins and outs of the witness protection program, and for critiquing pertinent chapters.

To my friend Tom Prothro for helping me understand the heart and the logistical workings of a church elder board.

To my sister and ever-faithful prayer warrior, Pat Phillips, for your ongoing commitment to pray on my behalf.

To Susie Killough, Judi Wieghat, Barbara Jones, June Lininger, Kim Prothro, and the ladies in my Bible study groups at Bethel, and my friends at LifeWay Christian Store in Tyler, Texas, for your heartfelt prayer support.

To my readers who encourage me continually with e-mails and cards and personal testimonies, thanks for sharing how God has used my words to touch you.

To my editor, Rod Morris, for catching the subtle things I missed and for making suggestions that tightened the story. Thanks for being gentle enough not to bruise my ego, yet thorough enough to leave no sentence unturned.

To Don Jacobson and Bill Jensen at Multnomah Publishers for believing in me and giving me the opportunity to write the Baxter series, and for your caring and capable staff whose hard work turned it into a reality. I'm so privileged to be part of the family.

And to my husband, Paul, who has been my labor coach as I birthed each of the stories in the Baxter series, thanks for your amazing patience throughout the process. With the release of each novel, it was as though we heard the cry of new life at the same time.

And to the Father of Lights from whom comes both my inspiration and my motivation to create, thank You for allowing me to be a vessel for Your healing touch in the lives of so many. I am awestruck by the life You breathe into the words I write.

"Above all else, guard your heart,

for it is the wellspring of life."

PROVERBS 4:23, NIV

PROLOGUE

Sheila Paxton looked in the rearview mirror at rows and rows of cars backed up on the Atlanta freeway. She glanced at her Rolex and heaved a sigh of disgust. If the pace didn't pick up soon, she would miss her plane. And the last thing she needed was to rattle Richard's chain by missing another of his precious dinner parties.

She assessed the traffic and quickly pulled into the middle lane. The driver behind her laid on his horn and she threw her hands in the air. "What's your problem? You're not going anywhere!"

At least it had been a profitable week. The Baxter City Council had unanimously voted to grant the permit for Thompson Tire Corporation to relocate there. Sheila had done the groundwork and had prepared persuasive answers to questions she knew would arise. And she had chosen to make her final presentation in a royal blue silk suit and three-inch heels. So the skirt was a little short. There were distinct advantages to being a woman. Richard wouldn't have liked it. But then, what Richard didn't know wouldn't hurt him.

Sheila reached for her cell phone and dialed Charlie Kirby's number.

"Mayor Kirby's office."

"This is Sheila Paxton. May I speak with the mayor, please?"

"Certainly. One moment."

A jet rumbled overhead, and Sheila turned off the radio. She surveyed the seemingly endless tide of Friday afternoon traffic and dreaded that she would have to rush to catch her plane.

"Sheila!" Charlie said. "Are you back in Raleigh already?"

"No, I'm in Atlanta, inching my way to the airport in this ridiculous traffic. I can't get you off my mind. I'm disappointed you didn't show last night. I hardly slept a wink."

Sheila could almost picture his mental stammering in the seconds of dead air that followed. "I forgive you *this* time. I'll be back next Friday to work out the final details on the Thompson deal, and I've already made arrangements to spend the entire weekend in Baxter."

"Oh? It shouldn't take more than a day to finish up."

"I know. I won't tell if you won't...ciao!"

Sheila disconnected the call, a smile on her face. She had his engine running and she knew it. There was something thrilling about going after a married man with seven kids, especially one that everyone thought was so religious.

She reached in her purse for a tube of lipstick, and pulled down the visor. In the mirror, she caught a glimpse of someone on a motorcycle angling his way through the stopped traffic. *He's got a lot of nerve, cutting in front of everyone else!*

She heard a loud popping noise, then looked in her side mirror and saw that the man on the motorcycle had a gun and was shooting into cars!

Sheila ducked. She reached across the console and opened her briefcase. She fumbled for her gun, then remembered she hadn't packed it because of airline regulations. More shots rang out. She grabbed her cell phone and pushed the auto dial for Richard's office.

It sounded as though the motorcycle had pulled alongside her. Sheila froze, her upper body still stretched across the console, the phone gripped tightly in her hand. She heard a gun blast and shattering glass, and felt an electric shock down her spine. Her arms went numb, and the phone fell on the floor.

"Sheila, is that you?... Sheila?... Talk to me!"

She heard Richard's voice, but couldn't make her mouth move. *So cold*, she wanted to say. *I'm so cold.*

Sheila stared at the phone until she couldn't focus, then closed her eyes, the sound of gunfire echoing in the distance, Richard's voice the last thing she heard.

I

Baxter Mayor Charlie Kirby sat in his office, looking over the building permit for the Thompson Tire Corporation. He winced when he heard something splat on the window and realized it was another egg thrown by angry protestors. Did they honestly believe that a few hundred new residents would change Baxter's culture, turn the town into a regional hub, blot out tourism, and put them all out of business?

Charlie sighed. The tire plant would create twice as many jobs as were lost in the closing of Logan Textile Industries. The increased population would present some challenges, but the pros far outnumbered the cons. The Thompson team had presented compelling reasons why the relocation was a win-win. Charlie's mind flashed back to Sheila Paxton writing on the marker board. She had looked more like a fashion model than a corporate lawyer. He entertained the image and realized he was blushing.

He glanced at the family portrait on his desk, then got up and stood at the window, his hands in his pockets, his eyes tracing the trail of egg yolks running down the glass and dripping onto the brick ledge. After the final plans were drawn up, he wouldn't see Sheila anymore.

Charlie was startled by his secretary's voice on the intercom. "Mr. Mayor, Ellen Jones is on line one."

"Okay. Thanks, Regina." He put a smile in his voice and picked up the receiver. "Hello, Madam Editor. How are you this fine day?"

"Charlie, don't patronize me. Have you looked out your window?"

"I can't see past the egg spattering."

"On the window—or on your face?"

"Come on, Ellen. It was a sound business decision."

"The city council couldn't have waited until the tension eased up?"

"We might have lost the window of opportunity. Thompson Tire was considering other sites. The tire plant will get this community back on its feet."

"At what price?"

"Sometimes it's necessary to sacrifice one thing to get another."

"That's hardly comforting to retailers on the square whose survival depends on the tourist trade."

"They're overreacting."

"Then convince them, Charlie. They're scared."

"I already tried. They don't want to be convinced. Look..." He took in a slow, deep breath. "More jobs means more people, which means more money to boost the local economy and—"

"The best positions at the plant are being filled by outsiders who will be transferred in."

"So what? The plant executives will be an asset to the community."

"Charlie, they're coming from Atlanta and Raleigh and are used to a big-city culture. That could have a dramatic impact on the way of life here."

"I've heard all this before."

"But did you *listen?* These people are used to Starbucks and restaurant chains and shopping centers and movie theatres and stores of every size and type. Do we really want to be a regional hub? That may be good for the overall economy, but what are we sacrificing to get it?"

"We need to grow, Ellen. Life moves on. Baxter has to keep pace."

"With whom?"

"Why are you being so arbitrary? When the new stretch of interstate is opened up, more businesses will start springing up.

There's no stopping progress."

"Maybe not. But don't dismiss the voice of people concerned about preserving our heritage. I'm trying to support you, Charlie. But even I'm not convinced that bringing in a big tire plant is necessarily the best answer for our economic woes."

"That's why you're the newspaper editor and I'm the mayor."

"Touché. But there's going to be trouble unless you do a better job of addressing concerns."

"Ellen, I already have. You can either rally the community behind me or fight me. It's your newspaper. But the deal's in concrete. Thompson Tire is coming to Baxter."

On Friday after school, Kevin Kirby sat on his heels in the Stedman's warehouse and started to light a cigar when he heard voices. His friend Ricky grabbed him by the arm and put a finger to his lips.

The boys moved behind an old washtub, closer to the railing, and peered down from the loft at Ricky's father and grandfather and several other shop owners who had walked in.

Ricky's grandfather held a stogie in his teeth and raised a hand to silence the others. "Thanks for coming," Lenny Stedman said. "I've got something on my chest and I'll cut to the chase: This new tire plant poses a serious threat to my business—and yours. I've always planned to pass the store on to Avery here. Unless we stick together, that won't happen now—"

"I don't know," Jack Weber said. "An authentic general store's a real novelty. You and Avery stand a better chance of making it than most of us. At least yours has a reputation."

"Won't be enough," Lenny said. "Tourists won't come here just to see Stedman's General Store. If the rest of you fold, I'm history."

"What a rip," Jack said. "Doesn't it tick you off that *we* have to pay the price so outsiders can line their pockets?"

Lenny shrugged. "We had our say. Just weren't persuasive enough."

"I'll give 'em persuasive," Avery Stedman said. "Maybe they need a two-by-four upside the head. They're not the ones about to lose a family business."

"Can't fight city hall, son. We're wasting our time."

"Yeah? And how am I supposed to raise *my* family? I grew up in that store and saw how hard you worked. Why should we lose it just because some sexy corporate attorney strutted her stuff at the mayor?"

"Stop it right there," Lenny said. "That's over the line and you know it."

Avery raised an eyebrow and looked at the others. "Am I the only one who's thought it?... Well?..."

"It crossed my mind," Jack said.

"Bunk!" Lenny puffed on his cigar. "Mayor Kirby's a man of integrity. I think he's wrong on this issue, but I don't believe some good lookin' attorney influenced his vote."

"Well, I do," Avery said. "Charlie's ball-and-chained to a wife and seven kids, playing the part of the 'good Christian man.' Maybe he wanted off the wagon for once. It's not hard for *me* to believe, the way she—"

"Enough said. You're out of line." Lenny looked from man to man. "What's done is done. I asked you here because the only way we're going to survive is if we dig in our heels. If any one of us on the town square closes up shop, it'll start a selling frenzy."

Avery nodded. "And it's anybody's guess what will go in. Nobody else seems to care about preserving what we've got here."

The men started talking among themselves again, and Lenny held up his hand.

"Some of our businesses have been on the town square as long as I can remember. If they go, a big part of our history will dry up. Can we agree to stick together on this?"

Kevin Kirby blinked the stinging from his eyes. He heard the mumbling and saw heads nodding, but all he could think about was making Ricky's dad take back what he'd said.

Kevin picked up a smooth, flat stone and skipped it across the glassy water of Heron Lake.

"My dad didn't mean it," Ricky Stedman said.

"He did, too. You just don't want me to feel bad." Kevin picked up another stone and hurled it as hard as he could. Why hadn't he done what his mother told him instead of going to the warehouse? Then he would never have heard Mr. Stedman's lies.

"Cool!" Ricky said. "Mine skipped four times."

Kevin stood facing the lake, staring at nothing.

Ricky reached down and pulled his bike upright. "I gotta go. If I'm late again, I'll be grounded. You coming?"

"Think I'll hang out here for a while."

"Look, Kev. Just 'cause he said it doesn't make it so."

Kevin looked into his friend's eyes and saw doubt staring back at him.

Ricky got on his bike and straddled it. "You gonna ask your dad?"

Kevin felt an aching inside he had never experienced before. He had always been proud to be part of a big family. Never once had it occurred to him that his dad might cheat on his mom—or might not care about the kids anymore.

"Well, *are* you?" Ricky said.

"Why should I? It's not true."

"Yeah. See you tomorrow."

Charlie put the storybook down. He got up and tucked his youngest daughter's arm under the covers. "Jesus loves you, and so does Daddy," he whispered. Charlie kissed her on the forehead, then tiptoed to the door and pulled it shut behind him.

"Is she out?" Marlene Kirby asked, a laundry basket in her arms.

"Like an angel. Here, Marlie, let me carry that." Charlie took the basket and walked down the hall to the laundry room and laid it on the counter. "I wonder how many loads you've done on this old Kenmore?"

She smiled. "Not enough. Want to sort or fold?"

"I'll sort."

"You were awfully quiet at dinner," she said. "Are you bothered by the reaction to the permit?"

"Somewhat. But it was the right decision."

Marlene folded a navy sweatshirt and put it on the stack. "Why are you so sure?"

"Because I've been an investor a lot longer than I've been a mayor. Down the road, people will remember this as a turning point in the growth of the town's economy."

Marlene shook a pair of blue jeans and smoothed out the wrinkles with her hands. "So, did you get all your paperwork done last night? I didn't even hear you come to bed."

"I made a respectable dent." Charlie felt the lie prick his conscience. "By the way, is something wrong with Kevin?"

"I don't think so. Why?"

"He didn't say a word at dinner. Looked like he'd lost his best friend."

Marlene smiled. "Hardly. Ricky was here after school, and the boys polished off half a package of Oreos before they rode their bikes to the lake. Would you hand me the white things?"

"Here, I'll do that." Charlie picked up the light-colored clothes he had sorted and put them in the washer.

Marlene poured in a scoop of detergent and turned the dial. "So much for laundry. Now I need to plan out the soccer schedule for tomorrow morning... Charlie, why are you staring at me like that?"

"I was just thinking what a marvel you are. Your day doesn't stop until you close your eyes, does it?"

"I've been doing this so long, I wouldn't know how to act if it did." Marlene kissed him gently on the lips and headed for the kitchen.

Charlie felt shame radiating from his face. He thought about another kiss: The one Sheila Paxton had initiated last night when he walked her to her car. It's not as though he hadn't seen it coming. But instead of resisting, he became a willing partner in an eager, passionate exchange that made him yearn for more...

Charlie had quickly moved Sheila's arms from around his neck, his eyes searching the dusk, hoping no one had seen them. "This is wrong."

"Oh, come on, Charlie. It was just a kiss. You enjoyed it as much as I did." Sheila's alluring eyes seemed to read his thoughts. "Ah, I should've known. You're not the adventurous type." Sheila smiled devilishly, a room key dangling from her hand. "Too bad. I absolutely hate sleeping alone." She inched closer and put her lips to his ear. "And I never kiss and tell." She dropped her room key in the pocket of his sport jacket.

Charlie watched her drive away, then went back inside and sat at his desk. He fought his conscience for several minutes and then called Marlene.

"Listen, Marlie. I've got hours of work to catch up on. I think I'll stay with it until I get tired."

"How were the meetings?"

"Long. We'll finish up in the morning. But I'm behind on everything else. Don't wait up."

"All right. I love you."

"I love you, too."

Charlie hung up the phone, Sheila's room key in his hand and Marlene's "I love you," echoing in his mind.

He got up and started pacing. He hadn't gone looking for this. And it wasn't as if Sheila meant anything to him. After the Thompson deal was closed, he'd never see her again. He picked up the receiver and dialed the number on the back of the room key.

"Good evening, the Parker House."

"I'd like to speak with Sheila Paxton in room 311," he said, making his voice sound deeper.

"One moment."

Charlie fiddled with the key in his hand and waited for what seemed an inordinate amount of time.

"Hellooo..." said a soft, alluring voice on the other end of the phone. "Where are you?"

Charlie's senses came alive with the taste of her lips, the scent of her perfume, the feeling of her body pressed to his. He hung up the phone, his heart pounding.

He paced for a few minutes, knowing what he *should* do. Instead, he picked up the phone and redialed the Parker House, then hung up before Sheila could answer. Seconds later, he sat staring at the ringing phone, glad when it was finally silent.

He didn't know how long he had stayed at the office after that, but he finally went home saddled with equal portions of guilt and desire, still unsure if he would resist if Sheila came on to him again...

Charlie heard Marlene singing in the kitchen and realized he was still standing in the laundry room. He went down the hall to the master bedroom and sat in the dark on the side of the bed. Why hadn't he just said *no* and put a stop to it?

2

On Saturday morning, Ellen Jones stood at the window in her office, her fingers wrapped around a warm cup of coffee, her senses enthralled with the magnificence of autumn. As far as her eyes could see, the trees were cloaked in rich shades of burnt orange, crimson, and gold. There was a knock and the door opened.

"Your newspaper's here," Margie said.

"You know, I could handle fall twelve months of the year."

"But then it wouldn't be so spectacular."

Ellen smiled, her eyes still fixed on the outdoors. "I suppose not. But I'd like to try it. How's the front page look?"

"Not bad, considering the subject matter. For those of us who wish the city council wasn't so *progressive*, it's not going to be an enjoyable read."

"Just leave it on my desk," Ellen said. "I want to enjoy this view before I leave."

Seconds after Margie left, Ellen's cell phone rang. She unzipped her purse and hit the talk button. "Good morning, love."

"Where are you?" Guy Jones said. "The cinnamon rolls are in the oven."

"I was just leaving."

"Have you heard the latest on the Atlanta freeway shooting? CNN just gave the names of the other five victims."

"Truthfully, I've enjoyed escaping the TV."

"Well, you'll never guess who died in the shooting: Sheila Paxton!"

Ellen switched the receiver to her other ear. "As in Thompson Tire?"

"One and the same. Did you know she was only thirty-five?"

"Poor thing. Did she have a family?"

"I don't know, honey. I just heard about it."

Ellen picked up the newspaper from her desk. "Turn the coffee on. I'm on my way."

Charlie Kirby sat in the bleachers at the second of three soccer games, losing the battle to concentrate on the event at hand. Sheila *dead?* It must have happened just minutes after she had called. He felt Marlene's arm slip in his.

"You don't have to do this," she said. "The kids will understand if you walk back to the house."

"No, I'm where I need to be."

Marlene gave his arm a squeeze. "Sheila's death has to be a blow to all of you who worked with her."

Charlie thought of Richard and wondered if he had any idea how easily Sheila was willing to give herself away.

"It's all so senseless," Marlene said. "My heart goes out to the families. Do you know if Sheila had a husband and children?"

"She mentioned someone named Richard, but I think he was a boyfriend."

"We should send flowers."

Charlie was aware of his head nodding. "All right."

"Do you know when and where the funeral will be?" Marlene asked.

"Monday. In Raleigh."

"You should go," she said.

"Let me think about it."

Marlene turned her eyes to the soccer field, then jumped to her feet, her hands cupped around her mouth. "Way to go, Kevin! Go! Go!"

Kevin Kirby raced down the field, his feet in complete control of the ball, and then delivered a powerful kick, sending the soccer ball whizzing past the goalie just as the clock ran out.

Marlene squealed with delight. "Charlie, did you see that? Kevin won the game! He won the game!"

"Great play, son!" Charlie shouted. "Good job!"

Kevin glanced up at Charlie and then turned the other way.

Ellen sat on the screened-in porch, knitting an afghan, and intently listening to the end of a CNN special report coming from the TV in the living room.

"Authorities are still investigating. But at this hour, it is believed the freeway shooting that claimed the life of Representative Gerald Landis and five others was a random act of violence.

"The shooter, Samuel Dwight Slover, twenty-nine, of Ellison had recently been released from the Hope Mental Health Center, though the center's spokesperson would not comment on the nature of Slover's illness or the length of his confinement. Family members were unavailable for comment.

"Authorities have been unable to determine where Slover got the automatic weapon used to kill six motorists, and which he later turned on himself. Slover had no history of violence and no criminal record."

"Guy, put it on mute. I can't listen anymore."

The sound went off and Guy appeared in the doorway. "Really a shame, isn't it?"

"It's terrible." Ellen exhaled loudly. "And the networks will play it over and over until we're all drawn into it."

"I wonder if the shooter was after Gerald Landis?"

"That's my guess. But people around here will be particularly interested in Sheila Paxton."

"I already see your wheels turning," Guy said.

"It's disgusting how the electronic media picks up on something and drives it into the ground. Gerald Landis wasn't the only victim. There are five other grieving families out there."

Dennis Lawton strolled with his wife, Jennifer, under the lofty trees along Acorn Street, marveling at the splendor of October and enjoying the warm breeze rustling the leaves.

"I missed all this color growing up in Denver," Dennis said. "We had one fall color: gold."

"Yes, but the aspen leaves looked like gold doubloons," Jennifer said. "I thought they were gorgeous."

Dennis felt a twinge as they stopped in front of a familiar brick bungalow. "Grandpa would turn over in his grave if he knew how this place has gone downhill."

Jennifer squeezed his hand. "Oh, I think Grandpa has a lot better things to think about now."

"Hey, you two," called a male voice from across the street.

Dennis turned and saw Lenny Stedman sitting on the front steps, lighting a cigar. "Hey, Mr. Stedman."

"Come over here and let me take a look at you."

Dennis took Jennifer's hand and walked across the street.

Lenny puffed his cigar. "Where're the twins?"

"Jen's folks took them to get their pictures taken," Dennis said. "We were glad for a chance to escape the 'terrible twos' for a few hours. So we decided to take a walk in Grandpa's old neighborhood."

"I sure miss Patrick," Lenny said, glancing across the street. "The new neighbors don't keep the yard looking the way he did. Aren't much for talking either." He turned his eyes to Jennifer. "You get prettier every time I see you."

"Thank you," she said, a pink glow coloring her cheeks. "How's Emma?"

"Happy as a lark—long as she doesn't see me smoking."

Jennifer smiled. "Maybe she'd like to keep you around a few years."

Lenny lifted his eyebrows. "That's what she says. You two hear any scuttlebutt about the new tire plant?"

"Oh, sure," Dennis said. "We know as many for as against. I heard the merchants association is divided. Is that right?"

Lenny nodded. "Some of us have a different mentality about what we do. Our businesses are second and third generation, and have been operating on the town square for decades. It's not just about money. It's about preserving this town's heritage."

"Yeah, the square is a great place," Dennis said. "I wish it never had to change."

"You say that like it's inevitable."

"Well, I hope not, Lenny. But there's a *lot* more involved than just Thompson Tire moving in. Once the interstate is opened up, business will probably concentrate closer to the off-ramps and away from downtown."

"Could've gone all day without hearing that," Lenny said.

"Yeah, I know. But it's smart to tackle the bad news before it sneaks up on you. Speaking of bad news: Did you hear that Thompson Tire's attorney was one of the victims in the freeway shooting?"

Lenny's eyes widened, his eyebrows arched. "No. Where'd you hear that?"

"It's been all over the news."

The front door opened, and Emma Stedman came rushing down the steps, her arms open wide.

"Oh, I was so glad to see you kids out here," Emma said, giving Dennis and Jennifer a hug. "Have you had lunch yet? I've got a big pot of chicken stew simmering on the stove, and I just took sourdough rolls out of the oven."

Dennis looked at Jennifer and then at Emma. "Sounds *great*."

"Of course, you can't leave until you've had a piece of peach cobbler," Emma added.

Dennis winked at Lenny. "We wouldn't think of it, would we, Jen?"

"Actually," Jennifer said, "Dennis hasn't stopped talking about your cobbler since the last time we were here. Maybe I can talk you out of your recipe."

Lenny laughed. "For a moment, I actually thought you kids walked up here just to see me."

Charlie lay stretched out on the couch in the family room, glad for a few minutes to himself. The kids were out playing—all but Kevin, who said he was tired and had gone to his room, not looking especially jubilant for a twelve-year-old who had just kicked the winning goal.

The splendor of autumn remained outside the window. And darkness flooded Charlie's soul with the realization that Sheila had died an unbeliever. He'd been so busy fantasizing what it would be like to sleep with her that he hadn't thought about her spiritual condition.

"There you are," Marlene said. "I didn't mean to startle you."

"That's all right."

She sat on the side of the couch. "I think you're right about Kevin. Something's bothering him. He left most of his lunch and didn't even call Ricky to tell him about kicking the winning goal."

"You sure the boys aren't at odds?"

"I really don't think so," she said. "This might be a 'guy' thing. Maybe you should talk to him."

"Okay, I will. But first, I'd like to just think for a while."

"Of course." Marlene stroked his cheek. "I'll take the two little ones with me to the grocery store and tell the others to play in the backyard until I get back."

Kevin heard footsteps in the hallway. He rolled over on his side and faced the window.

"Son?" Charlie whispered. "May I come in?"

Kevin lay still, his heart pounding.

Charlie came closer and stopped at the bed. Kevin didn't move.

"Something's bothering you, and I'd like to help. No matter

what it is, you can talk to me about it." Charlie began to massage Kevin's back the tender way he always did when Kevin was sick.

Kevin hugged his pillow, his eyes clamped shut, emotion tightening his throat. He felt the runaway tears splash onto his pillow and couldn't hold back the sobs.

"Son, what is it? Talk to me."

Kevin stiffened and then let the words spill out. "I'm glad she's dead!"

There was a long pause. Then he heard his father get up and close the door and pull a chair over to the side of the bed.

"Kevin, look at me..."

He didn't move.

"Son, turn around. Tell me what this is about."

Kevin sighed. He turned over and then sat on the side of the bed and faced his dad, avoiding his eyes.

"Are you talking about Sheila Paxton?"

Kevin nodded.

"Why in the world are you glad she's dead? You didn't even know her."

"Well, *you* sure did!" Kevin looked into his father's eyes and saw fear, not anger. A spanking would have hurt less.

"What does that have to do with anything?"

Kevin shrugged.

"Then I suggest you—"

"Mr. Stedman said Mom and us kids are a ball and chain—and that you wanted..." Kevin stopped, his chin quivering, the words forming a knot in his throat.

"That I wanted what?"

Kevin sighed. "I don't know."

"Yes, you do. Let's hear it."

Kevin looked down and ran his thumb and forefinger along the hem of his soccer shirt. "Never mind. It's probably stupid."

"Then just say it, son. You're not a baby. Talk to me like a—"

"Did you sleep with her?" Kevin raised his eyes, his heart pounding, and studied his father's reaction.

Charlie's face went blank, and he stared at Kevin as if he couldn't believe the question.

"Of course not! Where did you get an idea like that?"

"Ricky and I were in the warehouse after school when his grandpa and his dad and some other store owners came in. They didn't know we were in the loft. They were talking about you and Sheila Paxton."

"*What?*" Charlie turned red from the neck up. His jaw was clenched. "Who was?"

"Mr. Stedman."

"Which one?"

"Both. But Ricky's dad's the one who said it. His grandpa didn't believe it." Kevin told Charlie the whole story and wondered if he had ever seen him so angry. "What're you gonna do?"

"I'm going to confront Avery Stedman for starters. How dare he make such a disgusting accusation—and behind my back, no less!"

"Then it's not true? You aren't tired of us?"

Charlie's eyes brimmed with tears, and then his arms went around Kevin. "No, son. It's absolutely *not* true. I love your mother—and each one of you—more than you know. And I always will."

"Then why would Mr. Stedman say something like that?"

"I don't know. But I'm going to find out."

3

Charlie Kirby pulled his Lincoln Navigator up to a parking meter and turned off the motor. He looked over at Kevin and patted his knee. "Let me do the talking."

Charlie got out of the car and walked with Kevin to the front entrance of Stedman's General Store. He hurried past the clerk and flung open the door to the backroom, where he found Avery Stedman sorting freight.

"We need to talk," Charlie said.

"About what?"

"I want your dad in on this." Charlie looked around. "Is he here?"

"What's your problem, *Mr.* Mayor? Don't like eggs on your window?"

"Just get Lenny in here. I've got something to say to both of you."

Avery rolled his eyes. He stood up and cupped his hand around his mouth. "Hey, Dad!"

"What?" said a muffled voice from the loft.

"Could you come down here a second? Our honorable mayor has something to say to us."

Lenny Stedman appeared at the top of the ladder, then climbed down and stood next to Avery. "What's this about?"

Charlie put his arm on Kevin's shoulder and realized the boy was shaking. "My son was in that loft when you two decided to accuse me of having an improper relationship with Sheila Paxton. Just who do you think you are, making false accusations like that?"

"Now, hold on," Avery said. "We didn't know Kevin was—"

"What difference does it make if he was here or not?" Charlie's eyes collided with Avery's. "How dare you imply there is any impropriety between me and Sheila?"

"*Was*," Avery said. "Guess you heard about the shooting."

Charlie turned to Lenny. "You approve of this?"

"I told Avery he was out of line," Lenny said. "Tempers are hot right now. Sorry Kevin had to hear it."

"That's no excuse to malign my character."

Lenny nodded slightly. "Son, you owe the mayor an apology."

"Guess I'll just have to owe him one," Avery said. "I haven't changed my opinion."

"Kevin, would you wait in the car? Go on..." Charlie waited until Kevin left, and then stood nose to nose with Avery. "I'm warning you, back off. I've never been involved with Sheila Paxton and I'm appalled that you would even suggest such a thing. Do you realize how this kind of idle talk could hurt my family?"

"Should've thought of that yourself," Avery said.

"Meaning what?"

"I'm not the only one who thinks Miss Legs turned your head so you'd push the city council to rush the vote on the permit."

"There's no basis for this kind of accusation, and you know it! I'm not going to stand for it!"

"I'm entitled to my opinion," Avery said.

"Your *opinion* is slander!"

"So sue me."

Charlie suddenly felt powerless. What if someone had seen him kissing Sheila? Then again, if Avery knew, why wouldn't he have said so?

"Lenny, you'd better talk some sense into him. I'm not going to sit by and let him hurt my wife and kids because I made an economic decision he disagrees with!"

Avery scoffed. "Is that a threat? You always did think you were better than the rest of us. *Charlie* got the scholarship. *Charlie* got the prom queen. *Charlie* got the big bucks."

"So, that's what this is about?" Charlie said. "Jealousy?"

Avery took a step forward. "You don't even know what it's like to have to work for a living. You sit on your throne down at the mayor's office, deciding what's good for us *peons*. Well I'm sick of your holier-than-thou attitude and your—"

"Son, that's enough," Lenny said, grabbing Avery by the arm.

Charlie glared at Avery and let his ire burn. "I don't care what you think of me, I'm not going to let you hurt my family. I want this talk stopped right here, right now!"

"Or what?" Avery said. "You'll run us out of business? Isn't that what you had in mind all along?"

Charlie got in the car, his mind racing, his temples throbbing, and drove six blocks before he realized Kevin had been talking.

"Dad, are you all right?"

"I'm angry, that's all."

"Did Mr. Stedman apologize?"

"No, he didn't."

"Did you hit him?"

Charlie glanced at Kevin. "No, of course not. That wouldn't solve anything."

"Are you going to tell Mom?"

Charlie tightened his grip on the steering wheel. "I'll have to. I don't want her hearing it from someone else. But I need to pick the right time, so let's keep this between you and me for now."

"Yeah, okay, Dad. Mr. Stedman's a rotten person to say you were cheating on Mom, huh?"

Charlie felt his throat tighten, all too aware of the fine line between what never happened...and what almost did.

4

Assistant Manager Mark Steele opened the café curtains all along the east wall of windows at Monty's Diner and noticed the sky was starting to get light.

"Mark, it's almost six," Rosie Harris said. "Let's get this show on the road."

"Okay, Leo. Fire up the grill!" Mark went to the front window and turned on the Open sign, then unlocked the door. He bent down and picked up a bundle of newspapers, and had just brought them inside when Mort Clary walked in.

"Mornin' all," Mort said, hanging his hat and sweater on the hook. "Got my caffeine?"

"On the counter," Rosie said.

Mort grabbed a newspaper from Mark's hand and put a quarter in the jar by the register. He walked to the counter, his eyes fixed on the front page, and sat on a stool. "Too bad about this lawyer lady."

"Sure is," Rosie said. "People are nuts these days."

"Who's nuts?" George Gentry came in and sat at the counter, his wife Hattie next to him.

"The fella that done that freeway shootin'," Mort said.

"Wasn't that awful?" Hattie shook her head. "Sheila Paxton seemed like such a nice woman."

"*Nice?*" Reggie Mason walked to the counter, a grin stretching his cheeks, a newspaper under his arm. "That's not what I hear."

"Spare me," Rosie said.

Mort winked at Reggie. "There's all kinda rumors runnin' amuck."

"What rumors?" Liv Spooner came in and took her seat at the counter. "Did I miss something?"

"Just Mort and Reg running their mouths," George said. "Nothing worth repeating."

Mort snickered. "Don't be so all-fired sure, Georgie. I hear Miss Sheila What's-her-name put in a little overtime with the mayor, if ya get my drift."

George glared at Mort over the top of his glasses. "You're skating on thin ice."

"Charlie Kirby's a saint," Rosie said. "No one's going to believe that for a minute."

"Ain't what Avery Stedman thinks."

"Oh, did he finally learn to think?" George said.

"Just 'cause ya don't agree with his politics ain't no reason ta put him down."

George rolled his eyes. "But it's okay to cast aspersions on Mayor Kirby's character?"

"Wait a minute," Rosie said. "Go back to Sheila Paxton. Just because she's a knockout means she's not nice? Where do you guys get off with that kind of talk?"

"Settle down," Reggie said. "That's not it."

"Then suppose you tell me what it is."

"Ask Mort. He's the one who talked to Avery."

Rosie flicked Mort on the head. "You're a troublemaker, mister. Sheila Paxton was a class act—a beautiful, successful attorney. Why can't you leave it at that?"

"Never said she weren't all them things. Mayor Kirby musta thought so." Mort laughed his wheezy laugh.

Hattie got up and walked toward the ladies' room. "I'm not listening to any more of this."

"You just don't know when to quit, do you?" George said.

"Well, Georgie, before you start givin' me what for, maybe ya oughta check out the facts."

"What facts?"

"Avery said Tim Adler's boy seen her and the mayor smoochin' up a storm in the parkin' lot behind the city offices buildin'."

"Oh, well, then it *must* be gospel," Rosie said. "Isn't he the one who got suspended from school for vandalizing the gym?"

"Don't mean he's blind." Mort held up his cup for a refill. "Why would the boy make it up?"

"For attention," Rosie said. "Same as lots of other kids. If Mayor Kirby were going to cheat on Marlene, which I don't believe for a minute, he'd be more discreet than that."

Mort blew on his coffee, then took a sip. "Don't matter ta me one way or t'other. But folks are sure startin' ta wonder."

Charlie Kirby yawned, his eyelids heavy after his early morning flight to Raleigh. He drove his rental car down Sunderlin Boulevard, then turned into Sacred Heart Cemetery and followed the funeral procession, amazed at how few cars there were. The memorial service had been held at the funeral home, where he counted only twenty people in attendance. He hadn't been able to see how many were seated behind the privacy curtain, but figured there would be a respectable family showing at the gravesite.

He dreaded seeing Richard, and wondered if the man had any idea that Sheila was not only willing but eager to cheat on him. Charlie felt a pang of guilt and dismissed it. No point in beating himself for something that never happened.

But he still hadn't faced Marlene about Avery Stedman's accusation. After they got the kids to bed on Saturday night, Marlene started on her Sunday school lesson and didn't finish until after midnight. On Sunday after church they got busy with the kids, and by Sunday night, he had talked himself into waiting until after the funeral.

Charlie slowed and brought the car to a stop behind the others. He spotted TV cameras, and just beyond them, a green canopy covering a fresh grave. He got out and noticed a familiar white Lexus had pulled in behind him.

Charlie walked to the driver's side and waited until Guy Jones rolled down the window. "I was surprised to see you two at the funeral."

"It was a last-minute decision," Guy said.

Charlie bent down and looked in the window. "Hello, Madam Editor. Are you speaking to me?"

"Oh, come on, Charlie," Ellen Jones said. "When have you known me to hold a grudge?"

He smiled. "Good."

"I'm planning to write a feature story on Sheila. The networks are obsessing over Gerald Landis as if he were the only victim. People in Baxter want to hear about Sheila Paxton. Maybe her family and friends would like a chance to let their voices be heard."

"She has a boyfriend named Richard," Charlie said. "Maybe he'd like to talk to you."

Ellen looked out the window. "It's so strange. After a tragic death, I was expecting a lot more people than this."

"Come on," Guy said. "Looks like they're about ready to start."

Charlie walked with Ellen and Guy to the gravesite and saw a polished wood casket covered with a huge spray of fall flowers. He recognized several executives from Thompson Tire. His eyes moved from person to person and stopped on a tall, lean man about Sheila's age whose nose was red and whose eyes looked empty and desolate. *Richard.* Charlie felt a surge of guilt and quickly willed it away.

"If you'll be seated," the minister said, "we can begin."

Richard put on a pair of sunglasses once TV cameras were visible around the periphery.

Charlie studied him. Richard who? Charlie didn't even know his last name. The guy was decent looking. Thick hair. Italian suit. Rolex. He tried to picture Sheila at home with him, but found it too uncomfortable.

"Only You, O God, can make sense of such tragedy. We grieve for the tragic loss of this young woman..."

Charlie tried to think of something else...the elders meeting Tuesday night...his daughter's dance recital Thursday night...golf with Dennis Lawton Friday afternoon...the Falcons game on Sunday...propane for the grill...filters for the furnace...

Charlie was suddenly aware again of the minister talking. He glanced at his watch, surprised that five minutes had gone by.

"And so we entrust the soul of Sheila Anne Paxton to You, O Lord, and pray the words of Your beloved Son, who died so that those who believe in Him might live: Our Father who art in heaven, hallowed be thy name..."

Charlie recited the words to the Lord's Prayer, but they seemed empty. Afterward, Richard stood up, walked to Sheila's casket, and laid a red tulip on it. He lingered a few moments, and then returned to his seat. One by one, people got up and filed by the casket and placed a tulip on it. When Charlie's turn came, all he could think about was getting it over with.

The service ended with everyone singing "Amazing Grace."

Charlie turned to Guy and Ellen. "I should say something to Richard. Excuse me."

He walked over to where Richard was standing and waited until a small group of comforters thinned out. Two men stood near Richard and watched Charlie intently as he stepped forward and extended his hand. "Richard, I'm Charlie Kirby, the mayor of Baxter. I had the pleasure of working with Sheila on the Thompson relocation. I'm very sorry for your loss. We were all shocked and grieved to hear the news."

Richard removed his dark glasses and wiped his red-rimmed eyes. "Sheila mentioned you. Said she enjoyed working with you. Aren't you the one with seven kids?"

"That's me." Charlie forced a smile.

One of the men tapped Richard on the shoulder, then whispered something in his ear. Richard's face dropped. "I don't mean to be rude, but I need to leave. Thank you so much for coming, and for introducing yourself."

Richard turned and walked hurriedly between the two men toward two police officers leaning on a squad car. Richard and the two men got in a black sedan, then followed the squad car out of the cemetery.

"I wonder what that's all about," Charlie mumbled.

"Someone broke into his house."

Ellen's voice startled him and he turned around.

"How do you know that?"

"You want my *source*?" Ellen's eyes were playful, and then serious. "I overheard the officers talking about it."

Charlie shook his head. "Poor guy just can't get a break."

Ellen's eyebrows formed an arch. "Seems a little too coincidental, if you ask me."

5

Charlie pulled the Navigator into the garage. He pushed the remote and waited for the door to come down, glad to put the day behind him. All he wanted to do was sink into his leather chair and read the newspaper. He grabbed his suit coat and opened the door to the kitchen. Marlene was standing at the counter making lunches.

"Sorry I'm so late," he said. "Are the little ones asleep?"

She nodded. "Kevin and Kaitlin are doing homework. How was the service?"

"Tiring," Charlie said. "It's good I went, though. The only people in attendance were Sheila's boyfriend, some business associates from Thompson Tire, and a handful of friends."

Marlene didn't turn around or comment and continued making sandwiches.

Charlie walked up behind her, put his arms around her, and kissed her cheek. "Tell me about *your* day. How was Bible study?"

"Fine."

"And lunch with Rhonda and Mary Beth?"

"Fine."

"How'd Kaitlin do with the new ballet slippers?"

"Fine, Charlie. Just *fine*. Everything's just fine." Her hands were shaking.

"Marlie, what's wrong?"

Marlene put her hand to her mouth and started to whimper.

"Hey..." He tried to turn her around to face him, but she resisted. "What's got you so upset? Is Kevin in some kind of trouble?"

Marlene shook her head. When she finally turned around, the look in her eyes sent fear pulsating through him. "Not Kevin. *You.*"

"Come on," Charlie said. "Let's go to our room and talk."

"Not while Kevin and Kaitlin are up."

"They can't hear what we're saying."

"I'm not ready to talk about it!" Marlene said.

Charlie glanced at the clock. "I'm going to change my clothes. The kids will be in bed in forty-five minutes. We're not ending this day until we talk."

Her deep brown eyes welled with tears. She turned around and started spreading peanut butter on a row of bread slices.

Ellen Jones sat at the desk in her motel room, entering notes into her laptop.

"Guy, the whole thing is weird," she said. "What are the chances Richard Boatman's house would be ransacked while he was burying his girlfriend?"

"Any crook could have known who he was and where he'd be, Ellen. It's been in the news."

"Don't you think it's odd that Sheila didn't have family at the funeral?"

"What does that have to do with Richard's house being burglarized?"

"Nothing, my mind's racing. Tragic deaths usually draw a crowd. Only a handful of friends and a few business associates came out to acknowledge her. Seems odd to me."

"I think you're making too much of it."

"Hmm...maybe." Ellen got up and took two diet Cokes out of the small refrigerator and handed one to Guy. "I wonder who the man was with the binoculars?"

"Probably one of those nasty TV media people you loathe."

"I doubt it. Since when is the electronic media that subtle?"

"I was kidding, Ellen. Don't be so serious."

She smiled, and sat on the arm of his chair. "Sorry. I'm a bad sport. If I'm going to do a feature on Sheila, I guess I'll have to go looking for her friends and family."

"Sounds like you're not going to be ready to ride home with me on Wednesday morning. I can't stay any longer than that. I have to be in court all day Thursday."

"I can fly home."

"How long do you think you'll need to be here?"

"I'm not sure. But there's no point in leaving without a story."

Charlie sat on the bed reading the newspaper, a mound of pillows propped behind him. He heard footsteps coming down the hall and looked up in time to see Marlene walk into the room and quietly close the door.

"Have the kids gone to bed?" he said.

"Yes, but they're not asleep, so keep your voice down."

She went in the bathroom and a few minutes later came out wearing her pink terry bathrobe. She sat at the vanity table and let her hair down, then began to brush it vigorously.

"Are you going to tell me what's wrong?" Charlie said.

"I think you know."

"I can't read your mind, Marlie."

"Then suppose you just start at the beginning and tell me about your relationship with Sheila Paxton."

"What relationship? We worked together on the Thompson deal."

"A schoolmate of Kevin's says otherwise."

"Who, Ricky Stedman?"

"I was talking about Jeremy Adler."

"Jeremy? What does—"

"He claims he saw you, I think his exact words were 'mugging,' with Sheila Paxton in the parking lot of your office building—on the night you just happened to be working late. The kids in Kevin's school have been snickering about it all day. Kevin didn't tell me. His homeroom teacher did! Do you have any idea how embarrassing that was?" Her voice cracked.

"That's ridiculous!" Charlie said.

"So Jeremy just made it up—out of nowhere?"

"The kid's got problems. Why would anybody believe him?"

"You're saying he's lying?"

"I'm saying he's wrong. Look, Avery Stedman's mad about the Thompson deal. He's been shooting off his mouth, saying that there was something going on between Sheila and me. Kevin and Ricky were in the loft at the warehouse on Friday and overheard him talking to a few other merchants."

Marlene spun around and glared at him. "*They* were talking about this?"

"That's what was wrong with Kevin. I talked to him Saturday afternoon like you suggested, and then took him to Stedman's and confronted Avery in front of his dad. I told him it wasn't true and how dare he hurt my family by making false accusations. I told him I wanted the talk stopped right then and there."

"Well, that makes it all better," she said. "Once he stops trashing your reputation, everyone else in town will just forget the implications, right? This is so humiliating. Even my own son knew before I did!"

"I had every intention of telling you, Marlie. I waited up Saturday night, but you worked on your lesson until after midnight. And yesterday the kids were with us all day. It didn't seem right to drop this bomb on you last night before I left town."

"Thanks for your consideration. It was much better hearing it from Kevin's teacher." She put her face in her hands and started to cry.

Charlie got up and tried to comfort her, but she pushed him away.

"Marlie, please believe me. I wasn't involved with Sheila."

"Have you spent time alone with her?"

"Of course not."

"What about Thursday night when Jeremy said he saw you with her?"

"I was working."

"Alone?"

"You think I'm lying to you?"

Marlene plucked a Kleenex and wiped her eyes. She seemed to hesitate, then opened the top drawer of her vanity and dangled Sheila's room key from her index finger. "I found this in your sport coat. I called the Parker House and asked for Sheila Paxton in Room 311. They said she checked out Friday."

A bearded man sat in the dark behind the wheel of a blue Chevy Impala, his binoculars fixed on Richard Boatman's house. The lights were on inside, and every now and then he saw silhouettes move across the blinds. Boatman wasn't alone. He held the binoculars and moved his head slowly across the front of the house and stopped on the yellow crime scene tape draped across the front porch. He popped the last of the M&M's in his mouth, lowered the binoculars, and pushed the button on his watch: 9:20. He rolled his head from side to side until his neck popped.

Suddenly, the outdoor lights came on, and the garage door opened. A black Infiniti J30 backed out of Richard's driveway. The man raised the binoculars to his eyes and saw two people in the front seat and one in back. He waited until they were half way down the street, then started his car and slowly pulled away from the curb.

The Infiniti stopped at the corner, then pulled onto Woodland Avenue. He followed, leaving enough distance so as not to be conspicuous. After several blocks, the Infiniti slowed and turned into an upscale office complex. He drove the Impala around the block and pulled into the office complex parking lot, which was empty except for a cleaning service van and a black Infiniti parked near the entrance.

He got out and tried the door to the building, not surprised it was locked. He spotted a woman coming out of a utility door with a full trash bag. She put a block of wood in the door and then walked toward the Dumpster. He waited for a few seconds, then slipped in the door and hurried down the hall to the main lobby. He quickly scanned the directory. So, Boatman really *was* a CPA. Suite 208. He took the elevator up to the second floor, turned right, and walked down a long hallway. The lights were on in 208. He looked through the sheers on the door and saw Richard take something out of a safe and put it in a briefcase.

Two guys stood behind Richard—the same ones he had seen at the cemetery. He couldn't tell whether or not they were feds.

"Make it quick," one said. "This is against my better judgment."

"I just want the pictures," Richard said. "Nothing else matters now. Let's go." Richard stood and turned toward the door.

The bearded man ducked out of sight and hurried to the elevator. He stepped inside and pushed the hold button, then took his gun out of the holster and waited. He would get only one crack at this. He closed his eyes and focused intently on the sounds. The office door closed...the key turned in the lock...footsteps moved quickly in his direction. He took a slow, deep breath. Then stepped into the hallway—and with lightning precision got off two clean shots, dropping the men on either side of Richard Boatman before they had time to draw.

He laughed. "Surprised to see me?" He grabbed Richard by the arm and put the gun to his head. "How about you and me takin' a little ride?"

Ellen turned off her laptop. She yawned and rubbed her eyes, sure that the people in the next room could hear Guy's snoring. She got up and gently stroked his cheek. "They can hear you in Asheville, Counselor," she said softly. Guy mumbled something and then rolled over.

Ellen smiled and went into the bathroom. She got her cleansing cream out of her cosmetic bag and rubbed it on her face. As far as she could tell, Sheila Paxton was a self-assured dynamo who capably managed the legal affairs of Thompson Tire Corporation and who shared a luxurious home with a handsome CPA named Richard Boatman. She wore a Rolex and had a Saks Fifth Avenue air about her. How could a woman like that have drawn so little attention after being gunned down in a heart-wrenching tragedy?

There had to be more to Sheila Paxton's life than was reflected by twenty people gathered under a green canopy at her gravesite.

6

Charlie Kirby sat quietly through breakfast, listening to the happy chatter of his children. Marlene interacted with the kids as if nothing were wrong. But he had noticed the pan of burned oatmeal soaking in the sink.

Why hadn't he thrown out Sheila's room key? How could he have been so careless? All he could do now was hope and pray Marlene could forgive him for something that had never even happened.

Kevin pushed a slice of banana around the bowl with his spoon. One by one the other kids finished eating and got up and left the kitchen.

"Kevin, we need to leave in twenty minutes," Marlene said. "Don't forget your science report."

She hurried off somewhere, and Charlie and Kevin were left sitting at the table.

"Your mother told me what happened at school," Charlie said. "It had to be embarrassing for you."

Kevin's eyebrows scrunched together. "You should've told her."

"I'm sorry, son. I was ready to tell her Saturday night, but she was up until after midnight working on her lesson. We were busy all day yesterday. Time got away from me."

Kevin glanced up and then down at his bowl. "Jeremy says he saw you and Sheila Paxton, and you were—"

"I know what he *says*. You mother told me."

"Why would he say that?"

"I don't know, Kevin. Why would Avery Stedman shoot off his mouth the way he did? Once a rumor gets started, it's almost impossible to keep it from spreading."

"But Jeremy doesn't even know Mr. Stedman."

"Kevin, you and I have already been over this. What more can I say?"

Kevin shrugged. "Nothing. I gotta go."

"Son, come here." Kevin got up and stood next to his chair. "You know I tried to put a stop to this before it got ugly. Your mother's been hurt and it's going to take her some time to get over it. But I need you to be brave and stand your ground. Some people are mad about the tire plant coming here and are going to say things to get back at me."

"Jeremy's parents aren't mad about the tire plant, they're glad. So why would he want to get back at you?"

"Jeremy's got problems, Kevin. I don't know. But you're going to have to decide whom to believe. I'm not going to defend myself with you anymore."

"What about Mom?"

"Your mother's confused and humiliated. It was horrible having to hear such a private thing from your teacher. I'm angry with myself for not telling her, but I had no way of knowing this was going to happen."

Marlene Kirby leaned her head on the back of the rocker and glanced up at the mantle clock on the bedroom fireplace. She had an hour and half before she had to pick up her preschoolers.

She closed her eyes and began to rock slowly and rhythmically, her heart heavy with betrayal. She had been so sure that Charlie would have a logical explanation for Sheila's room key being in his sport coat! But when all he could do was insist he found it on the floor in the conference room and then forgot all about it, what was she supposed to think? Did he really think she was that naive? She had assumed his stylish new haircut and sudden preoccupation with working out were his way of dealing with turning forty-five. It never occurred to her there might be another woman.

Marlene ran her thumb along the row of tiny diamonds on her wedding band. Charlie had wanted to buy her a solitaire for their fifteenth wedding anniversary, but she wasn't ready to part with this one.

Their chocolate Lab came in and lay at her feet, his chin resting on her shoe.

"Are you sad, too, Hershey?" She wiggled her fingers.

The dog got up and nudged her hand with his cold, wet nose.

Marlene scratched his ears. "You always know, don't you—" The words choked her and she gave in to the silence, her eyes clouded, her face suddenly flushed.

In her best day, she had never looked as sexy as Sheila Paxton. But she wasn't dowdy either. Even after her seventh child was born, she got her figure back to a size ten. She had a cute hairstyle, a fashionable wardrobe—and still got a double take from time to time. If Charlie was unhappy with the way she looked, he had never given her a clue.

Marlene sighed. Had she neglected him? Been too involved with the kids? That wasn't it either. When they closed their bedroom door at night, the time was theirs. And whether they talked or held each other or made love, she had been as present to Charlie as she knew how to be. She was as crazy about him now as the day they married.

There was another possibility. She felt her throat tighten. What if Charlie didn't love her anymore? Marlene let the thought torment her for a few minutes, then got up and put in a load of laundry.

Charlie paced in his office, disturbed that Regina had avoided eye contact when she brought his mail. It was time to decide how he was he going to react to the rumors. He had seen what the media did to politicians who stray. He hadn't strayed—and what *almost* happened was nobody's business. He would deny everything, confident that his word would stand against the allegations of a mixed-up middle schooler and one disgruntled merchant.

But there was also the matter of his church family. Charlie had been an elder for the past four years. He knew the procedure: Once the elders had gotten wind of the rumors, they would choose someone on the executive committee to confront him privately. He was tempted to skip tonight's meeting, but that would only create doubt. He stopped pacing and looked out the window at the steeple of Cornerstone Bible Church. The elders would need assurance that he hadn't had an affair with Sheila Paxton. He could honestly tell them he hadn't.

But the situation at home was more complex. If he tried to explain to Marlene what had really happened, it would sound like an attempt to cover his trail. Plus the notion that he had considered cheating on her wouldn't hurt any less. It was just better to deny that anything had happened between him and Sheila.

7

Ellen Jones walked into her Raleigh motel room, tossed her keys on the bed, and collapsed in a chair. She pushed the curls away from her face and heaved an exaggerated sigh. "I might as well go home with you tomorrow."

"No luck?" Guy said, looking over the top of his reading glasses.

"I think I'm rushing it. I really wanted to put together a nice human-interest story on Sheila. But without Richard's input, I have precious little to work with. His friends don't seem to know as much about Sheila as I do. Is that not weird? The people at Thompson Tire have told me everything they know—and it's all related to her working relationships. The woman didn't strike me as an introvert. I wonder why the people closest to her don't know anything about her?"

"Maybe Sheila was a private person."

"Hmm...doesn't seem consistent. Anyway, I left two messages for Richard and don't feel right about intruding on his grief. He's obviously avoiding talking to me. Have you listened to the news today?"

"No. I'm working on Thursday's court case. I even forgot to eat lunch."

Ellen smiled. "You forget, and I indulge. What a team."

"Why don't you turn on the news and see if there's anything new on the freeway shooting?"

Ellen took two diet Cokes out of the refrigerator and handed one to Guy. She picked up the remote and pushed the "on" button.

"Something's going on. Look at this." She turned up the sound.

"WRLE News has been on the scene since early this morning after learning of a cleaning woman's grisly discovery of two men shot and killed in an office building in Haverly Heights.

"The FBI has made no comment. But according to local police, the men were killed between nine and eleven last night. Both victims suffered a single gunshot wound to the head, and both were armed. Names of the victims are being withheld pending notification of next of kin.

"The cleaning woman, who has asked not to be identified, told authorities she didn't see or hear anything unusual prior to eleven-thirty last night, when she got out of the elevator on the second floor and discovered two men shot in the hallway. She ran to get the other members of the cleaning crew, and then called 911.

"At this hour, Raleigh police have no witnesses, no suspects, and no leads in this baffling—"

The anchorman paused and appeared to be listening to something on his headset.

"We have some breaking news on the earlier report of a body discovered in Haverly Park... Sources now confirm that Raleigh police were led to the body of *another* murder victim, this one in Haverly Park, just blocks from the office building where two victims were shot last night.

"Chase Nicholson, a student at William Haverly College, told WRLE news that he was jogging on the east side of the park and had stopped to catch his breath when he spotted what appeared to be someone lying in a wooded area near the duck pond. He moved closer to check it out and was horrified to discover the body of a Caucasian man lying face down, hands tied behind him, and a gunshot wound to the back of the head. A message was stuck to the back of the victim's shirt. Nicholson said it was written in another language, possibly Spanish. Nicholson used his cell phone to call 911 and remained with the body until police arrived.

"Sources at Hope Presbyterian Hospital told reporters that the victim was positively identified as Richard Boatman, thirty-six, the boyfriend of Sheila Paxton, one of six victims in Friday's freeway shooting in Atlanta.

"Boatman's execution-style murder raises some troubling questions: Was his girlfriend the intended target of the Atlanta freeway shooter? Was Monday's break-in at the couple's Haverly Heights home tied to their murders? Does the message left on Boatman's back reveal the motivation for his murder? And, were the two men found shot this morning in a Raleigh office building a part of the equation—or was it coincidence?

"The FBI was unavailable for comment, and residents in Haverly Heights are shocked and nervous in the wake of the bloodbath that has rocked this upscale residential neighborhood.

"WRLE news will bring you breaking news as the details start to unfold."

Ellen put the TV on mute and turned to Guy, her eyes wide, her eyebrows arched. "So much for the private life of Sheila Paxton."

"Honey, you should tell the police about the man with the binoculars at the cemetery. It might be related."

"I can't offer a description. He was too far away."

"That's beside the point," Guy said. "Authorities need to know he was out there."

Charlie Kirby pulled his car into a parking place at Cornerstone Bible Church and sat for a moment, listening to the end of the news. He could hardly believe Richard Boatman had been shot and killed. The implications being batted around by the media sounded preposterous. But what if Richard *had* been executed. Is that what happened to Sheila? Were the murders linked? Charlie shuddered.

He got out and walked to the side door of the church. *Act confident*, he told himself. Nothing worth admitting had happened between him and Sheila. And certainly his private thoughts were no one else's business—not even the elders'. Now, more than ever, he didn't want his name linked to hers.

Ellen left the police station and walked a half block to her car. As she unlocked the door, she felt a sharp pain in her wrist and slowly opened and closed her hand a few times, bemoaning the ugly scar. Her mind flashed back a year and a half: Sawyer's upcoming trial...her poignant editorials...the rattlesnake in her knitting bag. She shuddered at the memory of that crude attempt to intimidate her. But there was no way she would take back one word she had written about Billy Joe Sawyer.

This was different. This wasn't Baxter's story. She could walk away.

She got in the car and locked her door, then dialed her cell phone.

"Hello."

"Guy, it's me. I gave the police my statement, and I'm getting ready to leave. I didn't want you to worry."

"You sound shaken. Are you all right?"

"I don't have a good feeling about this story. I'm not going to pursue it. I'm not willing to risk antagonizing whoever murdered these people by digging up facts on Sheila Paxton."

"I'm so relieved. I couldn't agree more. Come pack your things, and let's get to bed early. I'd like to be on the road by six."

The bearded man crept across the parking lot of the Luxury Inn Suites and squatted behind a white Lexus. He turned on a tiny flashlight attached to his key ring and jotted down the license number, then disappeared into the darkness.

8

The chairman of the elder board concluded with a prayer, and then dismissed the meeting.

Charlie Kirby started to get up from his chair and then sat down. "Wait. There's something I need to deal with tonight, something I'm sure you'll hear about—if you haven't already. I don't see any point in waiting for the executive committee to appoint someone to *handle* it."

Charlie looked around the table at eleven pairs of eyes and wondered if they knew. "There's been a development—some mean-spirited accusations—intended to pervert the nature of my business relationship with Sheila Paxton, Thompson Tire's attorney who was killed in the freeway shooting."

"You want to discuss this with the entire group?" Chairman Joe Kennsington said.

Charlie nodded. "I have nothing to hide. Let's get it out in the open. As you know, the city council's decision to bring Thompson Tire to Baxter has been divisive. I didn't realize just how divisive until my son Kevin overheard a disgruntled merchant insinuate there was a sexual relationship between Sheila and me—and that this alleged misconduct caused me to rush the town council to vote in favor of the tire plant. That's completely ridiculous. Clearly, this accusation was designed to smear me."

Joe's eyes moved around the table and then rested on Charlie. "If I'm hearing you correctly, Charlie, you're saying you're innocent."

"My relationship with Sheila was confined to business meetings—period."

"May I ask who made the accusation?"

"Avery Stedman."

Joe gave a slight nod. "The tension between you two goes way back."

"Some people never grow up," Charlie said. "Avery's resented me since high school. He's got some fool notion that I've had everything handed to me and have never had to work for anything."

"You think that's why he made the accusation?"

"That's probably why he reveled in it, but there's more to it. He's seething because the Thompson deal went through. He's convinced the plant will change the culture of the community and run him out of business."

Joe's eyebrows gathered. "But sexual misconduct is a serious accusation. Have you spoken with him about this?"

"Yes, on Saturday. I took Kevin with me to the general store and confronted Avery in the stockroom, in front of Lenny. It got ugly, so I sent Kevin to the car. But Avery refused to budge, even when his dad tried to get him to back off."

"So nothing was resolved?"

Charlie heaved a sigh. "Not a thing. Avery's convinced I'm trying to run him out of business. Says that I sit on my throne and decide what's best for the 'peons,' even though I don't have a clue, and that he's tired of my 'holier-than-thou' attitude. It's a little hard to reason with a guy like that."

"I'm sorry this is happening," Joe said. "Has to be embarrassing. How is Marlene handling it?"

"Not well." Charlie felt his face turn red. "It's partly my fault. I planned to tell her about Avery's allegations on Saturday night after the kids went to bed, but she stayed up to do her Sunday school lesson. After that, I couldn't seem to find the right time to broach the subject. So I decided to wait until Monday night after I got home from the funeral.

"Unfortunately, Marlie had parent-teacher conferences on Monday and was told by one of Kevin's teachers that a classmate of his has been telling everyone he saw me kissing Sheila in the parking lot behind my office building! Of course, that's the first Marlie had heard of it and she was completely humiliated. Kevin's pretty upset, too."

"Who's the classmate?"

"Jeremy Adler. He's the kid who got suspended for vandalizing the gym at the middle school."

"I remember that." Joe leaned forward, his arms folded on the table, and looked intently at Charlie. "What would possess a kid to say something like that? Seems kind of random."

"Who knows?" Charlie said. "Maybe he overheard Avery shooting his mouth off somewhere."

"Did you ask him?" Joe said.

"Not yet. I called his home several times today and got the machine. I left a message for his parents to call me. Regardless of what he *thinks* he saw, it wasn't me in that parking lot."

"Back to Marlene," Joe said. "She's pretty upset?"

"Of course, she is. Who could blame her?"

"Does she believe you?"

Charlie drew a line with his index finger in the condensation on his water glass. "She found Sheila's room key in my sport coat. I know how it sounds, but it's not what you think. Sheila must've dropped it. I found it on the floor next to the conference table, then forgot all about it. Look, I promise you, I didn't have an affair with her. You guys know me. Do you think I would cheat on Marlie?"

"Right now, I'm more worried about what she thinks," Joe said. "Do you know if she's open to talking to the executive committee?"

Charlie shook his head. "I doubt it. Maybe."

"Since you opted to bring this to the elders," Joe said, "is it all right with you if we open this up to questions?"

"Yes. Of course."

Joe moved his eyes around the circle. "Anyone?"

"I have a question," Bart Thomas said. "How are you going to handle this publicly? Ellen will be fair, but KJNX could be your worst nightmare."

"I'm still trying to decide that," Charlie said. "I know I'll be assaulted with questions. It seems the best approach is to be straightforward: Say that my alleged involvement with Sheila is unfounded, that perceptions can be distorted in the throes of anger, and that this is a political ploy to try to negate the Thompson deal."

"But what about the Adler boy?" Jed Wilson said. "How do his actions tie in politically? Aren't his folks in favor of the plant relocation?"

Charlie glanced up at Jed. "Yes, I think they are. But the boy's past misbehavior speaks for itself. His word isn't reliable. He's either lying or mistaken about what he saw."

Bart leaned forward on his elbows. "How does Kevin feel about all this?"

"He's hurting," Charlie said, blinking the stinging from his eyes. "It was pretty humiliating for him at school. But at least we're talking. Kevin's been in on this from the beginning, so it wasn't as big a shock for him as it was for Marlie." Charlie took a sip of water, then cupped his hands around the glass. "I should've never put off telling her. But I had no idea what a mess this would turn out to be. I've never been falsely accused of anything before."

"Any other questions?" Joe said.

Charlie pushed his glass aside and sat with his hands folded on the table, his heart pounding, confident he had revealed exactly what he needed to. There was a long, uncomfortable pause.

"All right, then," Joe said. "Let's pray for Charlie and Marlene. Heavenly Father, You've heard what Charlie has told us here tonight. You know what he means to each man around this table, and what an example he has been to the members of this church family. We ask that You would bless his honesty and openness by bringing healing to his marriage, to his family, and to his good name.

"We pray, too, for Marlene, that You would calm her spirit, and that she would be able to believe the truth about Charlie so that the enemy would not gain a foothold in this marriage. We pray for the children, especially Kevin and Kaitlin, that they would be protected from the lies and the hurt and that their relationship with Charlie would be strengthened.

"Lord, we pray that our community would allow this matter to be handled privately between Charlie and Marlene. We pray also that our church family would not engage in gossip or speculation, but would reach out in love to Charlie and his family with our support and prayers.

"Lord, we also ask that You silence Avery Stedman, Jeremy Adler, and anyone else who would make false accusations against Charlie. Protect him, Lord, in the shadow of the cross. Keep him from evil. It's in the name of Your Son, our Savior Jesus Christ, we pray. Amen."

Joe looked up at Charlie. "This isn't going to be easy. Keep us posted on what's happening. You know we'll be in prayer for you. I'll call Marlene and see if she'll agree to meet with us."

The group got up from the table and began to disperse, each man stopping to encourage Charlie on the way out.

Dennis Lawton lay on the couch in his in-laws' living room, watching TV, his son Bailey asleep in his arms. He heard the front door open and looked up in time to see Jed hang his keys on the hook. "How was the elders' meeting?"

"Good. I always love being with those guys." Jed turned and smiled at the sight of Bailey sleeping. "How long has this little guy been out?"

"Long enough for my arm to go to sleep."

"Where is everyone?"

"Ben's asleep on the bed in your room. Jen and Rhonda are in the kitchen, adding to the picture albums." Dennis laughed. "The twins are only two, and Jen's already filled an entire closet with photographs, negatives, videotapes, and other paraphernalia."

"If she's anything like Rhonda, be glad you built a big house. Anything on the news?"

"Not really." Dennis put the TV on mute. "But I heard some other 'news' that I find upsetting. Did you know someone is accusing Mayor Kirby of sexual misconduct with Sheila Paxton?"

"Says who?"

"Just a rumor going around. Did it come up at the meeting tonight?"

"You know I can't discuss that. But everyone knows there are folks who're mad about the Thompson deal. Maybe one of them mouthed off, hoping to bring Charlie down."

"Really a cheap shot, if you ask me," Dennis said. "Charlie's one of the good guys—a pillar of the community *and* the church. The idea of him cheating on Marlene is nuts."

Jed sat in the overstuffed chair. "Well, if this accusation gains any momentum, Charlie is going to suffer a lot of humiliation—not to mention Marlene and the kids. I don't want to see that happen."

"The poor dead woman can't defend herself either. KJNX could have a real field day with this one."

"Let's hope not... Dennis, didn't you say you and Jen stopped by Lenny and Emma's over the weekend?"

"Yeah, we had lunch with them."

"Did Lenny say anything about the Thompson deal—whether he was happy about it or not?"

"I think he's scared," Dennis said. "I tried to encourage him to prepare for change."

"Was he ugly about it?"

"Not at all. Jed, what's going on?"

"Oh, nothing. I'm just concerned about Charlie, that's all."

Dennis turned off the TV. "I wouldn't waste too much time worrying about him. He's squeaky clean. And a lot more shrewd than a handful of retailers who are living in the past and don't understand the bigger economic picture."

"They may be living in the past, but they have a lot to lose. And they're smarter than you think."

"Sorry, Jed. I didn't mean it the way it sounded. But sometimes people can't see past their own backyard. The city council's decision will prove favorable to everyone in the long run."

"Hmm...let's just hope that includes *Charlie.*"

9

At Monty's Diner, Wednesday morning's newspaper disappeared faster than Leo's blueberry pancakes. Mark Steele stood at the counter behind George Gentry and read over his shoulder.

SHEILA PAXTON'S BOYFRIEND MURDERED
AUTHORITIES LOOKING FOR CONNECTION

Richard Boatman, 36, was found murdered yesterday in a Raleigh suburb, just one day after burying his girlfriend, Sheila Paxton, who was fatally wounded in last Friday's freeway shooting in Atlanta.

Raleigh police are reeling today after yesterday's bloodbath that ended with three dead in the quiet, upscale neighborhood of Haverly Heights.

The grisly events began unfolding early yesterday morning when a cleaning woman reported finding two men shot and killed in an office building. Both victims suffered a single gunshot wound to the head. Police say both victims were armed.

Then late yesterday afternoon, Raleigh police were led to the body of a third victim, this one in Haverly Park, a few blocks from the office building where the two shooting victims were discovered...

Mark read slowly through the lead story, suddenly aware that the morning crowd was engaged in conversation.

"That's one couple that's not battin' a thousand," Rosie Harris said, making her way down the counter pouring refills. "Talk about lousy odds."

"Eerie," Reggie Mason said.

Mort Clary took a bite of pancakes. "Gotta be tied together somehow. Maybe this Boatman fella was her pimp."

"Oh, brother." Hattie Gentry rolled her eyes. "Just when we thought you were coming around."

"Pimp?" George Gentry said. "Mort, are you nuts?"

"Before you go name callin', Georgie, think about it. Maybe this Sheila Paxton was workin' fer Thompson Tire, tryin' ta close deals by usin' her feminine ammunition, if ya git my drift."

"Oh, we got your drift, all right—and it's offensive!" Rosie tapped Mort on the head. "That's about the meanest, stupidest accusation I've ever heard come out of you."

"Hold yer horses, I don't mean nothin' mean by it. But the lady was a looker, and—"

"*Looker*—not hooker." Mark threw a piece of peppermint at Mort. "Big difference."

Rosie pointed her finger at him. "Listen, mister. I resent the implication that Sheila Paxton was some kind of a vamp whose irresistible charms overpowered our defenseless mayor and caused him to make a bad business deal. Mayor Kirby is smarter than that. And the woman can't defend herself. Let her rest in peace."

"Just tryin' ta figure out how they fit together, that's all," Mort said. "You can bet them murders is related."

Reggie blew on his coffee. "Could be just a weird coincidence. Authorities haven't found a connection."

"Maybe they have, Reg. And they just ain't tellin'."

FBI Special Agent Jordan Ellis was taking a bite of an already soggy BLT when his cell phone rang. He washed the mouthful of sandwich down with a gulp of milk and hit the talk button. "This is Jordan."

"Well, Special Agent Ellis. This is a voice from your past."

"Brad? Brad Winston, is that *you?*"

"Hey, you haven't lost your touch. Good shot."

Jordan chuckled. "Let me guess: You're in charge of that mess up in Raleigh."

"Righto. And you're in Atlanta up to your ears in the freeway shooting. What's your spin—are the two are linked?"

"Proving it may be impossible," Jordan said.

"Was that a yes?"

"What's the skinny on Boatman?"

"Same old Jordan. Not going to offer me a crumb till you get something first."

"What do you know about him, Brad?"

"We're digging. He was a CPA. Did well, too. You should see his house and his bank accounts. Can't find anything that would lead us to his family, though. His friends have been cooperative, but when it comes right down to it, no one knows much about him beyond the obvious."

"And with all the media coverage, still no family?"

"Nada. But get this...the other two victims? They were *our* guys."

Jordan rubbed his chin. "Yeah, I figured. We ran up against a brick wall with the girlfriend, too. Went back to her law school and had them dig her college transcript out of archives. Showed she graduated from Ravenhurst College in New Hampshire with a 4.0. So we checked it out. Wanna guess what we found?"

"No record that Sheila Paxton ever went there?"

"You got it."

Brad laughed. "Think we're stuck in our own briar patch?"

"It's got our thumbprints all over it. If she was in the witness protection program, she was effectively erased."

"Well, Jordan, we *do* know how to make them disappear."

"Yeah, but this is one time when I wish we weren't so good."

Ellen Jones picked up her phone and dialed Charlie Kirby's office.

"Mayor Kirby's office."

"Hi Regina. It's Ellen Jones. May I speak with Charlie, please?"

"Of course. Please hold the line."

Ellen glanced out the window and relished the mosaic of fall color lining the street below. She would much rather have been out for a walk than doing what she was about to do.

"Hello, Ellen."

"Hi, Charlie. I trust you made it home from Raleigh without incident?"

"I did. No problem. What's on your mind?"

Ellen lowered her voice. "Charlie...we've known each other a long time. I'm uncomfortable doing this, but I need to ask you to comment on a rumor that's come to my attention."

"Which rumor? The one started by Avery Stedman that I had an affair with Sheila Paxton, or the one where Jeremy Adler says he saw me *making out* with her in the parking lot behind my office building?"

"I'm so sorry to have to even ask, but I felt an obligation to stop the rumor if I can."

"I doubt you can, Ellen. It's like chasing the wind."

"I take it you've been dodging bullets since last we talked?"

"That's putting it mildly. I'll tell you what I told the elders: I did not have a romantic relationship with Sheila Paxton. I saw her in office meetings—period. Avery Stedman is a sore loser and he's turned his anger into a personal vendetta to ruin me."

Ellen twirled her pencil like a baton. "What about the Adler boy. What's that about?"

"I went to his home and spoke first with his parents and then to Jeremy. Though he can't prove it was me he saw with Sheila, he won't recant. Said he'd rather be grounded. You should've seen him: the kid was eating up the attention. But what difference does it make now? The cat's out of the bag, so to speak. Good luck trying to put it back without getting clawed to death."

Ellen got up and shut the door. "You must be sick over this. How's Marlene?"

"Depressed. Can you blame her?"

"How're the older kids handling it?"

"Kaitlin doesn't quite grasp what's happening. Kevin's the hardest hit. No child should have to defend his father's honor. It's infuriating, Ellen. I'm innocent of these allegations."

"Why don't you make a public statement?"

"I shouldn't have to, that's the point."

"If you don't, this may get worse."

"And if I defend myself, it might be construed as covering my tail. What I'd like to do is wring Avery Stedman's neck."

"But you can't."

"I *know* that, Ellen."

She walked over and stood at the window, her eyes resting on Charlie's office building. "So why don't you let me report on this? I'm getting calls anyway. People trust what I print. I can help put a stop to it."

"How?"

"I'll talk to Jeremy Adler and Avery Stedman and find the holes in their allegations. I'll make sure it's reported in a way that's fair to you."

"I don't know...it's hard enough for Marlie knowing the rumors are circulating. But seeing them in print might send her over the edge."

"Charlie, I *have* to address this in some fashion, and preferably before KJNX gets wind of it. Heaven knows what spin they'll put on it."

"You're sweet to offer, Ellen. I hate to put you in such an awkward position."

"Don't worry. That's what I do. Besides, most people in town hold you in high regard. It won't be hard for them to believe the truth."

Charlie hung up the phone and caught a glimpse of dried egg on the window. He remembered an old saying, 'Always tell the truth so you won't have to remember what you said.' He leaned his head back and closed his eyes. He'd been consistent in his story.

How could he admit to Marlie how close he had come to having an affair with Sheila? He had always been careful to guard his heart against that kind of thing. One time he failed. What good would it do for Marlie to know he had wanted another woman? It would devastate her. Women never seem to understand the temptations men have. She'd probably never be able to forgive him. She certainly wouldn't trust him. And probably would never respect him again.

Marlie might come around if he stayed consistent. But could he find peace, knowing he hadn't been completely honest with her?

I didn't do it. That has to mean something. But even as he argued with himself, Charlie knew he was only justifying his thought life. That's where his sin had started. And for all he knew, the only thing that had kept him from acting it out was Sheila's death.

Confess your sins to each other and pray for each other so that you may be healed. The passage from James flooded his soul. Why should he confess his failing to Marlie—or to anyone else? Hadn't he asked the Lord's forgiveness? Hadn't he promised God he would never allow something like this to happen again? That should be enough.

Charlie rubbed his temples, then opened the top drawer and pulled out a half-empty bottle of water and two Extra Strength Excedrin. He popped the pills in his mouth and washed them down, then reached up to his in box and pulled out a stack of today's mail.

Dennis Lawton flipped on the *Six O'Clock News* and flopped on the couch. His twin boys, Bailey and Benjamin, ran giggling through the family room and crawled on top of him.

"Daddy! Daddy! Daddy!"

"Hey, you two, it's time for Dad to watch the news. Why don't you go ask Mommy for a cracker? After dinner, we'll go outside and kick the ball." Dennis smiled at the thought of their short little legs kicking furiously at the soccer ball. "Wait till after dinner and Daddy will play with you."

"Me kick ball!" Bailey shouted.

Benjamin climbed down from the couch, Bailey right behind him, and raced toward the kitchen.

Dennis picked up the remote and turned on the local news.

"Baxter Mayor Charlie Kirby was unavailable for comment following allegations that his clandestine affair with Sheila Paxton, Thompson Tire's corporate attorney killed in last week's Atlanta freeway shooting, caused him to pressure the city council to rush a yes vote on the Thompson Tire relocation.

"Reliable sources have confirmed for KJNX that allegations of sexual misconduct were made at a meeting of the merchant's association last Friday. Merchants who operate businesses on the town square have repeatedly objected to the tire plant and believe the decision was a poor one, and that the mayor's relationship with Ms. Paxton influenced the outcome.

"KJNX has also confirmed that a sixth grader at Baxter Middle School told teachers that on Thursday night of last week, he saw Mayor Kirby with Sheila Paxton in the parking lot behind the city office building, engaged in passionate kissing.

"KJNX is still trying to get Mayor Kirby to respond to these allegations, but as of this hour, the mayor is not talking. Back to you, Monica..."

Dennis put the TV on mute and walked to the kitchen. "Jen, did you hear anything today about this supposed affair Charlie had with Sheila Paxton?"

Jennifer looked up from the kitchen island where she was working. "Everyone at the grocery store was talking about it. Makes me sick. I can't believe it."

"Well, I *don't* believe it."

"You think he's innocent?"

"Don't you?"

"I don't know. Why would a middle schooler make that up? And after the allegations being hurled from the merchant's association, it's hard to know what to think."

"So, why not think he's innocent until proven guilty?"

Jennifer picked up a chicken breast and placed it on the grill. "How can you prove something like that?"

"Honey, that's my point. You can't. But look at Charlie's track record. He's never done anything like this. Plus, he loves the Lord—and his family. He's got too much to lose."

"It's hard for me to believe he'd do it either. But don't you think it's weird that two different allegations have been thrown out there?"

"Doesn't prove anything."

Jennifer placed two more chicken breasts on the grill and added the vegetable skewers. "You're right. Of course it doesn't."

"Your dad seemed somber when he came home from the elder's meeting last night. He's not at liberty to say, but I think the issue came up. He seems worried about what this will do to Charlie and his family."

"Poor Marlene. This must be horrible for her. But what if he *did* do it? Will he have to resign?"

"I imagine he'd opt to resign, Jen. He couldn't be effective if people don't respect or trust him."

"Has he made a statement yet? He hadn't earlier."

Dennis shook his head. "Not according to KJNX. Guess we'll have to wait to see how the newspaper reports it."

"Aren't you supposed to play golf with Charlie on Friday?"

"Yeah. Hope he doesn't cancel. I'd like to hear his perspective on this."

Jennifer took the rice off the stove and turned to Dennis, her eyebrows arched. "Oh, right. Like he's going to tell you if he's guilty."

"We've gotten to know each other pretty well, Jen. I'd like to think he'd trust me if he had something to get off his chest. And by Friday, he may be looking for a friend."

10

On Thursday morning, Mark Steele stood leaning on the wall at Monty's Diner, his arms crossed, his focus on the lively banter coming from the early crowd.

"Admit it," Reggie Mason said. "The mayor's goose is cooked. How much proof do you need?"

George Gentry held up the newspaper and shook his head. "Read the paper, Reg. These are allegations, not proof! Don't believe everything you hear on KJNX."

"Thank heavens the *Daily News* doesn't operate that way," Hattie Gentry said.

"Anyway you cut it, this thing is gettin' complicated," Reggie said. "And the mayor's in the middle."

Mark looked at Rosie Harris and nodded toward a bearded man sitting in the corner booth.

Rosie grabbed her green pad. "Sorry, I didn't see him come in."

Mark heard Mort Clary's voice, and turned his attention back to the counter.

"Wanna know what I think?" Mort said.

Mark shook his head. "I seriously doubt it."

"Let him talk," said George, rolling his eyes. "Words of wisdom await our hearing."

"No need ta be smug, Georgie all-powerful and all-knowin'. I ain't as dumb as ya think."

George turned and stared at Mort over the top of his glasses. "Okay, let's hear it."

"Well, supposin' this Sheila Paxton was workin' fer the feds—"

"You mean the FBI?"

"Yep. Maybe she ain't dead. Maybe the whole thing was phony—set up ta make someone *think* she got knocked off."

"Like who?"

"I ain't got all the answers. I'm still workin' on it."

George rejected the notion with a wave of his hand. "You're chasing the wind."

"Says you."

Rosie put a green sheet on the clip. "Leo, order!" She turned to Mark. "Did I miss anything?"

"Not really. Mort's had a brainstorm." Mark winked at her. "Thinks maybe Sheila was working for the FBI and her death was staged."

"Oh, brother," Rosie said. "Then how does he explain the other five victims? Were they just props?"

Hattie pursed her lips and looked at Mort. "I suppose you think the FBI created a huge traffic jam on the Atlanta freeway so they could make this happen?"

"They do all kinda stuff they ain't never gonna talk about," Mort said.

Liv Spooner stirred her coffee. "And just how do you think that theory ties in with the murders in Raleigh?"

"I said I ain't got it all figured out yet." Mort took a bite of pancakes. "But don't be so sure the feds didn't make it all up."

"Why would they do that?" Rosie said, shaking her head. "And how would they stage all those funerals? They would've had to get thousands of people in on it. The idea's nuts."

The bearded man in the corner booth coughed, his eyes fixed on the newspaper.

"Hey, let's keep our voices down," Mark said, nodding toward the man. "Not everyone can handle all this whining."

The bearded man reread the lead story in the *Baxter Daily News*, then let his eyes rest on the headline: "Allegations Hurled at Mayor

Kirby Unfounded."

"Can I get you anything else?" the waitress said.

"Uh, a little more coffee, thanks." He noticed her name tag. "Rosie, eh? I had a favorite aunt named Rosie."

"You live around here?"

"Just passin' through on my way to Florida. Thought I'd take a day or two and enjoy the leaves. Great color this year."

"I've got a sister in Fort Myers," Rosie said. "Ever been there?"

He shook his head. "Friends in Fort Lauderdale. I'm goin' down to hang out...enjoy a little vacation...soak in a few rays."

Rosie smiled and put his check on the table. "Sounds wonderful. Have a nice time looking at the leaves before you go. This is one of the prettiest autumns on record."

He reached in his jacket pocket and pulled out a diary he had found in a nightstand when he rummaged through Richard Boatman's house. He thumbed through a few pages, then glanced again at the headlines. What did he have to lose?

He downed the last of the coffee, then put the diary back in his pocket. He stood, picked up his check, and walked to the register.

Special Agent Jordan Ellis took a bite of cheeseburger just as his cell phone rang. "This is Jordan."

"It's Brad. Anything new on the Paxton woman?"

"Same brick wall. What about you? Any luck on Boatman?"

"His funeral was today. No family. *Lots* of press. Quite a few friends and business associates. But have I got a tidbit for you—a real shocker."

Jordan switched the phone to his other ear. "Well, spit it out, Brad. I'm listening."

"Seems Richard and Sheila weren't lovebirds after all."

"What do you mean?"

"Richard Boatman was gay."

"How do you know that?"

"A man came to us after the funeral: Pierce Goldman. Says

Richard was well-connected in the gay community—that his relationship with Sheila was just a cover-up for professional reasons."

Jordan shook his head. "Let me get this straight: Boatman and Paxton were just roommates?"

"According to Pierce Goldman. He gave us some names of men Richard's been involved with. We checked them out. They confirmed it."

"So how did Paxton fit into this extended family?"

"I was hoping you could tell me. She died on your turf."

Jordan mused. "Did Goldman say why he revealed this?"

"Yeah, he thinks Boatman's death could be a hate crime."

Jordan tossed his napkin in the trash. "Well, *I'm* starting to hate it. This thing gets more complicated by the minute."

The bearded man walked in the front door of the *Baxter Daily News* building and glanced at the directory. He started down the long hallway, savoring the old-wood smell of the wainscoting, then stopped at the first door and read the words inscribed on the opaque glass:

EDITORIAL OFFICES
ROOM 101

He pushed down on the old-fashioned brass doorknob, then walked inside. He returned the smile of an attractive blonde he guessed to be in her thirties. The rich wood paneling of the reception area reminded him of the Hotel Classico in Chicago.

"Good morning. May I help you?" she said.

"Yeah, I'm Tony English. My wife and I drove up from Hannon to enjoy the foliage trails. She's down shoppin' on the square, and I was wonderin' if it would be possible for me to meet Ellen Jones? I'm a big fan of hers. As long as I'm in town, I'd like to shake her hand."

The blonde smiled and picked up the receiver. "Ellen, there's a gentlemen here from Hannon who would like to meet you...Mr. English...says he's a fan...all right, I'll tell him."

"Mrs. Jones will be with you in a moment. Please have a seat."

The bearded man sat on a high-backed couch, then reached over and picked up a copy of *Time*. He thumbed through it, pretending to be reading. He heard a door open and looked up and saw Ellen Jones walk to the reception desk.

"Mr. English? I'm Ellen Jones." She offered her hand. "How nice of you to stop in."

He shook her hand and studied the woman who drove a white Lexus. Why had she been nosing around after Sheila Paxton's funeral? Did she know anything?

"It's nice to finally shake your hand. My wife and I really enjoy your features and editorials."

"Thank you," Ellen said. "Would you like to take a tour of the building—see the presses?"

He looked at his watch. "I promised my wife I'd pick her up at Slagel's at noon. Wish I'd thought of this earlier, before I piddled the mornin' away at the sporting goods store."

"Well, at least let me show you my office. Every *Daily News* editor for the past fifty years has occupied the same space. I don't think it's changed much in all that time."

"Thanks. I'd like that."

He followed Ellen into her office, then stopped and looked around, taking in everything. "Nice." He noticed her computer. "Guess you'll be doin' a feature on Sheila Paxton. Tragic what happened to her."

Ellen nodded. "Yes, it was."

"Then you're working on it?"

"Truthfully, I doubt I could add anything to what the other newspapers or the networks have reported."

"Get outta town! You run circles around those folks. That's what we like about you. You're real warm. Got a special style."

"Well, thank you. I appreciate your kind words. But Ms. Paxton's unfortunate demise doesn't really seem like Baxter's story."

"Really? After what I read about her and the mayor, seems like it hit real close to home."

"Those allegations are *false*," Ellen said, her voice laced with indignation.

"That's what the mayor said. I wonder if the FBI's buyin' it?"

Ellen's eyes widened. "The FBI? Why would they care? These allegations have nothing to do with Sheila's death."

"Maybe not. On the other hand, *if* Mayor Kirby was involved with her, it's hard tellin' what he knows. And if he's coverin' up an affair, he can't very well spill his guts to the FBI."

He studied Ellen's eyes and her facial expressions. She was plenty interested, all right.

"I've known Charlie Kirby for many years," Ellen said. "He's a man of integrity—always truthful."

He nodded. "Yeah, you're probably right. I get carried away playin' detective. What do I know? I never even met the guy." He turned, his hands in his pockets, and started perusing the numerous certificates on Ellen's wall, hiding the smirk on his face.

A lady's voice came over the intercom. "Ellen, Margie's on line one."

"Thanks." Ellen turned to him. "I need to take that call, Mr. English. It's been a pleasure. Thank you so much for stopping by."

"Nice meetin' you, too."

The bearded man shook her hand and went out to the reception area and left the same way he'd come in. If Ellen Jones knew anything about Sheila, she never let on. But if she hadn't questioned the mayor's truthfulness, maybe now she would. And it might cause her to dig just a little deeper.

Charlie Kirby sat at his desk, going over his speech for next week's Rotary Club luncheon, when he heard the intercom click on.

"Mr. Mayor, line one's for you," Regina said. "A Mr. English. He says Ellen Jones suggested he call you."

"Thank you." He read the last line of his speech and then

picked up the phone. "Hello, Mr. English. This is Mayor Kirby. How can I help you?"

"Well, Mr. Mayor. How nice to hear your voice."

Charlie tried to put the name with the voice and drew a blank.

"Tryin' to remember where you know me from? Not to worry, Charlie, my man. First things first. We have something in common."

"Excuse me?"

"The lovely Sheila Paxton."

"What about her?"

"We both feel *really* bad about what happened to her."

Charlie tried to hide his annoyance. "Everyone does. It was tragic. My secretary said Ellen Jones suggested you call?"

"I was glad you made it to the cemetery. I noticed you stayed and talked to Richard."

"Who are you?" Charlie said. "And how does this concern you?"

"Oh, it concerns me plenty. You see, I'd been lookin' for Sheila for a long, long time. Imagine my shock when I saw her face on the news. Then, I go to pay my respects and, lo and behold, Richard shows up at her funeral. Funniest thing: I'd been lookin' for him, too. Is that not a coincidence?"

"Is there a point to your call?" Charlie said. "I didn't know Richard. Sheila was a business associate."

"Business associate? That's not what *I* hear."

"I don't have to listen to this. I'm ending this conversation—"

"*Wait.* Better hear me out."

Charlie paused and held the receiver to his ear. "Get to the point, Mr. English. My patience is wearing thin."

The bearded man stood in front of the bathroom mirror and started cutting his dark beard. When it was as short as he could cut it with scissors, he lathered his face and began to shave the thick stubble. When he finished, he looked into the mirror and smiled, amazed at how different he looked with only a mustache.

He took off his glasses and opened the container of disposable contacts, then carefully placed one contact on his right eye and one on his left. He blinked a few times and then studied his reflection. Blue eyes...a nice twist for an Italian boy.

He patted some aftershave on his face and winced until the stinging stopped.

He walked to the table in the corner of the room where he had laid out the photographs he stole from Boatman. He picked up a sepia print of a man he hadn't seen since he was eighteen. He pounded his fist on the table. "Where are you, you lousy—"

There was a knock on the door and he jumped, his hand over his heart. "Yeah, who is it?"

"I've got a feather pillow for you, sir," said a female voice.

He opened the door and took the pillow from a lady in a maid's uniform. "Much better. Thanks."

"Did you get a map of the foliage trails, sir?"

"Sure did. I'm about to take a drive around the lake. It's real pretty out here. Never stayed at a lodge before."

She smiled. "Enjoy your stay."

He closed the door, tossed the pillow on the bed, and sat at the table. He sifted through the photographs until he found a snapshot of a husband, wife, and two kids—a boy and a girl. Mary Angelina couldn't have been more than ten or eleven in this shot. But there were those eyes...those dark, provocative eyes.

When he had seen her face plastered across the TV—the victim of some random freeway shooting—he couldn't get over the uncanny resemblance. He followed his hunch all the way to the cemetery. But the last person he expected to see there was Vincent!

He snickered. Vincent's murder must've frosted the old man. He studied the photograph and tried to imagine how the years would've aged the man's face. "I'm gonna track you down, Risotto, one way or the other. I'm afraid my friend the mayor's gonna wish he'd never gazed into your little girl's eyes."

II

Charlie Kirby walked in from the garage and laid his brief-case on the counter. He heard tiny footsteps racing toward him and turned in time to catch his youngest daughter, who jumped into his arms.

"Hi, sweetie."

The child squealed with delight, her arms tightly around him. He savored the moment.

"Dinner's almost ready, and Kaitlin's dance recital's in an hour," Marlene said. "You need to talk to Kevin first."

"Why, what happened?"

"You'll see."

Charlie kissed his daughter and put her feet on the floor. "Mommy wants me to talk to Kevin right now."

His daughter put her tiny hand around his finger and led him toward the hallway. "Kebbin gots a boo-boo. He cwying."

Charlie stroked her cheek. "You wait with Mommy." He walked down the hall to Kevin's room and knocked on the door. "Son, may I come in?... Kevin?" Charlie knocked again and cracked the door. "Kevin, I'd like to talk with you for a minute."

Charlie went in, pulled the computer chair close to the bed, then sat and began to rub Kevin's shoulder. "I know you're awake. Would you turn this way so I can see you? I hate talking to your back."

Kevin turned over on his side, facing Charlie, his eyes clamped shut.

"Better get some ice on that shiner. How'd it happen?"

"Doesn't matter."

"It does to me," Charlie said. "Were you fighting?"

"What do you think?"

"Son, please don't answer my question with a question. I'm not the enemy here. I'm trying to help."

"I don't need any help."

"Apparently you do."

Kevin opened his eyes. "I punched Jeremy Adler in the nose and he punched me back. We're even."

"You know I hate fighting. Never solves anything."

"Made *me* feel better."

"Did it?"

Kevin sighed, a tear rolling onto his pillow.

"I assume you were arguing about what he said about me?"

"He's a liar," Kevin said. "A big fat liar."

"Maybe he's just mistaken, son. You need to forgive him and go on. This is going to eat you alive."

Kevin glared at Charlie. "Look who's talking."

"Don't speak to me in that tone of voice."

"I don't see you and Mom forgiving Jeremy or Mr. Stedman or KJNX—not even each other. You slept in the recliner again last night."

Charlie arched his eyebrows. "You don't see Mom and me punching anyone either. The fighting has to stop." Charlie paused for half a minute. "I guess forgiveness is going to take time for all of us. I'm sorry you're caught in the middle. I know things at school are tough."

"It's all *your* fault."

"Son, I didn't start the rumors. And I didn't have an affair with Sheila Paxton. How is this my fault?"

Kevin shrugged, tears spilling onto his pillow. "Then why won't Mom forgive you?"

Charlie leaned over and pulled Kevin into his arms and let him sob.

"We'll get through this, son. Hang in there with me. God will get us through it."

But even as he said the words, Charlie knew his deception was a stumbling block to his prayers. He couldn't remember a time when God seemed so far away—or Marlie so detached.

And after being contacted by the mysterious Mr. English, he was in so deep he had no idea how to get out. The man seemed obsessed with finding Sheila's parents. Charlie finally convinced him that he didn't know anything about Sheila's background. But English would not be dissuaded. He said that unless Charlie convinced Ellen Jones to use her resources to dig until she found out where Sheila's parents are, he'd make sure KJNX got its hands on Sheila's diary.

Then English read him selected entries going back several months. What Sheila had written about her "affair" with Charlie made him blush—and made him angry. None of it was true! Yet Sheila must have written it because so many elements about the meetings with Thompson Tire were accurate.

Charlie felt tightness in his chest. He dreaded the thought that *anyone* would read what was in the diary—especially Marlene and Kevin. After all that had happened, how could he ever convince either of them Sheila had fantasized the entire affair?

Ellen Jones set a big bowl of pasta in the center of the kitchen table. "Be careful, it's hot."

"Mmm, what kind are we having?" Guy Jones said. "I see shrimp in there...and mushrooms."

She smiled. "All kinds of goodies: penne pasta with red, green, and yellow peppers; some zucchini; yellow squash; chopped onion; a little garlic; and some crushed red pepper. I tasted it. It's good."

"Smells wonderful."

Ellen sat down and silently blessed the food while she put two big scoops of pasta in a bowl and handed it to Guy, then filled another bowl and set it in front of her. "I'm famished. I forgot to eat lunch."

"How'd you do that?" he asked.

"A young man named Tony English came to the office to meet me. He told my receptionist that he was in town with his wife to see the leaves and just wanted to shake my hand, that he was a fan."

"How flattering."

She nodded. "Yes, it was. So, naturally, I went out to meet him. He mentioned that he was eagerly awaiting a feature on Sheila Paxton. I explained I hadn't planned to write one, that it wasn't Baxter's story. His entire demeanor seemed strange after that."

"Strange how?"

Ellen picked up the Parmesan cheese and sprinkled it over her pasta. "I can't explain it. But he manipulated the conversation and seemed to imply that Charlie might be guilty of the allegations and wondered if the FBI was buying his story."

"Why would the FBI care?" Guy asked.

"That's what I said. Mr. English said *if* Charlie was covering up an affair, it's hard to say what he might know, but he couldn't very well 'spill his guts to the FBI.'"

Guy took a sip of water. "Charlie says he's innocent."

"You say that like you don't believe it."

"Truthfully, I don't care."

"Oh come on, Guy, how could you *not* care? He's a married man with seven children."

"And he loves Marlene and those seven children. Whatever he may or may not have done is none of my business." Guy wiped his mouth with a napkin. "Look, honey. Men are wired differently than women. They have to fight temptations all the time. Women don't have a clue."

"Are you saying *you're* tempted to get involved with other women?"

"I'm saying opportunity knocks. I have to choose whether or not I'm going to open the door."

Ellen stopped chewing and stared at him. "*You've* never opened the door...have you?"

He smiled, then picked up her hand and kissed it. "Never."

"Why not?"

"Because I love you...and don't want to face what Charlie's going through. Besides, Madam Editor, you'd hang me out to dry."

"But you're tempted?"

"You're going to get paranoid about this, aren't you?"

"I'm not paranoid...just surprised, that's all. You've never led me to believe you might be attracted to other women."

"Ellen, men are attracted to females period. It has nothing to do with anything. A guy can love his wife, love his kids, and still find himself battling the attraction to someone else. Like I said, it's the way we're wired."

Ellen wiped the lipstick off her glass. "Well, I don't like it."

"It's not terribly convenient for us either."

"Do you think Charlie strayed? Be honest."

"How should I know? But I'm not going to stone him if he did. I'm sure he loves Marlene and the kids. He's a decent man. People make mistakes. Besides, everyone at that church of yours talks about forgiveness. Seems like a good time to walk your talk."

Ellen mused for a moment. She put down her fork and looked at Guy. "Do you suppose Mr. English's visit was deliberately staged to make me question Charlie's innocence?"

"Don't know. I wasn't there."

"Will you stop being so black-and-white, Counselor, and *speculate*?"

Guy half smiled and reached for the saltshaker. "I love it when you get passionate. Okay...it's possible Mr. English is opposed to the tire plant and took the opportunity to help sink Charlie's ship."

"Or?"

"Or he could be a fan who just wanted to shake your hand, and you got off on a rabbit track."

Ellen sighed. "Why do I do this? Why can't I just accept something at face value and go with it?"

"On the other hand, imagine how boring life would be without you playing Columbo."

Ellen smiled sheepishly. "You think I'm making too much it."

"Honey, I don't know. But give poor Charlie the benefit of the doubt unless you *know* differently. He's a decent man, whether or not he slipped up."

Charlie sat in his leather recliner, thumbing through the pages of *Fortune* magazine. Marlie had already shut the bedroom door. He was going to be spending another night in his study.

Had his life gotten this complicated just because he entertained the thought of sleeping with Sheila Paxton? Okay, he had kissed her—a flirt with temptation—but nothing he'd done was bad enough to warrant what was happening to him.

Lord, help me. Show me what to do. But Charlie had no sense of God's presence. His prayers had been stale for weeks.

Should he go to the police and tell them about the phone call? Should he involve Ellen Jones? Could he handle it if English followed through on his threat and made sure Sheila's diary ended up at KJNX? Charlie felt a twinge of nausea. He put the magazine down and turned off the lamp.

What was in Sheila's past that would cause a man to go to this extreme to track down her parents? Had her death been a murder? Charlie didn't want to be this close to it.

He reached down and pulled the afghan up to his neck. All he wanted was to go to sleep and forget it for a while.

The mustached man ordered a pizza, then flopped on the bed, his hands behind his head, and stared at the knotty pine paneling in his room at the Heron Lake Lodge.

His stomach growled, and his thoughts drifted back to Chicago, to the house on Marquette Road, and family dinners at the long table, where Mama would serve all his favorite meals. He closed his eyes and could almost taste warm oregano bread oozing with garlic butter...

"Giorgio, you want some more?" Mama would say. "You eat like your papa but you looka like a string bean."

His sisters laughed with delight as Mama filled his plate and he downed a third helping as if he had a hole in his leg.

"Eat hearty, Giorgio," Papa said. "You gonna be strong like your ol' man."

But one night Papa only picked at his food, and Giorgio sensed something was terribly wrong.

"I'm having seconds," Giorgio said. "If you don't hurry up, I'm gonna eat yours, too."

Mama kicked Giorgio under the table. She put her finger to her lips and shook her head.

"What'd I say?" Giorgio turned to Papa. "What's going on? Why are you so quiet?"

Papa looked up, his eyes heavy with sadness, and gazed deep into Giorgio's eyes. "I have to testify against Spike Risotto, or go to prison. That's the story."

Mama's lip quivered. Tears escaped down her cheeks.

Papa looked down at his plate. "You don't need me to spell it out."

A few days later, while the family was seated around the dinner table, someone kicked in the door, and deafening gunfire filled the room. Giorgio dropped to the floor and crawled under the table. He threw his body over two of his sisters. Everyone was screaming. He peeked out and saw blood splattered on the wall. Mama weeping. Papa dead...

Giorgio opened his eyes, his heart pounding, and swung his legs over the side of the bed. He put his face in his hands, and suddenly he felt vulnerable, exposed. He got up and splashed cold water on his face.

Spike Risotto never went to prison for gunning down Papa. Instead, the feds got Risotto to rat on the kingpin, then made him and his family disappear. But by some twist of fate, Mary Angelina and Vincent had finally surfaced. They had to have left a trail somewhere!

Giorgio would lean hard on the mayor to pressure Mrs. Jones into finding that trail. And if that didn't work? Giorgio twisted the coarse hairs of his mustache. The diary wasn't his only trump card.

12

C harlie Kirby walked in his office and laid his briefcase on his desk. He noticed his window had been washed. Outside, the Friday morning sky was streaked with blazing pink.

He checked the coffee pot to be sure Regina had it ready to go, and then turned it on.

He had hardly slept. English had given him until 6:00 P.M. to agree to lean on Ellen, or KJNX would get the diary. He shuddered at the thought.

Charlie sat at his desk. He took out his Palm Pilot and looked at today's itinerary. He had a city council meeting at eight o'clock, a ribbon cutting at nine-forty-five, and a conference call at ten-thirty. But his afternoon was free. He had agreed to play golf with Dennis Lawton and two big shots from the Rotary Club. Tee time was eleven-thirty. He wondered if he had the energy to swing a club.

He looked through his phone messages and noticed that the two men from the Rotary Club had canceled. Probably didn't want to be seen with him right now. Just as well. Golf with Dennis sounded relaxing. The media wouldn't be allowed on the course. Maybe he could forget about this whole ugly mess for a few hours.

Charlie's cell phone rang. What now? He had come to the office early for a little peace and quiet. He opened his briefcase, grabbed the phone, and pushed the talk button.

"Hello."

"Good morning, Charlie. This is your friend Mr. English, reminding you that the deadline is 6:00 P.M. By the way, I stayed up half the night reading the diary. You're quite a man."

"I told you, she made it up. I wasn't involved with Sheila."

"Right. I remember you said that. The fact is, Sheila says you *were,* and I've got it all right here. And if the media gets a hold of her diary, they'll have a field day. I can make all this go away if you get Ellen Jones to do some digging and find out where Sheila's parents are. People would tell her all kinds of stuff, if she was doing a feature story."

Charlie switched the phone to his other ear. "What if it's not possible to find the information you're asking for?"

"You better hope it is." *Click.*

Giorgio hung up the pay phone at Miller's Market, got back in his car, and hit the steering wheel with his palms. He hated having to rely on other people! But this was the break he needed. He'd exhausted every source he could think of, yet in eighteen years had never gotten to first base in his search for Risotto. Maybe the mayor *didn't* know anything—but he had the clout to get the Jones woman working on it, and the incentive to keep the details of his sleazy affair out of the news. It was worth a shot.

In the meantime, Giorgio could keep the feds at arm's length. If they figured out he had killed Vincent and the two agents, they would push his name even higher on the FBI's wanted list. That's the last thing he needed right now.

Dennis Lawton shut the rear door of his new Land Rover, then picked up his golf clubs and walked to the pro shop. He didn't see Charlie's name on the ledger. He signed in, then went outside and stood for a few minutes under the ivy-covered trellis. He glanced at his watch: 11:25.

He went in the snack bar, but didn't see Charlie there either. He ordered a diet Coke and sat where he could watch the door. What kind of shape would Charlie be in after the bad press he'd gotten all week? Dennis was surprised he hadn't canceled.

He looked around at the pastors who were starting to gather for their Friday afternoon ritual. It couldn't have been a more beautiful day. The sun felt warm, the air crisp. And the autumn color was at its peak.

"Sorry I'm late. Hectic morning."

Dennis looked up into Charlie's face and noticed the ridges on his forehead. "Glad you made it. Who's playing with us?"

"They had to cancel. It's just you and me."

"Okay. Walk or ride?" Dennis said.

"Do you mind walking? I could use the exercise."

As they left the snack bar, Dennis was aware of the stares.

"You sure you're up to this?" Dennis said. "I'll understand if you want to bug out."

Charlie shook his head. "It's the one thing I've looked forward to all week."

Dennis smiled and patted Charlie on the back. "Me, too. Let's get after it."

Giorgio stood in the woods, binoculars held tightly to his eyes, and watched Mayor Kirby and his golfing buddy walk down the eighteenth fairway. Charlie looked beat. And it didn't appear as though the two had said much since they teed off. He doubted the mayor was going to spill his guts about their little deal.

He lowered the binoculars and let them hang from his neck, then emptied the last of the M&M's into his hand and popped them into his mouth.

Giorgio wasn't about to be derailed. Though he'd had nothing to do with Mary Angelina's death, Spike Risotto didn't know that. And after Giorgio put a bullet in Vincent's head, and left a calling card on the poor sap's back, he knew Risotto would figure out who did it—and wonder if he was next. "*Nessun posto da nascondersi*, Risotto!"

Giorgio laughed, and headed back to the road where he had parked the car.

Dennis sat with Charlie in the clubhouse dining room and downed the last of a Perrier. They had been having such an enjoyable afternoon; he was reluctant to bring up Charlie's situation.

"Still can't believe I shot a seventy-nine." Dennis said. "Must be this great weather."

Charlie nodded. "I did better than I thought I would. An eighty-four is certainly respectable, at least for me. Thanks for a much-needed diversion."

Dennis started to say something and didn't, then decided to. "Charlie, how are you doing—really?"

"Oh, I'm dodging a few bullets, but I'll live." Charlie took his straw and pushed the ice around in his glass. "Who am I kidding? I'm terrible. This has been the worst week of my life."

"Yeah, I figured. I've been praying for you."

"Thanks, I'm not doing very well in that department either."

"Probably hard to feel spiritual when the fiery darts are flying. I'm praying you've got your shield up, though."

Charlie glanced up at him. "I don't even know who the enemy *is* anymore."

"That doesn't sound good."

"There's some weird stuff happening, Dennis. And, as the saying goes, 'it's lonely at the top.'"

"You need to talk to *someone*."

Charlie bit his lip. "I can handle it."

"Yeah, I can tell by looking at you you're the picture of peace."

"It's complicated, Dennis. It's hard to talk about it."

"Hey, I was a Class A rounder till I had the boys," Dennis said. "There's nothing you could tell me that I haven't already heard—or done myself."

Charlie gave him a questioning look. "You think I'm guilty? I'm not!"

"I believe you. But being accused has to be painful. If you need to unload, I'm willing to listen. Are you even sleeping?"

"Off and on. In my recliner. Alone."

"Marlene's not speaking to you?"

Charlie lifted his eyebrows. "Polite conversation geared around the kids. That's it."

"Have you taken this to the elders?"

Charlie nodded. "Tuesday night. I told them the allegations are false. Avery Stedman's ticked off about the tire plant and would love to see me resign. The Adler boy's got a history of behavioral problems." Charlie looked intently at Dennis. "Just so we're clear, I didn't have *any* sexual contact with Sheila Paxton. I swear it."

"I believe you, Charlie; take it easy."

"Sorry. I'm just so tired of having to defend myself."

"You don't have to say anything if you don't want to," Dennis said. "But I'm here if you need me. I want you to know that. Truthfully, you look like you could use a friend."

Charlie glanced over at the waitress taking an order at the table next to them. "No one in his right mind would get close to me right now. There's more to this situation than anyone knows about—much more."

"I thought as Christians we were supposed to bear one another's burdens."

Charlie paused, then looked up at Dennis, his eyes full of fear. "This one seems almost too big for God."

Special Agent Jordan Ellis sat at his computer going over the case notes on the freeway shooting. Earlier concerns that Congressman Landis had been targeted were ruled out.

Jordan had interrogated the shooter, Samuel Slover, a mental case who thought he lived inside a video game. The guy was completely out of touch with reality, incapable of targeting Landis or Sheila Paxton or anybody else.

Yet Paxton's and Richard Boatman's deaths were connected somehow. Jordan clicked open the Boatman case files and read them again. His senses told him Boatman had been in the witness protection program. So, why didn't anyone in the Raleigh field office know about it? He had a feeling the two dead agents had all the answers.

The shooter had to be a pro. Must've nabbed Boatman, hauled him to the park, got what he could out of him, and then executed him. Same gun. This case had Mob written all over it.

Jordan scrolled down and stopped at the message written on the back of Boatman's shirt: *Nessun posto da nascondersi.* Italian for "no place to hide."

He leaned back in his chair, his hands behind his head. Somebody sent a serious threat. Why wasn't Special Agent Winston beefing up the effort to find out who?

Charlie glanced at his watch: 5:05. He pulled into the garage, got out of the car, and hurried to the door. He stepped into the kitchen and almost bumped into Marlene.

"Leslie just arrived," Marlene said. "Why didn't you tell *me* you called and asked her to babysit? Do you have any idea how awkward it—"

"We need to talk."

"Charlie, I—"

"It's urgent, Marlie." He gently took her arm. "It can't wait. Are you ready?"

"Let me tell her we're leaving. When shall I say we'll be back?"

"I don't know. Tell her to order pizza and put it on my tab."

Charlie felt light-headed and wondered if he'd have the courage to go through with it.

Marlene came back with a sweater. "All right, I'm ready. Where are we going?"

"I don't know yet. I've got a lot to tell you. And not a lot of time."

Dennis Lawton walked in the side door of Cornerstone Bible Church. He walked down the center aisle and slid into the front pew. The only sound he heard was the beating of his heart. He bowed his head for a moment, and then looked up at the cross-shaped stained glass window that rose to the ceiling behind the pulpit. He remembered the first time he ever saw it. He didn't have a clue who Jesus was—or why he needed Him. Dennis had been running from God, running from his responsibilities to Jennifer and the twins—and running from his past.

A lot had happened since then. Jed Wilson got him involved with the men of FAITH. Through their acceptance, counsel, and example, he eventually had the desire to change. He accepted Christ, fell in love with Jennifer and his sons, and walked out of the sexual bondage of his past—a free man.

He joined the church and had never looked back on his sordid past. He had moved on with life, striving to grow in God, inspired by the example of men like Charlie Kirby, whom he considered to be a pillar of the church and the community. A family man. A rock. Dennis had assumed Charlie had it all together. But after Charlie admitted what almost happened with Sheila, Dennis realized that Charlie was as vulnerable to sexual temptation as he was.

Lord, I was guilty of much more than Charlie even thought about. He's such a good man. Please help him dig out of this hole. He's been lying to himself and he knows that now. Do what You need to do in his heart. Help him to be honest with Marlene. But please don't let this destroy them. Please don't let Satan have the victory in this.

Dennis blinked the stinging from his eyes, remembering what it felt like to be desperate. *Lord, if what's in that diary is revealed, lots of people will get hurt. The desire of my heart is that You'd prevent that from happening. But if You allow it, please use this to help Charlie and Marlene grow—and all of us who care about them. I ask this in Jesus' Name.*

Dennis sat for a few minutes and looked around the beautiful old church. This place was home. And the love of this church family had felt like the Father's arms around him ever since he became a Christian.

He rose to his feet and looked up at the stained glass cross. You forgave me so much, Lord. I'm going to stand by Charlie through this, no matter how ugly it gets. Give me the wisdom to help him any way I can.

13

Charlie Kirby turned onto Lake View Drive and drove up the winding road. He slowed at the family's favorite picnic spot, relieved to see no one else there. He pulled the Navigator into the gravel parking area, turned off the motor, and glanced at his watch: 5:25.

He sat staring out the windshield, trapped in silence, aware that Marlene hadn't said a word since they left home. How could he tell her? And yet, how could he not?

"There's no easy way to do this," Charlie said. "Please hear me out. I'm not going to make excuses. I'm in real trouble."

Marlene glanced over at him and then looked down at her hands folded in her lap.

"What I told you before was true: I never had an affair with Sheila. But—"

"Oh, please," Marlene said. "Either get real with me or take me home. You had the woman's room key, for heaven's sake."

"Please, just hear me out. I didn't tell you the whole story before."

"Which means you lied."

"I admit I was attracted to her. But I didn't want to be. It's not like I asked to be tempted."

"Of course not. The devil made you do it."

"I didn't *do* anything—except kiss her. She initiated it. I wish I could say I resisted, but I didn't."

"So Jeremy Adler *did* see you! You lied about that, too?"

"I was scared, Marlie. This looks so much worse than it was."

"Why did you have her room key?"

"I walked her to her car after Thursday night's meeting. She was all over me before I realized what was happening. We kissed. I admit that. But I pushed her away and said it was wrong. She laughed and said I wasn't the adventuresome type, then dropped her room key in my sport coat pocket. She said something about hating to sleep alone, that she wasn't the type to kiss and tell. Then she drove off."

Marlene folded her arms, her eyes fixed on the dashboard. "Why didn't you just give back the key and say no?"

"I've asked myself that question a hundred times. I don't know."

"You wanted to sleep with her, that's why!"

"I thought about it. I won't deny it. But I didn't, and that's the truth."

"Then why did Avery accuse you of having an affair *days* before Jeremy Adler said anything?"

Charlie shrugged. "He's had a grudge against me since high school. I think he just mouthed off because he was mad about the tire plant, then started to revel in it once the rumor mill got a hold of it."

"And why not? Heaven knows you supplied all the ammunition they needed!"

"I can't tell you how sorry I am. I never meant for this to happen." Charlie blinked the moisture from his eyes and glanced at his watch. "There's something else I need to tell you."

"I can hardly wait."

Charlie clasped his hands together to keep them from shaking. "A Mr. English called my office day before yesterday. He said we had something in common: Sheila Paxton. He said he'd been looking for Sheila for a long time, then saw her face on the news and went to her burial, shocked to see Richard—that he'd been looking for him, too. He also said he'd seen me at the cemetery talking to Richard. Everything the guy said seemed intrusive. I resented that he'd been spying on me. I started to hang up. But then he dropped a bomb."

Charlie turned and looked at Marlene, wondering if he could

get the words out. "He's got Sheila's diary. Apparently, during the months I worked with her on the Thompson deal, she wrote some pretty explicit details about an affair she supposedly had with me—"

"*What?*" Marlene glared at him.

"Honey, it's all fantasy. I swear it! I've told you everything. We kissed one time. That's it."

"Why would a woman like her fantasize about having an affair? She could've had any man she wanted!" Marlene began to cry. "I don't believe you, Charlie. God help me, I don't! You were sleeping with both of us! The diamond ring you wanted to buy me for our fifteenth...that entire song and dance was so I wouldn't suspect anything, wasn't it?"

"No, I—"

"I worked hard to look nice. I really did. After each baby, I got back to a size ten. But I can't do anything about the stretch marks." She put her hand to her mouth.

"Marlie, it's not—"

"Your sudden commitment to getting fit...your new hairstyle...all that was for *her*. How could I have been so blind?" Marlene put her face in her hands and started sobbing. "I've loved you with all my heart, Charlie! We've had seven wonderful children. When did that stop mattering?"

Charlie pressed his thumb and index finger to his eyes. "It matters, Marlie. It means *everything*. I'm so sorry. I'd give anything if I could go back and do things differently..." His voice failed.

Charlie turned away, afraid he would lose it. He felt more ashamed than he could have imagined. Above the sound of Marlie's crying, he heard the whistle of the six o'clock train from Parker. His pulse began to race.

"Honey, you need to hear the rest of this. I have a really bad feeling about this Mr. English. He's obsessed with finding Sheila's parents but won't say why. I finally convinced him I don't know anything about her background. But he won't drop it. He's pressuring me to get Ellen to use her contacts to find out where they are."

"You're not obligated to help him."

Charlie sighed. "If I don't agree to cooperate by six o'clock, he's threatened to give the diary to KJNX."

Marlene leaned back on the seat and rolled her head from side to side, tears streaming down her face. "Charlie, what have you done? KJNX will ruin you." She reached for a fresh Kleenex and wiped the mascara from under her eyes. "Why does this man need you to play detective? Can't he just hire a private investigator?"

"I asked him that, but he never gave me a straight answer. He's trying to use me because he thinks I've got no choice but to cooperate."

Marlene blew her nose. "He's got a point."

"I don't trust him. Who's to say he'd give me the diary even if I cooperated? I'm not going to be blackmailed."

Charlie's cell phone rang. Marlene jumped.

"That's probably him." Charlie glanced at his watch. "It's six o'clock." He put the cell phone on the dash, then reached over and covered her hand with his. "I'm not going to help him, Marlie. I've told you the truth. I'm not running from this anymore."

Giorgio stood at a payphone, the receiver to his ear.

You have reached Charlie Kirby. Please leave a message…beep…

He hung up and redialed, and let it ring until the recording clicked on. He paced on the sidewalk. Did Charlie think he was bluffing? Five minutes later he tried again and got the recording. He slammed down the receiver. "Bad move, Mr. Mayor."

Charlie stood leaning against the file cabinet in Police Chief Aaron Cameron's office, his legs crossed at the ankles, his hands in his pockets. "Isn't there some kind of law that would prohibit KJNX from revealing the contents of the diary?"

"Do you know for a fact KJNX has the diary?" Aaron said.

"No, but English sounded like a follow-through kind of guy. I don't think he was bluffing."

"The sheriff will be here in a minute," Aaron said. "Let's get his spin on this. It's a little out of my league." He turned to Marlene. "Can I get you some more coffee, Mrs. Kirby?"

"No, I'm fine. Thank you." She glanced up at Charlie and then looked away.

There was a knock on the door. Sheriff Hal Barker came in, took off his Stetson, shook hands with everyone, and then sat next to Aaron. "Start at the beginning. I need to know everything *you* know."

Charlie sat in the chair next to Marlene and told the story again—about his attraction to Sheila, his one indiscretion, and the phone calls from Mr. English.

Hal leaned forward, his elbows on his knees, slowly moving the brim of his Stetson in a clockwise motion. "Charlie, you said you never saw the guy. Did Ellen?"

"I don't know. I never asked her."

"Didn't you follow up with Ellen after English called you?"

"No. After he told me about the diary, I was afraid to even broach the subject with Ellen. I didn't want to set her curiosity in motion."

"I understand," Hal said. "But I think it's time to ask Ellen what she knows."

Charlie nodded. "All right. Let's get her on the phone."

Charlie folded a piece of computer paper and started fanning himself. "Is it warm in here—or is it me?"

"I don't think the heat's on," Aaron Cameron said. "You want something cold to drink?"

"Okay, thanks."

Aaron got up and looked in his small refrigerator. "I've got diet Coke and regular Orange Crush."

"Diet Coke," Charlie said.

"Anybody else?

Ellen Jones shook her head. "Nothing for me."

"No, thank you," Marlene said.

"Sheriff?"

Hal Barker wrote something on a yellow pad. "No, I'm fine. Let's get back to Mr. English. Ellen, can you describe him?"

"He was a few inches taller than I. Stocky. Dark hair. Dark eyes. Prominent nose. Short beard. Glasses. I'd guess him to be in his mid to late thirties. Oh, and he had a slight accent. Wisconsin, Michigan—something like that."

"Besides the beard, any distinguishing features?"

"His eyes were intense. Like I told you earlier, few people make me squirm, but he did. He seemed to be searching my thoughts and trying to stay a step ahead of everything I said."

Aaron took a sip of Orange Crush. "Did you suggest he contact Charlie?"

"No. Why would I do that?" Ellen twirled her pencil over and over like a baton. "What's going on?"

Aaron looked at Charlie. "You want to fill her in?"

Charlie got up and leaned against the wall, his hands in his pockets. He started at the beginning and told Ellen about the phone calls, Mr. English's obsession with locating Sheila's parents, and his threat to give the diary to KJNX if Charlie didn't cooperate.

"Good heavens," Ellen said.

"The diary's either a fabrication or a fantasy," Charlie said. "I didn't have an affair with Sheila. I know the deck is stacked against me, but I'm telling the truth."

"If KJNX gets their hands on that diary, it won't matter," Ellen said. "You know how they operate. What did you tell him?"

"I didn't," Charlie said. "He gave me until six o'clock tonight to make up my mind. I talked it over with Marlie. There was no way I was going to let this man blackmail me."

"And after I heard Charlie's story," Aaron said, "I got Hal in on it. Then we called you."

Ellen sighed. "I'm so sorry this is happening."

"Can KJNX reveal what's in the diary?" Charlie asked. "Even if it's untrue?"

Ellen looked at him, her expression somber. "You're a public figure, Charlie. If the diary's authentic, they have a very long leash."

14

Mark Steele stood near the east wall of windows at Monty's Diner and watched the morning sun spread like warm butter across the blue-and-white checkered floor. Saturday's customers weren't reading the newspaper. And gossip was stacking up faster than dirty dishes.

"Tried ta tell ya there was hanky-panky." Mort Clary laughed his wheezy laugh. "But ya negged me just like always. One of these days, you'll learn ta respect my instincts."

"I wonder who turned over the diary?" Reggie Mason said.

"The whole thing makes me sick." Rosie walked down the counter, pouring coffee refills. "I've always thought the world of Mayor Kirby."

"He's a politician, ain't he?" Mort said. "Can't trust none of 'em."

"Will you knock it off?" George Gentry blew on his coffee. "It's none of our business if the mayor slipped up. This is between him and the missus."

"Oh, like integrity doesn't mean anything?" Liv Spooner said.

"I suppose it would if he had any." Mort stifled his snickering.

"For all we know KJNX made it up." Hattie Gentry sighed. "Since when can they be trusted to tell the truth?"

"Yeah, but this'd be slander," Reggie said. "I know they exaggerate sometimes, but they couldn't report something this serious without proof."

"This isn't just about the mayor, you know." Mark folded his arms. "Mrs. Kirby has to hear it all—and his kids."

"But according to KJNX, they were being discreet in what they reported," Liv said.

George rolled his eyes. "Oh, is that what they call it?"

Charlie Kirby stacked the breakfast dishes in the dishwasher and turned it on. "What should we do about the kids' soccer games?"

"It's raining," Marlene said.

"It is?" He looked out the window. "I hadn't even noticed. I'm trying to keep things as normal as possible for the kids."

"You can forget that. Nothing will ever be the same."

He took a step toward her and she put her palms out. "Don't."

"Marlie, it's not like I didn't try. I couldn't stop them from running the story."

"We'll never be able to show our faces again in this town. We might as well put up a For Sale sign."

"I'm not as concerned about what everyone else thinks as I am that *you* don't believe me."

"I doubt if anyone in Norris County believes you after what Sheila wrote in that diary. You might as well have stuck a knife in my heart. It's so humiliating!"

"Hal's going to subpoena the diary."

"It's too late. The damage is already done."

Charlie paused and considered what he was about to say. "I called Joe Kennsington. I'm meeting with the full elder board this afternoon. I'm stepping down."

He couldn't remember a time when he hadn't served in the church. How many times had he been asked to preach? Or lead a committee? Or head up a project? And how many times as mayor had he used his bully pulpit to convey a Christian message to challenge this community to pull together? He had earned the people's respect. He cringed to think of how many spiritual casualties this scandal might inflict.

Marlie glared at him as though he deserved to have a millstone hung around his neck. She stifled her sobs with a Kleenex and hurried out of the kitchen.

Charlie walked over and stood at the sink, his hands gripping the edge of the countertop. He looked out into the black morning and felt deep remorse. *Lord, I'm sorry...I'm so sorry...*

Rain fell in sheets down the kitchen window. Charlie bowed his head, his chin quivering, and let his agony turn to mournful sobs.

Special Agent Jordan Ellis sat on a park bench, soaking in the Saturday sunshine, aware of the dark clouds approaching from the north. He felt his phone vibrate and turned to his wife, his eyebrows arched. "Duty calls."

He picked up his phone and hit the talk button. "Jordan Ellis."

"Jordan, it's Hal Barker."

"Good to hear your voice, Sheriff. What's on your mind?"

"I heard you were in charge of the freeway shooting investigation. Were you aware that Sheila Paxton kept a diary?"

"A *diary*? First I heard about it. Tell me what you know."

Jordan listened carefully as Hal filled him in.

"I want that diary, Sheriff. It might contain evidence that would help the investigation."

"Good. I want KJNX to lighten up on the mayor."

"No problem," Jordan said. "I'll get KJNX to surrender the diary as evidence in a murder case. If they pull that First Amendment garbage, I'll have a *subpoena duces tecum* ready to go. Our attorneys can duke it out. That's a battle we'll win."

"Truthfully, I don't know if there's anything in the diary that would help your case, or if *any* of it's true. Charlie swears he never had an affair with the Paxton woman. Says she made it up."

"Yeah, right. I've heard that before."

"I believe him, Jordan. I've known Charlie Kirby a long time."

"Well, all I'm looking for is something that could help us connect the dots. I want everything you've got on this guy English, too. I take it he's not a fan of Ellen's from Hannon?"

"Nah, the whole thing at Ellen's office was staged. We checked the motor vehicle department for picture IDs matching the name Tony or Anthony English. There were quite a few, but none in Hannon, and none that Ellen recognized."

"Did you dust her office for fingerprints?"

"Ellen was sure he didn't touch anything. But we dusted the reception area and the door handles. Do you know how many people come and go in a given day?"

Jordan paused, his mind racing. "Now, don't get territorial on me, Sheriff. But I'd like to send a couple of my agents up there to see what they can come up with. I also want to get an artist's sketch of English's face."

"Fine with me. You have a hunch who this guy is?"

"I know the *he's*, not the *who's*."

"Come again."

"I know what he's done and what he's planning to do. I just need to figure out who he is and who he's after."

Hal chuckled. "Too deep for me. Send your boys this way. It's all yours."

Charlie sat at the round table in the elders' meeting room. He told the other eleven men every detail of the dilemma he found himself in. He couldn't have felt more vulnerable had he been sitting there naked.

"I'm sorry I didn't tell Marlie the truth from the beginning. But I couldn't bring myself to tell her when all the facts pointed to the worst."

"Charlie, you need to get *completely* honest with yourself," Joe Kennsington said. "The facts pointed to the worst because you were actively entertaining the worst. Isn't that what hurts the most?"

Charlie sat staring at his hands. "Joe's right. It's hard to admit, but Sheila's fantasies weren't that different from mine. I wanted everyone to think I'm innocent because I didn't go through with the affair. But in my thoughts, I slept with her anytime I wanted to. Who was it hurting? It wasn't real. I wasn't being unfaithful." Charlie blinked the stinging from his eyes. "But I might as well have been. My heart was a long way from Marlie."

"I wish you'd have confided in one of us," Jed Wilson said. "We could've prayed you through it, helped you be accountable."

The others nodded.

"I was too busy lying to myself," Charlie said. "I can't believe how it's messed up my life."

"How are your kids reacting?" Pastor Thomas said.

"Kevin's hurting. He's clammed up. Kaitlin seems okay. The others are too little to understand. I guess that's a blessing. There's a lot of tension."

"I don't have to tell you the way this works," Joe said. "You need to do everything you can to make things right, starting with Marlene."

Charlie sighed. "I'm trying. But it's a little like moving an iceberg at the moment. You saw how she was when you tried to talk to her."

Charlie sat with his hands folded on the table, aware of eleven pairs of eyes watching him.

Joe took off his glasses. He cleared his throat, his hands folded in front of him. "This is a difficult situation, Charlie. I've known you a long time, and I'm willing to take you at your word that this alleged affair was a sin of intent and not action. But your influence goes way beyond your family and those in this room. Allegations of impropriety affect your church family and the entire community. It seems best if you step off the elder board until we get this resolved."

"I know." Charlie coughed to cover his emotion "Let me say again how sorry I am. You guys mean more to me than anyone except Marlie and the kids. I deceived you. I hope you can forgive me. It's hard enough to lose your respect..." Charlie put his hand to his mouth and choked back the tears.

"But if I'd had any idea that my lusting after a woman I hardly knew would destroy my relationship with the one I truly love, I never would've let my guard down. I could never have imagined the consequences...the price is so great." Charlie hid his face in his hands, unable to contain the tears.

Ellen and Guy Jones walked out of Monty's Diner and stood on the sidewalk under the striped awning.

"I can't listen to any more disgusting gossip," Ellen said. "Someone should hang the station manager at KJNX."

Guy took her hand. "Come on, let's walk off the chili and corn-bread."

The clock on the county courthouse struck two as they crossed the street and began walking arm in arm around the town square.

"Honey, I'm proud of you," Guy said. "You're actually not obsessing about the FBI nosing around the editorial offices."

"What good would it do? Besides, I know how Jordan operates."

Guy squeezed her hand. "Sounds like you've learned to respect him."

"I suppose I have. What is this, the fourth time in as many years he's graced us with his presence?"

"At least it's not serious this time."

Ellen mused. "Serious enough for him to want DNA evidence. His mind is probably on tilt, wondering what it is that's driving Mr. English to find Sheila's parents."

"Don't even go there."

"It was cruel of him to give the diary to KJNX. Don't you wonder what motivated him to do something like that?"

"It isn't as though he didn't warn Charlie. You promised to leave this one alone, Ellen."

She raised her eyebrows. "I know." Her cell phone rang. She took it out of her jacket pocket and hit the talk button. "Hello."

"It's Margie. Did you let the FBI in?"

"No, I told them you'd be close to the presses, working on tomorrow's edition. The agents were supposed to go to the side door and knock so you could let them in."

"That's what I thought. Looks like they've already come and gone. Your office door is unlocked and files are all over the place."

"Why were they in *my* office? I told them English didn't touch anything. They were going to gather evidence in the reception area."

"I have no idea how they got in. I'd feel better if you'd come take a look."

"All right, Margie. I'll be right there."

Ellen slipped the phone in her jacket pocket and looked up at Guy. "The FBI has a lot of nerve."

15

Ellen Jones set her purse on the kitchen table, then opened the refrigerator and took out two bottles of water and handed one to Guy. "I'm not even thirsty. I just want to get the bad taste out of my mouth."

"At least it wasn't the FBI who violated your space." Guy pulled out her chair and motioned her to sit.

"I can't believe Mr. English would be bold enough to go snooping in my office. He has to know Charlie reported him to the police. Talk about brazen."

"Maybe it wasn't him."

Ellen sighed. "Sure it was. And now he has my file on Sheila—all my notes, all my personal thoughts."

"Honey, you said yourself you didn't have much."

"That's not the point." Ellen took a sip of water. "This is getting scary. He sure knew how to pick the locks like a pro. Who is he? What does he want with Sheila's parents?"

"What you really mean is, who was *Sheila*? I see your wheels turning, Ellen. Forget it."

"It's a little late for that."

"Why? The guy can plainly see from your file that you don't know anything. He's not going to bother you anymore."

"There's a big story here. I can feel it."

Guy took her hand and gently turned it over, then ran his thumb across the scar on her wrist. "It's not worth it, honey. Leave it alone. This isn't Baxter's story. You said so yourself."

Ellen looked up and caught his gaze. "Tell that to Charlie."

FBI Special Agent Jordan Ellis sat in his La-Z-Boy, thumbing through Sheila Paxton's diary. He was surprised the TV station had coughed it up without a fight. Probably figured the story would draw more attention if the feds showed an interest in the diary.

Jordan turned to some of the more recent entries and shook his head. Too bad the media got a hold of this stuff. It was nobody's business.

He flipped back to the beginning and started to read.

January 1. Though I'm nursing the first hangover of the new year, it was fun going to Landon's party last night after another of Richard's boring dinner parties. I don't mind playing along since his business associates actually believe we're a couple. Keeps things a lot safer for us.

I'm flying to Baxter tomorrow to meet with Mayor Kirby and the city council about getting TT Corp's foot in the door. It's a win-win. Should be easy. Besides, Charlie the mayor can't take his eyes off me. That always gives me an edge.

Charlie is kind of sexy, in a Boy Scout sort of way. I found out he has seven kids and is an elder at his church. But under that straitlaced, goody-two-shoes facade is a tiger screaming to get out. I wore the fitted black dress at the last meeting and drove him crazy. It's just a matter of time.

Jordan's eyebrows gathered. The woman had no shame. He went back to the first paragraph. She didn't mind playing like they were a couple because "it kept things a lot safer for us."

Interesting choice of words. He laid the open diary facedown in his lap, then picked up his phone and dialed.

"Special Agent Winston."

"Brad, it's Jordan. Did you find a file on Boatman yet?"

"Uh, I was going to call you about that."

"Before the turn of the century?"

"Hey, don't get testy on me. Our two casualties didn't follow protocol on this one and it's a little hard to question them six feet under. We can't find anything on Boatman. I'm red-faced about it, okay? What about you? Any luck on Paxton?"

"No. If she's got a file it must be buried in the archives. But I've got something else that just might get this hare and tortoise race moving beyond a crawl."

"I'm for that. What've you got?"

"Paxton's diary."

"Whoa, how'd you get your hands on that?"

Jordan told Brad the story as it was relayed to him by Sheriff Barker.

"So the TV station dished up some juicy tidbits on the mayor before you even knew about a diary?" Brad said.

"Yeah, but we've got it now, and I'm thumbing through it as we speak."

"And?"

"I found something interesting on the very first page: Paxton wrote that posing as a couple had made things safer for 'us,' the obvious implication being she knew Richard was at risk, too. If they were just friends or roommates, then why would that be? There's only one way this makes sense: Paxton and Boatman were siblings."

"Hmm...honestly that never occurred to me."

"So who is Tony English, you might ask?"

Brad laughed. "You've got him figured out, too?"

"Not by a long shot. But once I do, we won't need a file to figure out who Sheila and Richard were. Ten to one, it's their old man English is after. Someone in the Mob who stepped on somebody's toes."

"Well, well, well," Brad said. "That would explain why we couldn't find a single family photograph in the house. The only picture we found was a framed eight-by-ten of the two of them—probably for show. Makes perfect sense."

Jordan tapped his pencil on the arm of his chair. "No telling how long ago they were put in the program. I'll get some of our people digging into past Mafia cases. Maybe someone will recognize these two.

⤙

Charlie Kirby got out of his recliner and started toward the bathroom, hoping to find something for his headache. He noticed the light on in Kevin's room. Why was he still up?

He walked to the end of the hall and listened outside the door. He faintly heard music playing. He knocked softly.

"Kevin?... May I come in?... Kevin, please...."

Charlie started to walk away and then decided he couldn't stand the silent treatment anymore. He knocked again and cracked the door.

"Son, I'd like to talk to you."

He pushed open the door and saw Kevin lying in bed, his eyes closed, earphones on his head. Charlie flipped the light off and on a few times.

Kevin's eyes flew open. He turned off the CD player, a sheepish look on his face.

"I knocked a few times, but you didn't hear me," Charlie said. "What are you listening to?"

"Nothing."

"You seemed awfully engrossed in *nothing*."

"Just a CD. No big deal."

"Then you won't mind if I take a look?" Charlie said.

Kevin sighed. He opened the player and handed Charlie the CD.

"Dream Slayer?" Charlie picked up the cover and tried not to overreact.

"So?"

"Son, where did you get this?"

"Ricky lent it to me. Why do you care?"

Charlie shot him a stern look and then let his face soften. He put the CD in the case and laid it aside. "Let's deal with that later. We need to talk."

"About what?"

"About the nightmare we're all trying to live through. I can't tell you how sorry I am you have to hear all the garbage. But

Kevin...look at me...I didn't have an affair with Sheila. I can't prove it. I don't even know how to defend myself—"

"Then don't." Kevin folded his arms and stared at the foot of the bed. "Doesn't do any good anyway. People already think what they want."

"I'm more interested in what you think."

Kevin didn't comment.

"I don't blame you for being angry. I'm angry, too. I wish I could make it all go away. But neither of us has control over the circumstances. We just have to trust God that it'll work out."

Kevin rolled his eyes. "Yeah, sure, Dad. Whatever."

"Son, God didn't do this. It won't do any good to be mad at Him."

"I'm not mad at Him, I'm mad at you! I called Jeremy a stupid liar—but you're the liar!" Kevin grabbed a pillow and covered his face.

Charlie blinked away the moisture and gently removed the pillow from Kevin's face. "I'd be a liar if I told you I did what I'm accused of. But I'd also be a liar if I let you think I'm completely innocent."

Kevin looked up, his eyes searching Charlie's.

"Son, you're old enough to understand temptation. Boys your age are exposed to all sorts of things they don't like to talk about: Cigarettes, beer, glue, drugs. My guess is there are even dirty pictures floating around your circle of friends..."

Kevin looked away.

"And this CD you've been listening to...the lyrics are violent and lewd. You know better. Why'd you listen anyway?"

Kevin shrugged. "Wasn't hurting anything."

"Maybe it was. Your mind gets used to what you feed it, same as your body. Do you understand what I mean?"

"I guess."

"Can you put it in your own words?"

"I don't know. Whatever you think about all the time is what you want to do?"

Charlie nodded. "But even grown men forget sometimes. That's what happened to me. Now I'm paying the consequences."

Kevin glanced up at Charlie and then fiddled with the hem on the pillowcase. "What do you mean?"

"As a Christian, I've always been careful to guard my mind, especially when it concerns the special relationship I have with your mother. We've talked about this before, that sex is God's gift to married people—nobody else. I've worked hard to avoid thinking of other women in a sexual way."

Kevin nodded. "You even turn the channel when the ladies' underwear commercials come on."

"Well, son, Sheila Paxton was a very pretty woman, and some of the clothes she wore made me want to look at her in a sexual way—sort of like those commercials. Only I didn't turn the channel in my mind. And pretty soon, the idea of being with her in the wrong way didn't seem wrong." Charlie took hold of Kevin's arm. "I'm not proud of what I was thinking. I've asked God's forgiveness—and your mother's. But I promise you, I didn't have an affair with her."

"Why did her diary say you did?"

"I don't know, son. There's not a thing I can do to prove otherwise."

"No one believes you. Mom doesn't."

"Well, God does. That's a start. I don't know how I can make this up to your mother."

Kevin's eyebrows gathered. "Are you getting a divorce?"

"Not if I can help it. I love your mom more than I can ever put into words. I made a mistake. But I never stopped loving her."

"She's pretty mad."

"I don't blame her. Having this turn into a scandal is humiliating. I don't blame you for being mad either."

"Do we have to go to church tomorrow?"

Charlie sighed. "I'd like to. But I'm not sure if your mom is ready to face the public yet. We might have to settle for Pastor Thomas's sermon on the radio."

"Good. I don't want to go either. I hate church."

Charlie started to say something, then decided against it. "Why don't you try to get some sleep? I think it would be a good idea if I kept this CD until you're ready to give it back to Ricky."

Kevin turned over on his other side and pulled the covers up to his nose. "Whatever."

16

Marlene Kirby woke up to a cold, wet nose nudging her hand. She opened her eyes just as Hershey's long pink tongue swiped her cheek. She put her arms around his neck and relished the affection, all too aware that sleep had done nothing to dispel her depression.

Hershey wiggled free and started running in circles in the middle of the room. He yelped and then sat, tail wagging, a look of anticipation in his eyes.

"All right. I'm coming."

Marlene looked over at the empty side of the bed, torn between missing Charlie and wanting him gone.

She got up and put on her bathrobe. She opened the door and Hershey shot out into the hallway, almost knocking Charlie down.

"I was hoping you were up," he said. "Can I talk to you before the kids get up?"

"I need to make the waffle batter."

"This can't wait."

"Well, Hershey can't either. Someone needs to let him out."

"I'll do it. Wait here. I'll be right back."

"Charlie, you already told me what you told the elders. What more is there to talk about?"

"Please." He turned and looked over his shoulder. "Give me five minutes."

Marlene went to the rocker and sat, her arms folded tightly in front of her. What was the point in rehashing what had happened? She didn't believe him anyway.

A minute later, Charlie came in and closed the door. He sat on the side of the bed, his elbows on his knees, his hands clasped together. "Honey, no matter how strained things are between us, we have to do something differently. Kevin is starting to act out."

"He's angry and depressed," Marlie said. "But I hadn't noticed him misbehaving."

"I got up at three o'clock to get some Tylenol and his light was on. I knocked on his door and he was in bed with the headphones on—listening to Dream Slayer full blast. I could hear from the doorway."

Marlene closed her eyes and shook her head from side to side. "He knows how we feel about that kind of music."

"Ricky let him borrow it. I think he's angry and trying to get back at me. So it seemed like a good time to use my situation to make a point. I had a heart-to-heart with him."

She listened as Charlie relayed the entire conversation he'd had with Kevin.

"I'm surprised you admitted all that to a twelve-year-old," Marlene said.

"I can't afford not to. We can't shield him from the gossip. He at least needs to hear the truth from me."

Marlene didn't say what she was thinking. "Did he believe you?"

"I don't know, Marlie. Kevin's more confused than anything. But he said something that kept me awake the rest of the night. He asked me..." Charlie paused, struggling to keep his emotions in check. "He asked if we were getting a divorce." Charlie caught her gaze and held it. "I told him not if I could help it. But I couldn't sleep after that. I need to know: Is that what you're thinking?"

She threw her hands up. "I don't know, I can't think straight! You have a lot of nerve expecting me to know *anything* about the future at this moment." Her chin quivered and she put her hand to her mouth. "You broke my heart, Charlie. I don't know if I can ever trust you again."

"But what about the kids? They need me."

"Well, I'm not sure if *I* do."

Marlene could tell by his face that her words had cut deeply. She didn't care.

"Do you want me to move out?" he said.

"Where would you go?"

"I don't know, Marlie. But I can't stay here under these conditions. I think it's doing more harm than good. Kevin knows I've been sleeping in my study. What kind of message does that send?"

"It's your own fault."

"That's beside the point. Our son is not handling this well. No matter how upset we are, we can't let this throw Kevin into a tailspin. Twelve is too tender. He can't handle the pressure inside the house *and* out."

Marlene realized she was rocking too fast. "I don't know what to tell you, Charlie. I'm a long way from resolving this. Do what you have to do."

"I suppose I could stay at Morganstern's until this blows over," Charlie said. "Maybe we could get some counseling."

"What for? I'll never know for sure whether or not you're telling the truth." Marlene started to sob. "I still don't believe you. I've tried, Charlie. God knows I have. But you lied. How can anyone believe you after the diary?"

Kevin moved away from his parents' bedroom door. He turned and tiptoed down the hall, went back to his room, and shut the door. He took Dream Slayer II and slid it into the CD player, put on his headphones, and turned up the volume.

On Sunday morning, Mark Steele turned on the Open sign at Monty's Diner, and then unlocked the door and held it open, not surprised to see a crowd already gathered outside.

"Mornin'," Mort Clary said, squeezing past him. "Need my caffeine." Mort put a quarter in the jar and took a newspaper off the top of the stack.

"Wonder what Ellen's got ta say about the mayor?"

"She's giving him the benefit of the doubt," Mark said.

"Really?" George Gentry came into the diner, his hand holding his wife's. "After what KJNX revealed?"

"Revealed is right!" Reggie Mason stepped inside.

Liv Spooner nudged Reggie forward. "Move it, Reg. I already know what you think."

The early crowd sat at the counter and Rosie Harris poured the first round of coffee.

Mark waited until the other patrons were seated and then stood behind Reggie and reread the lead story.

DIARY UNDER SCRUTINY

Myerson's KJNX-TV has surrendered a diary to the FBI that allegedly was written by Sheila Paxton, and supposedly contains details of an illicit relationship she had with Baxter Mayor Charlie Kirby.

The diary first came to the forefront on Friday evening when KJNX received an anonymous tip from a man who not only revealed the whereabouts of the diary, but also stressed that it would be "a shocking eye-opener for the people of Baxter."

KJNX station manager Hutch Evans arranged for the diary to be picked up at an undisclosed location and, after reviewing the contents, made the decision to run the story. "We have every reason to believe the diary is authentic," Evans said. "Mayor Kirby's involvement with Ms. Paxton may have influenced the controversial decision to allow the relocation of Thompson Tire's regional plant in Baxter. Therefore, we believed it was in the best interest of the citizens of Baxter that this information be made public."

Mayor Kirby denied the allegations of impropriety with Paxton.

"The diary cannot be authentic," Kirby said, "because I had no such affair with Ms. Paxton. Something is very wrong here." The mayor also stated that, prior to KJNX running the story, he received several calls from a man threatening to give the diary to KJNX unless the mayor convinced *Baxter Daily News* editor Ellen Jones to use her sources to dig into Paxton's background for information that has not been made public. The mayor reported the blackmail attempt to local authorities, who then informed the FBI.

The FBI refused to comment, and has asked Mayor Kirby to refrain from making further comments during its investigation.

Mark lifted his eyes and tuned in to the conversation already underway at the counter.

Reggie blew on his coffee. "Man, this is big-time stuff. Who would've thought the diary would end up at the FBI? Think the mayor knows somethin'?"

Mort nodded. "Probably a lot more than he's lettin' on."

"Honestly, you two always look for the worst," Hattie Gentry said.

Rosie's eyes widened. "You have to admit this doesn't look good."

"Well," Hattie said, "I think we should give the mayor the benefit of the doubt."

"Yep, doubt has benefit." Mort elbowed Reggie and laughed his wheezy laugh. "Works fer me."

Liv shook her head and let out a sigh. "Oh, let's be honest. There's not a person here who believes the mayor is telling the truth."

Giorgio pushed open the door to his room at the Heron Lake Lodge and went inside. He shut the door with his foot, then carried a cup of coffee and two doughnuts to the table and sat down.

He wasn't giving up because the mayor had failed to cooperate. That two-bit TV station had ruined Charlie's chances for reelection. Giorgio laughed. Served him right. On to Plan B.

He took a bite of doughnut, then opened the file he had taken from Ellen Jones's office. He read through her notes on Sheila Paxton one more time to see if he'd overlooked anything. He hadn't. Jones had no plans to pursue the story. She was reluctant to dig into Sheila's background and risk opening herself up to whoever killed Richard. He let out a laugh. Too late for that!

Ellen walked into the house and heard a wolf whistle from the other room. She smiled and walked into the family room, where she saw Guy sitting in his favorite chair reading the Sunday paper.

"You look wonderful in that dress," he said. "Let me feast my eyes for a moment. How was church?"

"Good. Especially the sermon," Ellen said. "Charlie and Marlene weren't there. I'm not surprised."

"Me either. Christians shoot their wounded."

"That was unfair."

"Tell me people weren't whispering about it—how they're appalled and disgusted."

Ellen's eyebrows gathered. "People *care*, Guy. We're all concerned for the Kirbys. It's a horrible situation. No one should have their private life exposed that way."

"I agree with that. I'm just wondering how long before they're asked to leave the church."

Ellen sat on the couch and studied Guy's face. "No one is going to ask them to leave the church."

"Wanna bet?"

"What's eating you?" Ellen said. "You're deliberately antagonizing me."

He folded the newspaper and put it in his lap. "Sorry. I just know how self-righteous Christians can be. They're not going to accept Charlie after he fell from grace."

Ellen paused for a few seconds, careful to hide her annoyance. "I hadn't noticed the church trying to stone him. So far, it's been Avery Stedman, Jeremy Adler, and KJNX."

"Okay, that's fair. But brace yourself for the reaction from the pews because there's going to be plenty, believe me." He held up the front page. "I will give *you* credit for not being one of those who shoot their wounded."

"Well, thank you, Counselor. I was wondering if you'd noticed."

"Of course I noticed. I thought it was fair and factual. You didn't put a spin on it."

"Thanks. It's getting harder to stay objective. I honestly don't know what to believe about Charlie's guilt or innocence. But this whole thing with English gives me the creeps."

"I'll feel better when they find him. You gave them a good description."

Ellen nodded. "The artist's sketch was excellent. I can't imagine they won't find him soon."

17

Dennis Lawton tiptoed out of the twins' room, a finger to his lips. "They're asleep," he whispered to Jennifer. "Let's go out on the deck and enjoy the sunshine. The lunch dishes can wait."

He walked to the family room and slid open the glass door. The crisp October breeze was wrapped in warmth radiating from the cedar deck. He walked to the railing and looked out over a patchwork of autumn color to Heron Lake beyond. "What a gorgeous day."

"Why does Sunday always feel different?" Jennifer said.

He smiled, slipping his arm around her. "I don't know, but it does, doesn't it."

"The last time the leaves were this pretty was the day you proposed."

Dennis let his eyes glide slowly across the splendor of the forest's golds, reds, and oranges. "Three years today."

"I thought you forgot."

He kissed her cheek. "No way." He reached in his pocket and took out a ring box and put it in the palm of Jennifer's hand.

"What in the world?"

"Go ahead, open it."

She opened it and drew in a breath. "Dennis, it's gorgeous."

"Try it on."

Jennifer held the platinum band between her thumb and forefinger, then slid it on the ring finger of her right hand. She blinked several times to clear her eyes.

"I had it custom made. See the cross, the heart, and the three vines intertwined? That's to symbolize that our marriage is a cord of three strands, not just two. The rubies represent His sacrifice that made it all possible."

Jennifer held out her finger and studied the ring. "It's beautiful. I love it! What a wonderful thought." She threw her arms around Dennis. "I love you so much."

Dennis gave her a soft, lingering kiss. "I hope we're always this happy."

"You say that like you're not so sure."

Dennis took her hand. "I was just thinking about Charlie and Marlene. I could never have imagined their lives taking such a horrible turn."

"It's his own fault," Jennifer said.

Dennis started to say something and then didn't.

"Come on, you can't possibly believe he's innocent—not after the diary."

"He's really heartbroken."

"As well he should be. His life is in shambles."

"I know. But it's wrong to assume he's guilty. Only Charlie knows the truth." Dennis paused, then decided to say it. "He talked to me about the diary and the guy trying to blackmail him before it ever hit the news."

"You're kidding? When?"

"After Friday's golf game. I encouraged him to tell Marlene and to go to the police."

"*You* did? I can't believe you didn't tell me. Why are men so closed-mouth about everything?"

"It wasn't my place to say anything about this."

"Charlie actually told you he was innocent?"

"He told me he didn't have an affair."

"And?"

Dennis turned and fixed his eyes on Heron Lake glimmering in the midday sun.

Jennifer sighed. "You're not going to tell me anything, are you?"

"I will tell you this: I'm committed to never getting into a mess like this."

"You'd better not."

"Honey, do you have any idea how vulnerable men are?"

"No more than women."

"Different than women."

He tilted her head until she was looking into his eyes. "You need to pray for me every day. Don't ever take for granted that I'm not vulnerable because I'm a Christian. In some ways, that makes me more vulnerable. Do you think the enemy wants our marriage to be strong? He'd love to bring us down."

"I hadn't thought of it that way."

"Honey, men don't have to go looking for temptation. It's everywhere they turn. They have to learn how to guard themselves. The men of FAITH taught me that."

"I'll never understand it. I'm never tempted to cheat on you."

"Jen, it's not like all men are looking to cheat. We were created to be visual. And a lot of women are either oblivious to that fact—or they deliberately capitalize on it. The way they dress is distracting to men, even in the workplace."

"Oh, come on, Dennis. That's a cop-out. Whatever happened to self-control?"

"I'm not disagreeing with you. But men are barraged with sex on TV shows and commercials. Then there're the invitations to pornographic websites, and sexy models on the covers of lingerie catalogs. Sometimes a guy's day is a minefield. I'm not sure even wives realize."

"Hearing you talk this way scares me."

Dennis stroked her cheek. "You don't have to be scared. Just be aware. And pray. Even good men are susceptible. We're all made of clay."

Special Agent Jordan Ellis heard a jet fly overhead and wondered how long he had been staring at the Sunday comics.

He had stayed up half the night reading Sheila Paxton's diary from cover to cover, and hadn't found a single clue to help him figure out her true identity—or that of Richard.

About the only thing he was sure of was that Paxton was conniving and promiscuous. Being raised in an environment of organized crime could certainly account for her cold disregard for men. She'd recorded six conquests since January. Jordan thought it odd that her encounters with each lover sounded remarkably alike. What was she, some kind of serial seducer?

He got up and paced. He hated it when he hit a brick wall. Paxton and Boatman were siblings—he'd bet his life on it. So, who was their old man? And who was English? All he needed was one or the other, and he could put this case to bed.

Ellen sat knitting a sweater on the screened-in porch, Guy sitting next to her on the wicker couch. The trees in the backyard were a breathtaking mosaic of crimson and gold against a bluebird sky. A downy woodpecker worked its way around the tree trunk closest to the porch.

"What are you smiling about?" Guy said.

"That little woodpecker working up a storm. Too bad he can't take Sunday off and enjoy this pretty day."

Guy put his arm around her and pulled her close. "I'll miss you when you're gone. Remind me what time you leave for Knoxville tomorrow."

"I'd like to be on the road by noon. That'll give me the evening to rest. The editor's conference doesn't actually start until Tuesday morning."

"Are you ever going to finish that sweater for Dennis's sister?"

"Angie won't be home until Thanksgiving break. Jennifer said she's thriving in the university setting. She got a 4.0 the first quarter."

"And everyone thought she was a lost cause. Just proves you can't judge a book by its cover."

"I never do that."

"Never say never."

"Honestly, Guy...you and your clichés."

"I've got a better one: An apple a day keeps the doctor away."

Ellen laughed. "All right, O subtle one. The pie should be cool enough to slice. But you have to skip the cheddar cheese. Too much saturated fat."

He wrinkled his nose. "You sound like the doctor."

She smiled at him and pinched his middle. "Well, Counselor, an ounce of prevention is worth a pound of cure."

Charlie packed as much as he could get in the big suitcase and zipped it. Never had he felt such profound sorrow. What would he do without Marlie and the kids—even temporarily?

He sat on the side of the bed and picked up the framed wedding photo that had been on Marlie's nightstand almost as long as he could remember. The happiness in his bride's eyes was so evident—and so different than today. He had crushed her spirit. How well could he live with that?

He looked at the face of the groom...fresh out of seminary, eager to find a church to pastor. But God had other plans. It was soon evident that the Lord was calling him to an entirely different vocation...

"Charlie, God's closed every door," Marlie had said. "He must have something else."

"But I was so sure he was calling me to preach. I honestly haven't considered anything else."

A week later he got a call from an old college friend who had gotten into serious financial trouble after buying up some land. He offered to sell it to Charlie at a ridiculously low price. He and Marlie prayed about it and then approached Charlie's grandparents for a loan. They bought the land and, within a year, sold it to a developer and made ten times what they had paid for it. Charlie went back to his friend and split the profit so he could get his life together.

Charlie continued to make real estate investments—and more money than he would ever need. He learned early on to be a good steward of what God had given him. He established a foundation and gave a generous percentage of his earnings to a variety of worthy causes.

He also learned that his presence in the financial world afforded him unique opportunities to live out his faith in honest business dealings and to encourage those around him. He took seriously the words of Francis of Assisi: "Preach the gospel at all times. If necessary, use words." And over the years, he'd had more opportunities to let his light shine at business lunches than he ever would've had in the pulpit...

Charlie let out a sigh of agony. The same Christ-loving man who had been a light was now a dark blot, a stumbling block. His witness was ruined. His marriage was ruined. His example was suddenly worthless.

He heard footsteps approaching the door. He blinked the tears from his eyes in time to see Marlie open the door just far enough for her to fit in the doorway.

"Are you going to say good-bye to the kids?" she said.

Charlie felt his throat tighten. "Uh, not tonight. I'll wait until they're in bed before I leave. If it's all right with you, I'll come back tomorrow when they're home from school and talk to them. This isn't a good time—" His voice cracked and he put his fist to his mouth. "Give me a minute, and I'll come tell them goodnight."

Special Agent Jordan Ellis hung up the phone, his jaw clenched, and dropped his pencil on the desk. So, the bureau in Washington wanted the diary and for him to back off the case? They confirmed that Paxton had been in the witness protection program, and told him to let it go—not to concern himself anymore with Paxton's connection to the diary, the blackmailer, or the mayor. They would handle it.

Jordan crushed the paper he had doodled on and threw it in

the trash. He got up and paced, then sat down and dialed the phone.

"Special Agent Winston."

"Brad, it's Jordan. Washington wants my hands off the Paxton case. They know something, but they're keeping it hushed."

"I just got a similar call. They told me Boatman's case is a matter for the witness protection program and to stay out of it. You had that figured right."

Jordan tapped his pencil on the desktop. "We were starting to get warm on this one, Brad."

"Yeah, and that's probably the reason they want us to back off."

18

Ellen Jones heard the cuckoo clock strike twelve. She slipped on a navy blazer, pulled her purse strap up over her shoulder, and picked up her briefcase. With her free hand, she extended the handle of her weekender and started to roll it toward the kitchen.

"Here, let me help you with that," Guy said, coming down the hallway.

"Thanks. I've got it."

"Come on, Madam Editor, humor me. It makes me feel macho."

Ellen smiled. "All right. It's all yours."

She let him have everything but her purse, then followed him out to the garage and waited while he loaded it into the trunk.

"I hope your Avalon turns out to be a good road car," Guy said. "You haven't had it out on the highway yet."

"I'm sure it'll be just fine."

Guy came over and put his arms around her. "Enjoy the conference. I'll miss you." He kissed her softly. "Don't run off with some handsome young stranger."

"No chance of that, Counselor. I've finally got you trained." She smiled and slipped in behind the wheel. "I love you. See you by dinnertime on Thursday."

Ellen backed out of the driveway, pushed a praise and worship tape into the CD player, then headed for the main highway.

Charlie Kirby walked into Pastor Thomas's office and closed the door. "Thanks for seeing me on such short notice, Bart."

The pastor's arms went around him and Charlie swallowed the emotion.

"Please...sit down," Pastor Thomas said. "I'll get us coffee. You like yours black, if I remember right."

Charlie nodded. "Thanks."

The pastor poured two cups of coffee, handed one to Charlie, then sat in the chair next to him. "You and Marlene have been in my prayers day and night."

"Thanks. I never knew anything could hurt this much. I have no defense against the diary. Marlie and everyone else will think the worst and there's absolutely nothing I can do about it."

"She still doesn't believe you?"

"No. But that's not why I'm here. I need you to know that I've checked into Morganstern's for a while."

"You've separated?"

"Not officially. And if I can help it, not permanently. But the tension level at home is off the charts. Kevin is starting to act out. I'm as worried about him as I am Marlie. I saw his light on late Saturday night and checked in on him. He had his earphones on, but I could hear the volume clear over to the door. He was listening to Dream Slayer."

"Oh, my. Blake and Melissa have cautioned our middle school kids about that group."

"Kevin knows better. He's just crying out for help. He's been smoking, too. And he's starting to lie. I'm afraid he's on a downward spiral."

"Do you want me to talk to him?"

Charlie sighed. "I think before we can do anything to help Kevin, Marlie and I need to decide where *we're* going as a couple."

"Do you think she'd divorce you over this?"

"I don't know...neither of us has ever believed divorce to be an option for Christian couples."

"But that was before she thought you cheated on her?"

Charlie nodded. "I'm scared, Bart. What can I do?"

Pastor Thomas paused for several seconds, then looked into Charlie's eyes. "The best advice I can offer is: Take the lead. Love her. Woo her back. Show her by your actions that she means everything to you. And no matter how angry she acts, no matter what she throws back at you, no matter how many times she rejects your efforts, do it anyway. And be consistent."

"She won't believe it's genuine."

"Charlie, it's going to take a long time to build back trust. And consistency is your best ally at this stage. I've learned something over the years: women are really not that difficult. Their deepest desire is to be loved. Find out what sorts of things touch Marlene's heart and do them—consistently, lovingly, genuinely, unselfishly. It seems one-sided, but you'll start to reap the benefits. If you invest your energy into loving her, meeting her needs—expecting nothing in return—*eventually* she won't be able to resist you. And a happy woman will meet your needs better than you ever imagined. It's a win-win. I've seen it happen many times."

"How do I start?"

"That's going to be an individual thing. Only you know what pleases her and what really moves her. If you're not sure, ask the Lord to show you."

"I've got to tell you, Bart, it feels hopeless. I'm trusting God to pull this off. If He doesn't, my marriage is doomed."

Ellen saw the green highway sign for Knoxville and moved over into the right lane just as the interstate split into a Y.

The patchwork of color lining the freeway made her regret she hadn't taken the weekend to enjoy the trees around Heron Lake before they peaked out.

Her cell phone rang and she groped the passenger seat until she found it. She picked it up and hit the talk button.

"Hello, this is Ellen... Hello, is anybody there?... Guy?... Margie?..."

"Listen to me carefully," said a man with a New York accent. "Sheila Paxton is alive."

"Who is this?"

"Just think of me as Lucky Day."

Ellen sighed. "How did you get my cell number?"

"Wanna know something else? The diary's a fake. The mayor didn't do it."

"You should be talking to the FBI," she said.

"Why? They bury everything to do with Sheila Paxton."

"Why would they do that?"

"Good question. You tell me."

"Look, I don't have any business getting involved—"

"Oh, you'll wanna check *this* out: Twenty years ago. Linwood Heights, Illinois. Our Lady of Lourdes High School. Mary Angelina and Vincent Risotto. That's R-I-S-O-T-T-O."

Click.

Ellen turned off the phone, her heart pounding. Where had the man been calling from?

She looked in her rearview mirror and saw a freeway full of cars. She took the next exit and pulled over onto the shoulder. She took out a three-by-five card and jotted down what the man had said.

She opened her briefcase and looked down a couple of rows of Post-it notes until she found Jordan's cell number. She held it in her hand for a few moments, fighting the temptation not to tell him. Finally, she dialed and waited, twirling her pencil over and over like a baton.

"This is Jordan."

"It's Ellen Jones. Uh—I'm following up to see if you found any DNA evidence in our offices."

"Nothing we could match at NCIC."

"Was the diary useful?"

"Not to me."

"But you're looking for Mr. English?"

"We've turned it over to your local police," Jordan said. "Chief Cameron will take it from here."

"I thought this was part of your ongoing investigation on Sheila Paxton?"

"Off the record? The case has been pulled. Washington is handling everything from here on out."

"Why?"

"I don't ask why, Ellen. It's not my case anymore."

"Oh dear." She leaned her head back on the seat. "I'm not quite sure what to do."

"About what?"

"I just got an anonymous tip from a man who claims that Sheila Paxton is alive. How's that for piquing one's interest?"

"Not mine. It's not my case anymore."

"Well, whose is it?" Ellen tried to hide her annoyance. "The caller also said the diary is a fake and that Charlie didn't do what he's accused of."

"Couldn't prove it by me. Far as I could tell, Paxton wrote it and the mayor's guilty."

"Why do I get the feeling you're brushing me off?" Ellen said.

"Look, I'm no longer in charge. I'm not really free to comment on this."

Ellen paused. Should she tell him the rest of it? What was the point if it wasn't his case?

"All right, Jordan. Thanks for your time."

Giorgio felt sure Ellen Jones would take the bait. His New York accent sounded real enough, and how could any newspaper-woman pass up a tip like that? *Lucky Day.* He laughed.

After all the years of thinking Risotto was out of his reach, things were starting to gel. Giorgio wasn't about to pack it in now.

He didn't need the mayor. With a little prompting, Jones would come up with something to put him back on Risotto's trail.

One way or the other, he was going to fulfill his vow to end Risotto's life the same way Risotto had ended Papa's.

But he needed to be patient—stay low-key. Nowhere could he leave a clue that it was he who was after Risotto. He wanted to take him down and then spend the rest of his life gloating in the victory of vengeance, not rotting in some sorry prison cell.

Charlie went out in the backyard and found Kevin leaning against the privacy fence, a cigarette butt on the ground near his foot.

"Give me the cigarettes," Charlie said.

Kevin took them out of his pocket and gave them to Charlie. "I can get more. Who's going to stop me?"

"Kevin, look at me. It's important that you understand what your mother and I are trying to do. I'm only leaving temporarily. There's too much tension in the house. We all need time to let our feelings settle down."

"If you're getting a divorce, why don't you just admit it?"

"Because we're *not*, that's why."

"McKenna Wyatt's dad left. He never came back."

"Well, I'm your father, and I'll be back."

"Yeah, sure."

Charlie took in a breath and let it out slowly. "Son, I'm not sure how much you can understand of what your mother and I are going through. Adultery is a horrible violation of marriage vows. Even though I didn't have an affair, your mother believes I did and so her pain is the same as if I had. I understand that. But there's not a lot anyone can do to make her feel better. She's going to have to work it out within herself, and it's going to take time. And prayer. But I'm committed to winning her back."

Kevin looked up at him. "She'll never know for sure if you're telling the truth."

"I know. That's the most difficult part of all. In the meantime, while she and I are trying to work this out, I need you to help your mother with the younger kids. Can I count on you?"

"I guess."

"Kaitlin and Kelly are old enough to understand some of this," Charlie said. "I took them aside and talked to them a few minutes ago. They cried, but I assured them that I'm only going to be gone for a while. Plus, I'll see you on weekends. It's not as though your mom and I aren't speaking. We just need a little space."

"Mom cries all the time. What am I supposed to do?"

"Just give her a hug. She needs to let go of the pain. That's part of the process."

"It's all your fault."

Charlie nodded. "I should've told the truth from the beginning." He moved closer to Kevin and put a hand on his shoulder. "I hope you'll pray for your mom and me. And I hope you'll stop smoking...and stop listening to music you know is objectionable. If we all do the right things, we'll get through this without more hurt."

Kevin folded his arms and looked at the ground.

"I'm not leaving you. And I'm not leaving your mom. I'm just trying to get some of the tension out of the house. It's important to me that you understand that."

"Yeah, sure, Dad. Whatever."

Marlene Kirby sat in her rocker and reached for her Bible. She noticed a pink rose on her pillow. Her heart stirred and her eyes brimmed with tears. She got up and held the rose in her hand, her eyes closed, and inhaled the sweet fragrance. It took her back to the days when she and Charlie were newlyweds and he used to bring her one every day.

How dare he think he could march right back into her heart with such a ploy? She tossed the rose into the trash and sat in her rocker. She started to pick up her Bible and then didn't.

How could she ever take him back? And yet, how could she not? *Lord, what am I supposed to do? In my mind, I see him with her. I wonder if I'll ever be able to give myself to him again. I feel so betrayed.*

Neither she nor Charlie had been intimate with anyone else before their wedding night. That exclusivity had been a special part of their relationship. She could hardly bear the thought of him being with another woman.

Marlene heard the youngest child cry out for the third time tonight. She got up and headed for her daughter's room, experiencing both the aloneness of a single parent and the indignation of a woman scorned.

Ellen sat at the table in her hotel room, questioning whether she should leave the Sheila Paxton story alone. What was it about this woman's background that the FBI was hiding? Was she alive? And if so, could she clear Charlie's name? How could anyone dispute that Sheila's story was relevant to the community now?

Ellen knew if she told Guy about the call, he'd insist she not pursue it. She picked up the conference brochure listing tomorrow's editorial workshops. Most of the sessions suddenly seemed similar to others she'd attended. A morning workshop by the senior editor of the *Denver Post* had piqued her interest. But how badly did she need to be there?

19

Ellen Jones awoke to a loud ringing noise and couldn't remember where she was. She finally realized it was the hotel telephone. She turned over and felt around on the nightstand until she had the receiver in her hand. "Hello?"

"Good morning, Mrs. Jones, this is your 5:00 A.M. wake-up call. The current temperature in Knoxville is forty-two degrees. Today's forecast calls for clear skies, high near seventy. Have a nice day."

Ellen put the phone back on the cradle. She lay quietly for a few minutes, trying to remember if she had booked a flight to Chicago or if it had been a dream. Her eyes flew open. Her flight was for eight o'clock! She threw off the covers and stumbled toward the bathroom, stopping to turn on the coffeepot.

She stood in the shower, letting the warm water wash the sleep from her eyes, and wondered if she was being naive to check out a tip from someone known to her only as Lucky Day. How could any newspaper editor worth his salt ignore such a potentially big story? Her mind was racing with possibilities. What if Sheila Paxton was alive and Charlie could be exonerated?

But what if she got to Linwood Heights, Our Lady of Lourdes High School, and nothing clicked. Then what?

What did she have to lose? The lead would either pan out or not. Either way, she should have plenty of time to find out, then get back to Knoxville and drive home on Thursday.

Marlene Kirby walked in from the garage and laid her sweater on the kitchen counter. She had three hours to herself before it was time to pick up her preschoolers. The phone rang. She almost let the machine pick it up and then relented.

"Hello."

"Mrs. Kirby, this is Mildred Ames at Baxter Middle School. I'm calling to double check on Kevin. I don't show you called saying he would be absent."

"I didn't. Kevin's in school today."

There was a long pause.

"His homeroom teacher marked him absent this morning. I have the pink slip in front of me."

"It must be a mistake." Marlene glanced up at the clock. "He's in math this hour. Would you mind checking and calling me back?"

"Not at all, Mrs. Kirby. Probably just a mix up. I'll call you right back."

Marlene hung up, then grabbed a handful of Toll House cookies and sat at the table, her back to the windows. The morning sun flooded the breakfast nook with relaxing warmth. She took a bite of cookie and got up to get a cup of coffee when the phone rang again.

"Hello."

"Mrs. Kirby, it's Mildred Ames again. Kevin isn't in math class. I had the janitor check the boys' lavatories and I also checked with the school nurse. He's not here."

"Are you saying he's truant?"

"Quite possibly."

"But he's never skipped school before. I—uh—what do you suggest I do?"

"If you have any idea where he might have gone, it would be a good idea to check there. Don't be too alarmed. We deal with this all the time. Most kids will try it once or twice and then realize the consequences aren't worth it."

Marlene sighed. "I'd like to paddle his behind! I suppose he's too big for that. My guess is he's off somewhere with Ricky Stedman."

"Actually, I thought of that," Mildred said. "I checked, and Ricky's in class."

"All right, Mrs. Ames, thank you. I'll take care of it."

Marlene hung up harder than she meant to. She didn't need this! She popped the rest of the cookie into her mouth and grabbed her keys. So much for a quiet morning.

Kevin Kirby laid his bicycle on the ground and climbed up on a smooth boulder. He hugged his knees and looked out over Heron Lake. This was cool—and a whole lot better than putting up with the snide remarks and the snickering at school.

He lay flat on the rock, his knees bent, and let the sun bake him. He reached in his jacket pocket, took out a cigarette, put it between his lips, and flicked the lighter. He took a puff and started coughing. So what if he hated the taste? It felt good getting away with it, having a choice for a change. He was tired of everyone else making his life miserable.

He knew his parents were getting a divorce. He didn't need Ricky to keep reminding him. Did they think he was dumb enough to believe the separation was only temporary? They were just giving him time to get used to it.

He inhaled and defiantly blew a stream of smoke up toward the sky.

"Hello over there."

Kevin sat up, his heart pounding, and quickly crushed the cigarette. He saw a man in overalls sitting in a lawn chair at the water's edge, holding two fishing poles.

"I—I didn't see you sitting there."

"Just plopped my chair down. Name's Josiah. You're welcome to join me."

Kevin jumped off the rock and walked over to the man. His eyes looked like two lumps of coal sticking out from under the brim of his straw hat. His face was dark and leathery, but his smile was whiter than the egret flying overhead.

"What's your name, boy?"

"Kevin."

"Like to fish?"

"I don't know. Maybe. I've never done it."

"Nothin' like it. Good eatin', too."

"What are you trying to catch?"

"Catfish. They go for that stinky bait. Seems to draw 'em right up. Here." Josiah handed him a pole. "Hang on to that."

"What do I do?"

"If that red bobber disappears, pull up and start reelin' like nuts." Josiah put his hand on Kevin's and moved the reel forward a few times. "That's it."

"How will I know it's a bite?"

"You won't hafta ask!" Josiah's laugh was deep and inviting.

Kevin smiled without meaning to. "Do you live on the lake?"

"All day long."

"I live in town, but I like riding my bike out here. Sometimes I come with my friend, Ricky. But not today."

"Playin' hooky, are you?"

Kevin glanced at Josiah out of the corner of his eye. "You're not going to tell, are you?"

"Think I should?"

"Won't do any good. I'm not going back to school."

Josiah took off his straw hat and wiped his shiny head with a red kerchief. "Gettin' away can be good for the soul. Gives a man room to think."

"Like anyone cares what *I* think."

Josiah gave a slight nod. "Feels that way when you start to grow up."

"I'm twelve. They treat me like I'm a kid."

"Your folks?"

"Yeah. They're going through some stuff, and expect me to believe everything's gonna be all right. But what if it's not?"

Josiah turned, his forehead creased. "Your folks splittin' up, are they?"

Kevin bit his lip. "My dad moved out. He said he'll be back, but he won't. They never come back."

"Had a lot of experience with this, have you?"

"Some of my friends' parents are divorced. They fight all the time over who gets who when. It's a bummer."

"Scared that's what's fixin' to happen?"

Kevin shrugged. "I guess so."

"Your folks fight a lot, do they?"

"Not really. But my mom doesn't trust my dad anymore. Nothing's ever gonna be the same for us kids."

Josiah looked out over the water. "You been prayin'?"

"Doesn't do any good. They're not gonna get back together."

Josiah scratched the white stubble on his chin. "It's a mistake to decide the Lord can't do somethin' about it."

"Then why hasn't He?"

Josiah turned to him, a knowing look in his eyes. "It's all in the timin', boy. Keep tellin' the Lord what you're hopin' for. He cares what you think. And He's got the answers."

Kevin felt the line tighten and saw the rod bend until he thought it would break. "I've got one! I've got one!" He dug in his heels and gripped the pole tightly with both hands.

Josiah got out of the chair and stood next to him. "Look out yonder. The bobber's clean disappeared! Keep your line tight, boy, and reel. Reel! That's it! Whooooeee...looks like a monster!"

Ellen drove her rental car through the old business district of Linwood Heights. Getting out of O'Hare had been a madhouse, but she still had time to check out the high school before the school day was over.

She drove through the intersection of Main and Jefferson, then glanced at the directions the man at the service station had drawn for her. The school should be three blocks south. She looked up and read the street signs: Polk...Harrison...Adams. She spotted the stone building on the west side of the street.

She parked her car out front, then walked up the sidewalk and front steps of the old school. It reminded her a little of Baxter High, but without the ivy-covered front. The trees on the school grounds were almost bare, autumn's only souvenir the crunchy blanket of dried leaves left on the grass.

Ellen went inside and found the office. She opened the door and was met with the smile of a gray-haired woman.

"May I help you?" the woman asked.

Ellen handed her a business card. "I'm Ellen Jones, editor of the *Baxter Daily News*. I wonder if I might speak to whoever handles student records?"

"You can start with me. I'm Evelyn Morley, administrative assistant to the principal. Won't you please sit down?"

"Yes, thank you. I'm gathering information for a human-interest story, and would very much like to find two students who attended here about twenty years ago: Mary Angelina Risotto and Vincent Risotto."

"I'm afraid I can't help you." The woman seemed to shut down, her eyes avoiding Ellen's. "Even *if* I could locate their files, the information would be outdated."

"That's all right," Ellen said. "Even an old address is a start."

"It's never been our policy to give out personal information on students."

Ellen put a smile in her voice. "But these students are adults now. An old address could hardly be considered confidential. It's not as though I'm asking for their SAT scores or transcripts. Please, it would really save me a step."

Ms. Morley's eyes searched hers. "Help yourself to some coffee. I might be a while."

"Thank you," Ellen said, curious as Ms. Morley walked away that she hadn't bothered to ask the spelling of the last name.

Charlie Kirby hung up the phone and hit the intercom button. "Regina, I'll be out for a while. Take messages."

Charlie went out the side door and down the hall, then exited the building in the back. Marlie was waiting by her van.

"Where have you looked?" Charlie said.

"Everywhere I know to look: the woods behind the house, the soccer fields, Monty's."

"Maybe he's with Ricky."

She shook her head. "No, he's not. Ricky's at school. Charlie, I'm scared. This isn't like him at all."

"Maybe he rode out to the lake."

Marlie raised her eyebrows. "He might've. But I wouldn't know where to begin looking. What are the odds we would spot him?"

"Poor. Unless he wants to be found."

"You think he does?"

"Maybe," Charlie said. "He's obviously screaming for attention."

"Well, we can't just wait for him to come home."

"I think that's exactly what we *should* do."

"It'll be dark by six," Marlie said. "What if he's not back by then?"

"Let's not overreact to this. I'll call Hal and ask him to have his deputies keep their eyes open. But I think Kevin will come home on his own."

"Sure, when he's good and ready. So what am I supposed to do, go home and worry?"

Charlie looked beyond her at his three youngest children smiling and waving from the van. He waved back. "Honey, in another half hour, there'll be six kids at home who need their mother. Let me handle this."

Marlie sighed. "All right. I don't have much choice."

20

Ellen Jones looked at her watch. How long could it take to find records on two former students with the same last name?

She got up and walked out in the main corridor and began perusing the photographs, ribbons, and awards framed along the wall. She stopped in front of a glass case filled with football and basketball trophies, noting the first state trophy had been won in 1934.

To the right was another glass enclosure, displaying prom and homecoming memorabilia. She smiled at how the styles had changed through the years. For a moment she was transported back to her senior year and stood waving atop a maroon-and-white mum-covered float. Her thoughts were interrupted by the sound of Evelyn Morley's voice.

"Mrs. Jones, if you'll come back in the office, I'll show you what I found."

Ms. Morley quickly ushered Ellen into the office.

"Here are the files." She handed Ellen both files, something stamped in large letters across the front of each.

"Deceased?" Ellen said.

Ms. Morley nodded. "They were brother and sister, I remember that much. But for the life of me, I can't remember how they died."

"Is there an old address or phone number?"

Ms. Morley's face turned red. "I—I'm sorry. The files are empty. It appears the contents have been lost."

Lost or removed? "Oh, dear," Ellen said. "I had so hoped to find these two. Could you make an educated guess at which Catholic grade school they may have attended?"

"There were only two back then: Saint Joseph's and Saint Jude's. I'm so embarrassed about this."

"Please don't be," Ellen said. "I put you on the spot dropping in without calling first. I really appreciate your effort to help me."

Kevin Kirby sat next to the campfire and warmed himself. Josiah had cleaned four catfish they had caught during the afternoon, then had gone to get what he needed to fry the fish.

Kevin heard footsteps and looked up. He saw Josiah trudging through the dusk, pulling something.

"Got what we need for some fine eatin'," Josiah said, his smile bright in the light of the fire.

He opened a cooler and took out a bottle of cooking oil, a plastic bag of flour, salt and pepper shakers, and two cans of baked beans. Also two oven mitts and a spatula.

"I brought us some paper plates and plastic utensils. And some Oreos for dessert."

"My favorite!" Kevin said.

Josiah smiled. "Never met a boy that didn't like 'em. Oh, and I brought a couple of root beers. You like root beer?"

"Yeah, thanks," Kevin said.

Josiah handed him the can. "I'm gonna cook us a fine dinner. Then I'm gonna put you and your bike in that old pickup of mine and haul you home to your mama."

"She's gonna be mad. I'll be grounded."

"Can't blame her, boy. She's thinkin' somethin' awful mighta happened to you. Course, that's what you wanted her to think."

"I didn't say that."

Josiah shook his head. "Nope. You didn't." He poured cooking oil in the skillet and put it on the fire, then squatted next to the cooler and started to coat the fish with the flour.

"How come you let me stay this long?" Kevin said.

"I got my reasons."

"Like what?"

Josiah picked up the cans of baked beans. "You want yours heated up or cold out of the can?"

"Cold's fine. I eat them that way at camp. So why'd you let me stay?"

"You ever tasted catfish, boy?"

"Uh—yeah, sure. My mom's."

"Well, you're about to discover mine's the best there is, that's all there is to it."

"I don't know. Hers tastes great. She's a good cook."

"And a good mom, would you say?"

Kevin nodded. "Yeah, my friends like to come to my house. She's always baking something for us or taking us somewhere. She even lets us make pizza. They wish their moms were cool like mine."

"Does she read to you?"

"When I was younger. Now we have devotions every night, and she and Dad let me read to them."

"Go on!"

"My mom and dad pray with me, too. At least, they did before all the trouble started. My dad says he'll be back. Doesn't mean he will."

"Don't mean he won't." Josiah placed the first fish fillet in the hot oil and drew back when it popped.

"You have more faith than I do," Kevin said.

"Nah, I'm just usin' mine, that's all."

"Using it, how?"

"The Lord said we don't have 'cause we don't ask. I'm just thinkin' we oughta ask more—in His will, of course."

Kevin shrugged. "How am I supposed to know what that is?"

"You read the Bible, don't you?"

"Uh-huh."

"Then you know for sure it's His will that married folks stay married. Seems to me your folks are nice people who need a touch from God. Why don't we start askin' Him for that?"

Kevin sighed. "I guess we could. Maybe I need it, too."

Josiah smiled. "*That's* why I let you stay so long."

Ellen walked out the front door of Saint Jude's Grade School and heaved a sigh of frustration. Everyone here had seemed conveniently ignorant.

"Did I overhear you askin' about the Risotto kids?"

Ellen turned and saw a white-haired janitor in coveralls standing in the doorway. The name *Hank Sweeney* was embroidered above his pocket.

"Yes," Ellen said. "I'm an old friend of the family. I've lost touch and would like to reestablish ties."

"There were cousins—last name Stassi. Used to live across from me on Washington. I think their house number was 214. Maybe the aunt and uncle still live there."

Ellen smiled. "Thank you."

She walked down the front steps and out to her rental car. She pulled out the city map of Linwood Heights and looked for Washington Street, then took a pencil and marked it. Only six blocks from here. Why not?

Marlene Kirby saw lights flash on the living room drapes. She peeked out and saw a pickup truck pull up out front, then Kevin get out on the passenger side.

"Charlie, Kevin's home!" she shouted.

She rushed outside and threw her arms around Kevin. "I don't know whether to hug you, paddle you, or ground you for a year. Where have you been? Why didn't you call?" She choked back the emotion. "I've been worried sick."

"Sorry, Mom. I know I'm in trouble."

Marlene looked up and saw Charlie shaking hands with the driver. She walked over and stood next to them. "I'm Marlene

Kirby, and you are?..."

"Name's Josiah, ma'm. I was tellin' your husband here that Kevin spent the day at the lake with me. Sometimes a little space to think can clear a young man's head."

"He was playing hooky," she said.

"Yes 'm, I figured that out."

"Then why did you wait till now to bring him home?"

"He wasn't goin' nowhere nohow. Figured he was safe with me. We just sat and talked, did a little fishin'. Kevin caught us some catfish, so we fried 'em up for dinner."

"That's just great," Marlene said. "Kevin skips school and has a ball out at the lake. That's some deterrent not to do it again."

"Marlie, why don't you take Kevin inside and let me talk with Josiah for a few minutes?" Charlie said. "Son, put your bicycle in the garage and wait for me inside. You've got some explaining to do."

Ellen slowed the car as she turned onto Washington, her eyes searching for numbers on the houses, mailboxes, or the curb. She spotted 214 under a porch light and pulled over in front of the house and turned off the motor.

The old house was part frame and part stone, with a long front porch. She got out of the car and walked up the steps to the front door. The porch swing was in need of paint and the screens were torn. She straightened her blazer and rang the bell.

An elderly woman cracked the door, leaving the chain lock in place.

"Are you Mrs. Stassi?" Ellen said.

The woman nodded slightly, her eyes searching. "Yes."

"My name is Ellen Jones. I just spoke with Hank Sweeney who used to live across the street. He thought you might be able to assist me in finding the Risotto family. We lost contact some years ago."

A short, burly man with thick, white hair stepped next to the woman in the doorway. "Who are you? Why are you nosin' around here?"

"I'm sorry if I gave you the impression I was nosing around. I'm Ellen Jones, an old friend of the Risottos, and—"

"Is that so? How long since you talked to 'em?"

Ellen felt herself blushing. "I don't remember exactly. But it's been many years. The children were young."

"How young?" he said.

"I—I truly don't remember. I'm just an old friend who would like to reestablish contact. Do you have an address where I might find them? Or a phone number?"

He laughed. "Either you're one gutsy lady, or you ain't got a light on in the attic. We ain't seen my brother-in-law or the family for eighteen years."

"I'm sorry; I didn't know."

"Stop with the dumb broad act. Everyone knows the feds made 'em *disappear*."

Ellen wondered if he could hear her heart pounding. "Then I guess you can't help me."

"If you're nosin' around after Spike, *no one* can help you. I suggest you watch your back. Now get outta here."

He slammed the door in her face.

Ellen suddenly felt chilled. She hurried back to the car, got inside, and locked it. What had she walked into?

Marlene Kirby went in her room and shut the door, both grateful for and resentful of Charlie's help. She spotted another pink rose on her pillow, and heard a soft knock. "Come in."

Charlie opened the door and stepped inside, then sat on the side of the bed next to her.

"Did Kevin go to bed?" she asked.

"Yes. After he surrendered two packs of cigarettes and Dream Slayer II. Apparently, he's been holding out."

"Charlie, what are we going to do with him?"

"A better question is, what are we going to do with us? Kevin isn't going to straighten up until we do."

"Look who's talking." She folded her arms tightly to her chest.

"There's nothing more I can say in my defense," Charlie said. "I've been completely honest, though I realize you may never believe me. But regardless, we're responsible for seven great kids who need us both. That seems more important at the moment than how we feel about each other."

Marlie turned and picked up the rose. "Why do you keep doing this? It's not going to change my mind."

"What about your heart?"

She sighed. "I never said I didn't love you. I don't trust you."

"That's *my* fault."

"Yes, it is."

Charlie put his hand on hers and she didn't pull away. "Marlie, I'm so sorry I hurt you. I've never loved anyone the way I love you..." He paused to gather his composure. "I offer no excuse for flirting with temptation. But I'm going to spend the rest of my life making it up to you."

"I don't know if that's possible," she said.

"I think it is."

She pulled her hand away. "Pretty sure of yourself for a man who's hanging by a thread."

"I'm not sure of anything except the Lord's faithfulness. He can fix this, Marlie. I can understand you not trusting me, but you can trust Him. He's faithful."

"Yes, *He* is." She tossed the rose in the trash can. "What did you say to Kevin after I left?"

"I let him talk mostly. He knows what he did was wrong, and he feels bad about what he put you through. I grounded him for the week."

"What if he does it again?"

"Let's hope he doesn't. I'm grateful for Josiah. He's a strong believer and seemed like a good influence. The Lord was watching out for Kevin." Charlie turned to her. "But he needs a stable home life, and that's our responsibility. That'll be the biggest deterrent to his misbehaving."

"Charlie, I can't make myself feel what I don't. No matter how pleasant I act, Kevin will see through it."

"Then let Bart Thomas counsel us. Let's pray together that God would change us and restore our marriage. Marlie, it's not going to happen unless we commit to it."

She rolled her eyes. "And we all know what commitment gets you."

21

At 5:58 Wednesday morning, Mark Steele stood in the doorway of Monty's Diner, taking in a breath of crisp autumn air. He picked up the bundle of newspapers and went inside, cut the twine, and stacked them by the door.

"Rosie, Leo, I'm turning the sign on."

Mark turned on the Open sign and through the front window spotted Mort Clary and Reggie Mason coming to the entrance. He picked up two newspapers and waited at the door.

Mort came in and tipped his hat. "Mornin', Mark." He took a newspaper, then hung his hat on the hook, dropped a quarter in the jar, and walked to the counter.

Mark handed Reggie a newspaper and whispered, "Since when does he call *me* by name?"

Reggie shrugged and put a quarter in the jar. "He's actin' weird."

Mark followed Reggie to the counter where Rosie Harris stood with the coffeepot. She filled Mort's cup. "There you go."

"Much obliged."

"Uh, you're welcome." Rosie looked at Mark, her eyes wide.

George and Hattie Gentry came in, grabbed a newspaper, and went to the counter.

Mort glanced up. "Mornin' to ya, Georgie, Hattie."

"Same to you." George looked questioningly at Rosie.

Mort opened his newspaper and began to read.

Mark caught George's eye and mouthed the words, "What's up with him?"

"Might as well say it outright," Mort said.

"Say what outright?" Liv Spooner took her place at the counter.

"That yer wonderin' why I'm bein' so nicey-nice."

George smiled and pulled down the newspaper, exposing Mort's face. "Okay, why are you?"

"Just feel like it."

"Come on," Reggie said. "Fess up."

"Can't a guy be nice without drawin' a crowd?"

"Not if his name's Mort Clary," Rosie said.

Mort took a sip of coffee, then folded his newspaper and set it on the counter. "I seen somethin' that's got me bothered."

"You bothered?" Rosie said. "This I've got to hear."

"I ain't all bad, ya know."

"Come on," George said. "Let's hear him out. What gives?"

"Well, I was down at Miller's Market yesterday afternoon, loadin' groceries into the back of my truck, when I spotted the mayor's wife out in the parkin' lot—cryin' her eyes out."

"I imagine she cries a lot these days," Hattie said.

Mort folded his hands. "It's one thing ta wonder about it, another ta see it firsthand. All them kids was misbehavin'. She just put her head on the steerin' wheel and started ta sob. Can't imagine tryin' to handle all them young'uns without their daddy around."

"Well, Mort Clary," Hattie said. "You *have* got a heart in there."

Mort's face turned red. "Just felt bad for the missus, that's all."

"I heard the mayor's moved out and is staying down at Morganstern's," Reggie said.

Mark moved closer to the counter. "Where'd you hear that?"

"I don't remember, but I think it's true. I saw him pullin' out of there yesterday morning."

"Ain't no little thing breakin' up a family," Mort said. "I been there."

"You?" Rosie said.

"Forty years ago. My wife left me. Took the three kids. I'd been runnin' around, actin' like a fool. I didn't love her no less, but she never could see it in her heart ta forgive me. Ain't never seen 'em since."

"I had no idea you've been carrying that around," Rosie said. "How awful not to know what your kids look like."

Mort nodded. "Still wonder about 'em every day."

George sighed. "Sometimes we talk about the mayor's situation like it's a movie. But these are real people with real pain."

Reggie blew on his coffee. "Bet they'll get a divorce."

"I doubt they believe in divorce." Rosie poured Mort a refill. "They're strong Christians."

Reggie snickered. "Yeah, I could tell that by the mayor's behavior."

"Well," Hattie said, "even nice people make mistakes. It's how they handle the mistakes that determines the outcome."

"That's right," Mort said. "A man don't have ta give up on livin' 'cause he slipped up. Grace ain't about holdin' grudges."

Rosie arched her eyebrows, a hand on her hip. "I've never heard *you* talk that way."

"Did ya think I ain't never been ta church?"

George patted Mort on the back. "How about if Hattie and I buy your breakfast today?"

Ellen Jones sat in the back row at the closing session of the editor's conference, grateful to be back in Knoxville and anxious to get home tomorrow.

She was unable to concentrate on anything the speaker was saying. All she could think about was how deceitful she had been, going to Chicago without even telling Guy where she was. What if something horrible had happened to her? Even when she had called him from the airport, she never let on that she wasn't in Knoxville.

And now she was in the middle of something big, and probably dangerous, the very thing she had wanted to avoid. Plus, she had lied to the Stassis about who she was, violating her own code of ethics.

She couldn't stop wondering who Lucky Day was and when

he would call again, maybe this time in person. What had he expected her to learn beyond the obvious—that Sheila Paxton and Richard Boatman were Mary Angelina and Vincent Risotto? Did he want her to find out who killed them—and why?

Lord, I really stepped over the line on this one. I'm so sorry. I promise to make things right with Guy. I'm so ashamed that I deceived him. Father, protect me. I think I'm in over my head.

Special Agent Jordan Ellis was sitting at his desk finishing up the day's paperwork when the phone rang.

"This is Jordan."

"It's Ellen Jones. I need to bend your ear about something."

He sat back in his chair. "Okay. Go."

"Hear me out before you chew me out," Ellen said. "Remember I called you the other day and said I'd gotten a tip that Sheila Paxton was alive? Well, I didn't tell you all of it, mostly because you said it wasn't your case anymore. But I've done something I may regret, and I need your advice."

"Go on."

He listened as Ellen told him everything, beginning with the telephone tip from Lucky Day and ending with her strange encounter with Mr. Stassi.

"How do you expect me to respond to this?" Jordan said.

"Just tell me if my hunch is correct."

"You know I can't comment on this case! You're a newspaper-woman, for cryin' out loud! This is the last thing we need to show up in print!"

"Then it's true?"

"I didn't say it was true. I *said*, I can't comment!" Jordan took in a breath and breathed out slowly. "Look, the best thing you can do is go home and forget it. Push the entire case out of your head and get on with your life."

"How can I do that realistically?" Ellen said. "This Lucky Day will be back in touch. He's expecting to get something. After all, he gave me a hot tip."

"And you never wondered why?"

"Of course I did. He knows Sheila's supposed affair with Charlie is a local scandal; and since KJNX was privy to the diary, I must be itching for a piece of the story. He's probably after the same thing English is: To keep me digging until I figure out where Sheila's parents are. Do you think they want to harm them?"

"I can't comment. But feel free to make that assumption. If you're smart, you'll bail on this story before we end up bailing you out of Heron Lake."

There was a long pause.

"It's really that serious?" she said.

"More than you know. And you need to get out of it as gracefully as you got yourself into it. You didn't find out anything this Lucky Day didn't expect you to find out. Just tell him you aren't interested in doing a story."

Ellen sighed. "I should just drop it?"

"Like a hot potato."

Jordan hung up the phone and started to pace. Couldn't this woman ever leave well enough alone?

He was supposed to be off this case. How could he tell her they had found a fingerprint match on Mr. English, that his real name was Giorgio Antonio Merlino, wanted by the FBI in connection with several Mob-related executions? Giorgio's old man, Papa Merlino, had agreed to testify against Spike Risotto, but had been gunned down before he ever took the stand. The Risottos were put into the witness protection program shortly after that when Spike Risotto helped the feds build a case against the big boss.

Jordan sighed. If Giorgio Merlino was after Risotto, Ellen was safe only as long as she was useful.

Ellen sat in her hotel room, picking at her dinner, her mind racing. She was scared. No point in kidding herself. But the unanswered questions of this story wouldn't leave her alone. Was Sheila alive?

Was Richard? Had their deaths been staged by the Department of Justice's witness protection program? Who was English? Who was Lucky Day? Did they both want Risotto dead? If they couldn't find him, what made them think she could?

Her cell phone rang. She jumped, her hand over her heart. "Hello."

"I understand you made a little trip to Chicago."

Ellen recognized the New York accent. "How do you know that? Are you following me?"

"I knew you couldn't ignore a story this big. So I went over to Washington Street and had a little talk with Benny Stassi. He told me you dropped by—and how you knew where to find him. Of course, I had to kill Benny and the missus. And the old janitor—your buddy, Hank."

Ellen's heart beat so fast her voice was shaking. "W-why would you do that? All I did was follow up on the tip you gave me. They didn't even tell me anything."

He laughed. "Now you know I mean business. I want to know where Risotto is. Give me that and I'm outta here. Oh, and don't make me wait too long—or you're next." *Click.*

Ellen hung up the phone, her entire body trembling. She sat for a few minutes, trying to think. Finally, she dialed the phone.

"This is Jordan."

"It's Ellen again."

"You sound shook."

"I got another call on my cell phone from Lucky Day. He knows I went to Chicago. He said he paid Benny Stassi a visit—and had to kill him and his wife and Hank Sweeney, the janitor I told you about. I don't know if he's telling the truth or not. I'm really scared. He said he wants me to find out where Risotto is or I'm next."

Jordan started yelling. Ellen held the phone out until he quieted down.

"I know I'm in deep trouble," she said. "Tell me what to do."

"I ought to let you hang by your thumbs."

"I know. You can yell at me later. But I'm stuck here in Knoxville, and I'm terrified."

Jordan combed his hand through his hair. "As well you should be. I'll call Tennessee and have them send a pair of agents to drive back with you tomorrow. In fact, I'd feel better if someone stayed with you tonight. You okay with that?"

"Whatever you say."

"In the meantime, I'm going to find out if our Lucky Day really killed the three in Chicago." Jordan let out a sigh of disgust. "Do you have any idea how much danger you're in?"

"I'm sure I do," Ellen said. "After this, I may retire from the newspaper and write novels."

"Let's hope you live that long."

"Please, I'm scared enough."

"Good. Maybe you'll listen for a change."

22

Ellen Jones drove down the interstate, FBI Agent Terri Farber riding in the passenger seat and Agent Michelle Taft seated in back. She wondered how Guy would react to her arriving home hours early—and with two unexpected guests assigned to keep her safe.

"Are you feeling any more relaxed?" Agent Farber said.

"I feel safer," Ellen said. "Relaxed isn't a word that comes to mind."

"We're not being followed," Agent Taft said from the backseat. "I'm sure of that."

Ellen looked in the rearview mirror at the face of Agent Taft. She looked seasoned, her short, moussed hair prematurely salt-and-pepper. Yet she couldn't be forty.

"How much further to Baxter?" Agent Farber brushed the blond bangs from her forehead and took a sip of water.

Ellen smiled without meaning to.

"Did I say something funny?"

Ellen shook her head. "No, it just reminded me of my boys when we took car trips—always wanting to know if we were there yet. They're grown now. It's just Guy and me."

"Guy's your husband?" Agent Farber said.

"Yes, if he's still speaking to me. The attorney side of him is going to be so put out with me I can't believe it."

"Well, you took a big chance. The newspaper people I've been around act like they're invincible when it comes to getting a story."

"I didn't start out trying to get this story." Ellen heard the defensive tone in her voice. "The perp, as you refer to him, contacted me. I have no idea how he got my cell number." Ellen sighed. "But I took the bait—hook, line, and sinker."

Agent Farber's cell phone rang and she hit the talk button. "This is Farber. Uh, yes, sir, we left Knoxville a couple of hours ago... Agent Taft's with me... You did?... And?..." She glanced over at Ellen and then turned her face toward the side window. There was a long pause. "You want me to pass that along?... Okay, sir. Thanks." Agent Farber put the phone back in her pocket.

"What was all that about?" Ellen said.

"Special Agent Ellis said to tell you the three people in Chicago are confirmed dead, each with a clean shot to the head."

A few seconds passed before Ellen could find her voice. "Then it's true? H-he actually murdered three people, just because I followed up on the lead? But that's exactly what he *wanted* me to do. Why would he do such a despicable thing? Those poor people..." Ellen blinked the stinging from her eyes. "Do you think he killed Richard Boatman and his two bodyguards?"

Agent Farber looked at her questioningly. "Bodyguards?"

"Yes, the two men found shot in Richard's office building."

Agent Farber started to say something and then didn't.

Ellen's mind was reeling with pieces of the puzzle. *Of course, how could I have missed it?* "They weren't bodyguards; they were FBI agents! Vincent Risotto alias Richard Boatman was being relocated after his sister died. And somebody got to him before the FBI could get him out of Raleigh. Right?"

"I wouldn't want to venture a guess," Agent Farber said, her eyes fixed on the road ahead. "I wasn't assigned to that case."

"I think we can cut the guessing game," Ellen said.

"Not my call, ma'am."

"Well, could we at least cut the *ma'am* and go with *Ellen?* First names would make me feel less like a potential victim."

Jordan Ellis hung up the phone and sat back in his chair, his hands clasped behind his head. Washington had agreed to put the Paxton case back in his court. Now he could roll up his sleeves and figure out how to nail Giorgio Merlino before he got to Risotto—or worse yet, to Ellen.

He shook his head. What kind of hate made a guy capable of executing a trail of innocent people just to prove a point?

He pulled out his cell phone and dialed.

"Baxter Police Department. How may I direct your call?"

"This is Jordan Ellis. I need to speak with Chief Cameron, please."

"Yes, sir. One moment."

Jordan unwrapped a stick of spearmint gum and stuffed it in his mouth.

"This is Chief Cameron."

"Aaron, it's Jordan. I don't mean to rain on your parade, but Washington has given me the green light to get back into the Paxton case. I'm going to set up shop in Baxter for a while. Can you handle that?"

"Sure. We haven't made any headway in finding English."

Jordan doodled on a yellow pad. "Well, I've got a hot tip I'll share with you when I get there. This case is multilayered. Better get the sheriff in on it."

"It's starting to feel like the norm, having the FBI in Baxter."

Jordan chuckled. "What scares me is I'm actually starting to like it there. Okay, Aaron, keep the coffeepot on. I'll see you sometime tomorrow."

Ellen pulled into the garage and saw Guy's Lexus. She had hoped he would be at work until dinnertime. She got out of the car and saw the door to the kitchen open.

"You're home early," Guy said. "I wasn't..." His eyes went from

Ellen to Terri to Michelle—and back to Ellen.

"Meet Terri Farber and Michelle Taft," Ellen said. "They're FBI agents. And they're going to go outside for some fresh air while I fill you in on what's been happening."

The two women shook hands with Guy and then turned and walked away, leaving Ellen and Guy standing in the garage.

"Let's go sit at the kitchen table," Ellen said.

Guy looked at her questioningly. "What *is* this?"

"This is Ellen Jones throwing herself on the mercy of the court. Come on, Counselor. Let's get it over with."

She walked inside and sat at the table.

Guy sat facing her, his elbows on the table, his hands folded. "This had better be good."

Ellen paused until she could find her voice, then told him everything that had happened from the time she left Baxter until she pulled into the driveway.

"Well, don't just sit there," she said. "Say something."

"I don't know what you expect me to say. I'm incredibly disappointed in you, Ellen."

"I didn't actually lie. You never asked where I was calling from."

Guy shot her a look. "A fine line, don't you think?"

Ellen felt her throat tighten. "I can't tell you how sorry I am."

"This isn't like you! You're the one who can't handle telling a white lie. How did you justify *this?*"

"Obviously, not very well."

Guy exhaled loudly. "This is so beneath you, Ellen." He pushed back from the table, his face flushed. "I'm so angry I can't think straight!"

"You certainly have a right to be. I'm ashamed I deceived you. But I can't undo what's done."

Guy put his hand on the back of his neck. "I don't know if I can go through this again. How do you think I felt when Wayne Purdy was threatening you? And when Sawyer held you at gunpoint at Saint Anthony's? And when you almost died after the rattlesnake bite? This makes all that seem like a cakewalk!"

Ellen nodded and blinked the moisture from her eyes. "I know."

"I can't believe you got yourself mixed up in this! I am *not* going to lose you! Do you hear me? I'm not!" Guy bit his lip. He paused to gather his composure. "So, is Jordan handling the case?"

She nodded. "Apparently. He'll be here tomorrow."

"Are the two lady agents staying?"

"Yes. Jordan doesn't want me to be alone."

Guy stood up and walked to the kitchen window, his hands in his pockets. "He'd better be on top of his game. And you'd better do everything he says."

"I will."

"That would be a nice change."

"Badgering won't help, Counselor. I'm a little fragile over here."

"That's great, Ellen. But so am I! If you get killed, *I'm* the one who'll suffer! You, on the other hand, will be 'at home with the Lord.' Isn't that nice?"

She started to comment, but chose instead to sit quietly while Guy continued to let out his anger. Finally, he stopped talking and put his palms down on the countertop and lowered his head.

"Are you all right?" Ellen said.

"Of course I'm not all right! This maniac executed three innocent people just to prove he means business. It's hard telling how he'll react when he finds out you called the FBI."

"There's no way he could know I've been in touch with Jordan. For all he knows, I'm still digging to find out where Risotto is."

"Ellen, you are in so deep..." Guy's voice cracked. "I don't believe in God. But if I did, I'd be praying."

Ellen walked in the front door, agents Terri Farber and Michelle Taft behind her. She kicked off her running shoes and flopped on the couch. "That felt good. Thanks."

"No problem," Terri said. "It's part of our normal routine."

Michelle nodded. "It feels like it's dropped thirty degrees since dinner. I wish I'd brought my heavier sweats."

"You can borrow some of mine," Ellen said, aware of the phone ringing.

Guy came into the living room and handed her the cordless phone. "It's Pastor Thomas."

"Hello, Pastor," Ellen said.

"I hope I'm not disturbing you."

"Not at all. I just got back from a good run."

"Is everything all right?"

Ellen paused. "More or less. Why do you ask?"

"For some reason, Penny and I can't get you off our minds. We've felt led to pray for you all day—to the point where I felt compelled to call and tell you."

Ellen looked up at three pairs of eyes and three pairs of ears. "Pastor, excuse me a moment." She got up, her hand over the receiver. "I'll take this in the kitchen. The TV remote is right there on the coffee table."

Ellen walked out to the kitchen, aware that Guy was following her.

"Pastor, I can't tell you how much I appreciate your prayers. I am dealing with something, though I'm not at liberty to share my situation at the moment. *Please* keep praying."

"I don't mean to pry," Pastor Thomas said, "but rarely have Penny and I been led this strongly. We're concerned."

Ellen glanced up at Guy and debated whether to talk about spiritual things in front of him.

"I appreciate your concern," she said. "And your prayers. All I can say for now is please don't stop."

"All right, Ellen. We'll be praying. And we're here if you need us."

She hung up the phone and it rang again.

"Hello?"

"Ellen? It's Rhonda Wilson. Is everything all right with you and Guy?"

"Uh, more or less. Why?"

"Jed and I have had the strangest prompting to pray for you. Is there something specific we can pray for?"

"Rhonda, I can't say too much at the moment, other than you're hearing the Lord right. Please keep praying."

"Okay. Call if you need us."

Ellen hung up the phone.

"Rhonda Wilson, too?" Guy said. "Didn't Jordan tell you not to say anything?"

Ellen looked at her hands, trying to find an answer he could accept.

"Are you just going to ignore my question?"

"You won't like the answer."

Guy rolled his eyes. "I can't believe you told them anyway!"

"I didn't say a word. Sometimes the Lord impresses a person to pray for someone else."

"What do you mean by 'impresses'?" Guy said.

Ellen looked up at him and saw his dark eyes full of skepticism. "It's difficult to explain. It's like a continual nudging to pray for someone."

"You've had this experience?"

"I know a number of people who have. I believe it's valid."

"And I believe it's baloney."

"Fine, then you explain it." Ellen sighed. "Look, what difference does it make why they decided to pray? We need all the help we can get!"

Charlie Kirby sat on the porch swing at Morganstern's, his jacket collar pulled up around his ears, his hands in his pockets. The only thing colder than his nose was Marlie's rejection.

He sighed. How empty the starry night seemed without her! They had always loved the night sky, ever since that mountain retreat in Colorado...

Charlie had taken Marlie by the hand and trudged through the powdery snow until they were far from the artificial lights of the retreat center. Suddenly, the snow seemed to have light of its own, dispelling the darkness, and giving the landscape an almost magical quality.

"It's gorgeous," Marlie said. She dropped down in the snow and lay on her back.

Charlie lay next to her, staring up at the heavens. "Are you cold?"

"No, I'm *amazed*. Look at the stars! I've never seen them like this."

He squeezed her hand. "I know. Blows my mind to think that God did this just by speaking a word."

Marlene turned her head and looked at him, her face full of wonder. "How many people go their whole lives without realizing all this is out here?"

"Probably a lot. Thanks to the lightbulb."

She smiled. "I guess in a roundabout way, God created that, too." She looked up and didn't say anything for a long time. He saw a tear run down the side of her face and wiped it with his glove.

"Hey, what's wrong?"

"Nothing. I'm just overwhelmed with God's goodness—and His glory. I never dreamed I'd love anyone the way I do you. And to be here with you, seeing all this...I feel so blessed."

Charlie inched closer and slid his arm under her neck, and then let his lips melt into hers until every thought he couldn't put into words flowed from his heart to hers. "I love you so much," he finally whispered.

Marlie looked at him, the sweetest smile on her face. "I have something wonderful to tell you."

He stroked her cheek. "What's that?"

"The test was positive."

Charlie stared at her trying to let the reality sink in. "You're pregnant? For real? Are you sure?"

"Dr. Harmon confirmed it."

Charlie jumped up and pulled Marlie to her feet. "I can't believe it! I'm going to be a dad!" He laughed. He cried. He took her in his arms and waltzed in the snow.

She looked up at the sky as he whirled her round and round. "I can't think of a more appropriate place to tell you. Just think: God knows every one of those stars by name, and He knows this child of ours..."

Charlie got out of the porch swing and walked to the railing, a north wind nipping at his face, tears stinging his eyes.

Lord, I know I sinned. I flirted with temptation, and I'm not even sure I would've said no to Sheila the next time. I suppose, technically, I left myself open for what's happened to me.

But Marlie and Kevin shouldn't have to pay for my mistake. Lord, You are the only One who can make this right. I know You've forgiven me. But if they can't, we're going to lose each other.

23

Special Agent Jordan Ellis got out of his car and buttoned his topcoat, relishing for a moment the brilliant reds, golds, purples, and oranges adorning Baxter's town square. Part of the courthouse was hidden behind the golden branches of a huge oak tree, but the clock tower rose above the treetops, crisp white against a bluebird sky.

He walked up the courthouse steps and went inside, then took the elevator to the second floor. When he got out, Police Chief Aaron Cameron and Sheriff Hal Barker were standing in the hall in front of the sheriff's office.

"Well, look who's here," Hal said.

Jordan extended his hand. "Good to see you, Sheriff. You too, Chief."

"Your agents have your temporary office ready to go," Aaron said. "Third door on the right. Deja vu."

"Great." Jordan looked at his watch. "When do you want to meet?"

"I cleared my calendar," Aaron said. "Hal's got a deputies' meeting at three-thirty."

"All right, give me thirty minutes, then come down to my office." Jordan looked at Aaron, and then at Hal. "Any chance we can get the Joneses and Kirbys to join us?"

"I'll see," Aaron said. "If not, do you want to wait?"

Jordan shook his head. "We don't have any time to waste."

Marlene Kirby walked in from the garage and put her coat and purse on the countertop. All she had thought about for the past twenty minutes was a hot cup of coffee, a Toll House cookie, and the quiet that awaited her with all seven kids in school.

Hershey scratched on the door, and she let him in.

"Too cold for you, too?" She rubbed his ears and stroked his fur. "Okay, go find a place to curl up. This is my quiet time."

Hershey sat at her feet and whined, his tail wagging.

"Oh, all right." Marlene went to the pantry, picked up the box of dog biscuits, and took out two. "This is all you get."

Hershey devoured them and then went and lay in the sun in the corner of the breakfast nook. Marlene was thinking Kevin could learn a lot about obedience from Hershey.

She walked to the coffeepot and saw a pink rose next to her coffee cup. She picked it up and put it to her nose, the fragrance filling her senses. Why was Charlie doing this? Did he really think it would mean anything now?...

Marlene had awakened to the sound of Charlie's voice, and from her hospital bed, she saw him sitting in a rocker, Kevin cradled in his arms, their noses almost touching.

"Well, son, you're our firstborn," Charlie said softly. "I've always wondered what you'd be like. God knew, but He didn't let me and your mother in on it till now."

Charlie's eyes seemed to trace Kevin's facial features. The joy on her husband's face brought tears to her eyes.

"Can I tell you a little secret, man to man? You've got the best mother there is, bar none. She loves children. In fact, she wants a whole houseful of them. But for a while, we get her all to ourselves. She's about the gentlest, kindest, sweetest woman that ever was." Charlie reached over to a vase of flowers and pulled out a pink rose and held it up. "She's as sweet as this rose. And just as intricate.

And out of the millions and millions of women in the world, God picked her just for us..."

Marlene dropped the rose in the trash can and poured herself a cup of coffee just as the phone rang.

"Hello," she said, harsher than she meant to.

"Marlie, it's me. Are you all right?"

"Yes, I'm fine. What is it, Charlie?"

"Chief Cameron and Sheriff Barker are joining with the FBI in an effort to find Mr. English. They want Ellen and me to come to a meeting at the courthouse in forty-five minutes. I think you should be there."

"I have to pick up the preschoolers at eleven-thirty."

"I'll bet Jennifer Lawton would do it for you."

"Charlie, why do I need to be there for this? Haven't I been through enough humiliation?"

"It sounds serious. Jordan Ellis thinks you ought to be there. Guy Jones is coming, too."

Charlie was standing in the temporary FBI office making small talk with Ellen, Hal, and Aaron when he saw Marlie come in. He walked over to her, resisting the urge to put his arm around her.

"Thanks for coming," he said. "Did you get the kids squared away?"

"Jennifer's going to pick them up and keep them till I call. Who are all these people?" she whispered.

"FBI agents. Why don't we sit over there next to Ellen and Guy? Jordan's ready to begin."

"I'm glad we were able to get everyone here for the meeting," Jordan said. "I'm telling you up front, the information I'm about to share is sensitive. I'd like each of you to listen carefully. If you have questions, let's get them answered before you leave. I must insist you don't discuss the details of the case with anyone else.

"Each of you knows the events that led to our search for Mr. English, but I need to fill in the blanks. Some of what I'm going to say will make you uneasy. But I also want to assure you that my agents are trained to keep you safe. If we work together, we'll get this guy before he hurts anyone else."

Jordan went on to explain the violent history between the Risottos and the Merlinos, and about Mary Angelina and Vincent being placed in the witness protection program. He gave details of the three killings in Raleigh and the three in Chicago, and said the execution-style murders were probably done by the man who blackmailed Charlie and was threatening Ellen: Giorgio Merlino. Jordan warned that this man was desperate to get Risotto and would stop at nothing to achieve that end.

Charlie glanced over at Marlie and felt about an inch tall. He thought back on Sheila's sleek dark hair, her deep brown eyes, and her olive complexion. Her Italian heritage was evident. But he couldn't comprehend that a woman so sophisticated, educated, and articulate had grown up in the Mob.

Jordan cleared his throat and took a sip of water. "My agents are going to be working with Chief Cameron and Sheriff Barker to conduct a search of the area to see if we can retrace Merlino's steps. Ellen's description gave us an artist's sketch that closely resembles his mug shots. Someone has to have seen him. *If* he's here, we'll find him.

"But truthfully, it's hard to say where he is. The phone records show Merlino's calls to Ellen's cell were made from a pay phone in Linwood Heights, Illinois. And the ones to Charlie's cell were made from the pay phone at the Quick Stop in Baxter."

Charlie held open the door to the kitchen and followed Marlie inside. "Want me to go to the Lawtons' and pick up the kids?"

Marlie shook her head. "No, I'll go get them in a few minutes. I need time to assimilate this."

Charlie threw his London Fog jacket over a chair and sat at the table across from Marlie, his hands folded. "It *is* mind boggling. I'm shocked about Sheila's background. Hard to believe the man who tried to blackmail me was a gangster."

"Then you can imagine how terrified Ellen must be."

"Don't worry, Marlie. The FBI will get this guy. They won't let anything happen to Ellen."

Marlie shot him a look, her eyes brimming with tears. "Of course, if you'd kept your hands to yourself, none of this would've happened."

Charlie started to defend himself and then decided it was pointless. "At least Jordan doesn't think this Merlino will threaten me anymore."

"Why would he?" Marlie said. "He's already destroyed you—he didn't have to use a gun."

"Well, it didn't work. I'm fighting back."

She rolled her eyes. "It's a little late for that."

"Marlie, honey, please look at me. I'm deeply sorry for my inappropriate thoughts about Sheila. But my battle with temptation had absolutely nothing to do with my feelings for you. I love you. I will *always* love you. If only I could make you understand that."

She glanced at the clock. "I need to pick up the kids."

"Are you okay with being here alone with them?"

"I'm not asking you to come back, if that's what you think."

"I know," Charlie said. "But wouldn't you feel safer with me in the house? I'll sleep in my study."

"What about Kevin? You're the one who said the tension in the house was causing him to act out."

"Well, he's acting out anyway. I might as well be here to help you deal with it."

Marlie looked up at him, her eyebrows furrowed. "You're wasting your money on the roses."

"Not from my perspective."

"I've thrown them in the trash—all of them."

"I know."

"If you think you can soften me, you're wrong."

Charlie pushed away from the table and stood. "I've got a city council meeting at three o'clock. Shall I check out of Morganstern's?"

Marlie looked at him, her eyes full of questions. "Suit yourself. Just don't think coming back here is going to make any difference in how I feel."

Giorgio heard a knock on his door at the Heron Lake Lodge. He jumped up from the table and looked out the peephole. Two men, each wearing a badge and a Stetson, stood at his door.

Giorgio grabbed his pistol and looked out the back window, his eyes surveying the grounds behind the lodge. He didn't see any sign of law enforcement.

He hid the gun in his waistband, then opened the door, appearing sheepish. "Sorry. You caught me in the bathroom."

"Mr. Aldridge—George Aldridge?" said the man on the left.

"Yes, sir. That's me. What can I do for you?" Giorgio said, putting forth his best Carolina accent.

"I'm Deputy Hines and this is Deputy Sloan with the Norris County Sheriff's Department. We were wonderin' if you've seen this man?" Deputy Hines held up a color sketch of a bearded man with brown eyes and glasses. "Take your time, sir."

Giorgio was careful not to touch the paper. He shook his head. "No, sorry. Is he in trouble?"

"We just wanna talk to him, sir. Here's my card. We'd appreciate a call if you spot him. It's real important."

"Sure thing. I'll be here a few more days, enjoying the foliage. I'll keep my eyes open."

"Much obliged." Deputy Hines tipped the brim of his Stetson.

Giorgio shut the door, a grin stretched across his face. He felt the adrenaline coursing through his veins. He loved the thrill of danger! Trying to blackmail Charlie Kirby had been fun. Blowing away six people to make a statement, completely entertaining. But muscling Ellen Jones to find Risotto would prove the most exciting of all if he could stay a step ahead of the feds.

Charlie walked through the wrought iron gate and up onto the wood porch of a gray-and-burgundy Victorian house. He rang the bell.

A female FBI agent opened the door and then stepped aside. "It's Mayor Kirby."

"Charlie!" Guy Jones said. "Come in out of the cold."

Charlie stepped inside and slipped off his coat. "Sorry to drop by unannounced. I won't stay but a minute."

Charlie followed Guy into the family room where Ellen was sitting by the fire, her feet on an ottoman.

"I'm glad it's you," Ellen said. "I'm nervous as a kitten. Want some decaf? I brewed a fresh pot of hazelnut."

"All right, thanks. Black is fine."

"I'll get it," Guy said.

Charlie sat down on the sofa, aware that two female FBI agents were in the next room.

"Quite a meeting we had today," Ellen said.

Charlie nodded. "Sobering."

Guy came in and handed Charlie a cup of coffee, then sat in the chair next to Ellen's.

"I feel a little responsible for the trouble you're in," Charlie said.

"Nonsense." Ellen sipped her coffee. "I made my own choices."

"Even so, I—"

"Ease your mind, Charlie. None of this is your fault. You have enough to worry about. How're things with Marlene?"

"Not good. I'd been staying at Morganstern's since Sunday night, but after today's meeting, I thought I should move back in so she and the kids won't be alone. I'm headed there now."

Ellen sighed. "I don't understand what this Giorgio Merlino hoped to gain once he gave the diary to KJNX."

"I think he did it for spite," Charlie said. "He doesn't strike me as the type of guy who takes no for an answer."

Guy arched his eyebrows. "Don't remind me."

"Were you as surprised as I was to find out Sheila's background?" Charlie said. "I feel so stupid."

"You're not alone," Ellen said. "After Richard was murdered, my instincts told me I had no business getting close to this story. I left Raleigh with Guy and decided not to do a feature on Sheila. And I would've left it at that, but—"

"But that would've been too simple," Guy said.

Ellen sighed. "But when the diary surfaced, and Merlino attempted to blackmail you, it suddenly became personal. How could I have known that following up on a tip that Sheila was alive would land me in the middle of some Mob-related vendetta...and get three more people killed to boot?"

Guy smiled wryly. "Nothing like a little trip to the Windy City."

"I can't comprehend that Merlino murdered the people Ellen talked to," Charlie said. "You two must be terrified."

"That about covers it," Guy said. "It's unsettling that Jordan doesn't know where he is."

"Charlie, is there anything we can do to help you?" Ellen said. "You and Marlene look weary."

"Pray. If Marlie and I stand any hope of resuming a normal life, God's going to have to intervene."

"He's got all kinds of people praying for Ellen," Guy said sarcastically. "Go ahead. Ask her."

Charlie took a sip of coffee and noticed Ellen's pained expression. "I hope they're praying for me, too. It's going to take a whole lot more than my own strength to get Marlie and me back together."

The mantle clock chimed eight times.

Charlie took the last sip and put the cup and saucer on the end table. "Thanks for the coffee. I really need to be going." He got up from the couch. "Never thought I'd be nervous about going home."

Guy put a hand on his shoulder. "Hang in there."

"Thanks, I will. You, too."

Ellen hugged him a little longer than usual. "It'll be all right," she whispered. "You two are going to make it."

Charlie sat on a park bench near the courthouse, the wind nipping at his ears, his hands tucked in his coat pockets, and listened to the leaves whirling in the darkness. Sometimes it seemed as though this place had a heartbeat.

He looked up at the white rounded pillars on the front of the courthouse and thought of how many times he had hidden behind them, playing hide-and-seek as a boy.

His eyes moved along the empty streets around the square, and he could almost hear the marching band in the Fourth of July parade—and the barbershop quartet. His mouth watered for fried chicken, watermelon, and homemade ice cream...

"Come on, Charlie," Avery Stedman had said. "We're gonna take some cherry bombs out to the pond and scare the ducks." He laughed. "It's gonna be so cool."

"My dad's singing in the quartet."

"So?"

"I think he'd like me to be here."

Avery rolled his eyes. "Everybody who's anybody is gonna be there."

Charlie knew better. And before an hour was over, the volunteer fire department was called out. Avery Stedman and a few trouble-makers from school had "accidentally" burned umpteen acres of valuable farmland...

Charlie shook his head. Avery hadn't gotten any wiser or any more truthful with age.

On the corner under a streetlight, he noticed Father Donaghan shuffling down the sidewalk holding his sweater-clad Chihuahua on a leash. For a split second, he could almost feel Hershey's cold nose nudging his hand.

The tower clock struck nine. All the kids would be in bed. He got up from the park bench and walked to his car, wondering if this awful feeling would ever go away.

24

Charlie Kirby awakened, aware of Kevin standing in the doorway of his study. He opened his eyes wide and blinked several times to get the sandy sensation to go away, then sat upright in his recliner.

"When did you get home?" Kevin said.

"Uh, just after you went to bed." Charlie brushed the hair off his forehead. "Come sit for a minute."

Kevin came in and flopped in a chair. "Are you staying?"

"I'd like to. Your mother and I have some things to work out. Things won't feel normal for a while."

"I'm getting used to it."

"I don't want you to get used to it." Charlie got up and stretched. "I'm going to work hard to make things right."

"How're you going to do that? Mom's still mad."

"I know. But I love her. And I love you kids. I'm going to do everything I can to help us get back to normal."

"She's depressed," Kevin said.

"I think we all are, son."

"Why do you keep giving her roses? All she does is throw them away."

"Someday she won't," Charlie said. "That's how I'll know—"

Charlie heard bare feet running down the hall, and looked up just as a headful of dark curls came charging through the doorway.

"Daddy!" His youngest daughter squealed with delight and leapt into his arms.

Charlie kissed her repeatedly, and then lifted her up high,

enjoying the sound of her laughter.

A few seconds later, the other five children were all over him, vying for his attention. Even Hershey yelped and ran in circles. Charlie relished the pandemonium. He fell back into the recliner and let them climb all over him.

"Children, I need your attention." Marlie stood in the doorway until all eyes were on her. "Everybody wash your hands. Breakfast is ready. We've got three soccer games today. I need you guys to hustle."

One by one, the kids squeezed by her and raced toward the kitchen.

Marlie remained in the doorway, her eyes colliding with Charlie's.

"Don't think that just because you're home, all is well," she said. "The children have missed you, and I wouldn't do anything to squelch their excitement. Just don't expect me to feel the same way." She reached in the pouch of her apron and pulled out a crumpled pink rose, its stem folded in half, and pitched it in his lap. "Stop trying to manipulate my feelings, Charlie. It won't work."

Dennis Lawton came into the kitchen and slid his arms around Jennifer and nuzzled her neck. "What have you got planned today, Mrs. Lawton?"

Jennifer rested against his chest. "I offered to keep four of the Kirby kids so Marlene could take the others to their usual Saturday morning soccer marathon. I don't know how she keeps up with it."

"Charlie helps her, that's how she does it."

"That doesn't seem to be going very well. She looked miserable yesterday when she picked the kids up."

"Well, it's only been a week since she found out about the diary," Dennis said. "It'll take a lot longer than that to get over it."

"If she ever does. Do you really think Charlie's innocent?"

"Doesn't matter what I think." Dennis turned her around in his arms. "Remember what Pastor Thomas keeps driving home, that

God calls us to be witnesses, *not* judges?"

"I know. I'm concerned about Marlene. I'm not sure I could get over it."

"You're right, *you* couldn't. But the Lord could do it through you. Sometimes that's the only way it's possible."

Jennifer laid her head on his shoulder. "I always considered the Kirby's marriage to be the perfect model."

"Yeah, it would be tragic to see them get a divorce. I hope they're going to Pastor Thomas for counseling."

"Marlene didn't say, and I didn't ask."

"When is she bringing the kids?"

Jennifer looked up at the clock. "In twenty minutes. I need to get the boys dressed. It's going to be an absolute zoo."

"Don't worry, I'm not leaving you alone with six kids," Dennis said. "We've got enough here to entertain them for a while, and then maybe we can get pizza or something later on."

She kissed his cheek. "You're a prince."

Jordan Ellis sat in his office, his feet on his desk, perusing the contact reports the sheriff's deputies and police officers had submitted. They had checked out every bed and breakfast, motel, and lodge in the area—even apartments. Giorgio Merlino was not registered. No big surprise.

The day manager at the Heron Lake Lodge remembered checking in a man who resembled the artist's sketch, but she didn't recall his name or the dates he had stayed there. The sheriff's department pulled the guest registry dating back to Sheila Paxton's death, but found nothing of interest. They were in the process of checking out all the out-of-state license plate numbers.

Jordan sighed. Where had Merlino stayed? Where was he now? Not that he cared what happened to him—or to Risotto. They were both creeps who didn't deserve the time of day.

But what happened to Ellen Jones was of utmost concern, and he still didn't know where the enemy was.

His phone rang and he picked it up. "This is Jordan."

"This is Hal. Aaron and I want to show you something. We're heading your way."

"Good, I'm going nuts down here."

Ellen Jones savored the last bite of cinnamon roll, and then chased it with a swallow of coffee.

Guy handed her a warm, wet cloth with a pair of tongs, and she wiped her hands.

"Well, ladies," she said, "you can see for yourselves how he spoils me."

"Does he have a brother?" Agent Terri Farber said, pressing together the crumbs on her plate and popping them into her mouth.

Agent Michelle Taft looked at Guy and then at Ellen. "You guys really do this every Saturday?"

Ellen nodded. "It's a fun ritual. He's got it down to a science."

A cell phone rang and everyone got quiet.

"It's yours," Terri said, her eyes wide. "If it's him, I want to listen."

"Hello, this is Ellen...hello?..."

"Well, well, well. I thought maybe you'd decided to avoid me," Giorgio said. "Which would be a very stupid thing to do."

Ellen motioned Terri to put her ear close to the receiver.

"What exactly do you want from me?" Ellen said, trying to sound calm.

"You know what I want: Find me Risotto. Unless you'd like to end up like poor Mrs. Stassi."

Terri mouthed the words, "Tell him you need time."

"I need a little time," Ellen said.

"That's all I'm givin' you, lady—a little time. Time's almost up."
Click.

Ellen hung up the phone, her hand shaking.

Guy put his arm around her and pulled her close. "It's all right. He can't get to you."

"I'm going to find out where the call originated." Terri took her cell phone out of her pocket and left the room.

"What did he say to you?" Michelle said.

"He wants me to find Risotto. How does he think I'm going to do that? He said time's almost up."

Michelle raised her eyebrows. "Yeah, for *him* maybe."

Jordan heard footsteps and looked up as Sheriff Hal Barker and Police Chief Aaron Cameron walked into his office and placed a form on the desk in front of him.

"Look at this," Hal took his index finger and pointed to the name George Aldridge. "This guy's a guest at the Heron Lake Lodge. Drives a blue Impala with Illinois plates."

"I read the report," Jordan said. "Your deputies talked to him yesterday and he seemed cooperative. Doesn't match Merlino's description."

Hal's eyes narrowed. "But the license number he gave on the guest check-in form is registered to a Jillian Majors, a nurse at the University of Chicago Medical Center. She was reported missing two weeks ago."

Charlie took the remote and flipped from channel to channel, then turned off the TV. Not even college football sounded appealing.

He walked out to the kitchen, but didn't know why. He smiled at the pictures of the kids on the refrigerator and could hardly wait until they were home.

He could understand Marlie rejecting his offer to go to the soccer games with her. But why had she been reluctant to let him stay with the younger kids? Was she trying to punish him?

The doorbell rang and Hershey started barking.

Charlie went out to the entry hall and looked through the peephole. It was Pastor Thomas. He opened the door.

"Bart, what a nice surprise."

"Sorry to come by unannounced. I was in the neighborhood and hoped it would be okay."

"Sure, come in," Charlie said. "I'm here by myself. Marlie and the kids are at soccer—well, the three oldest anyway. Jennifer Lawton has the little ones."

"I'm glad you decided to come home," Bart said. "You looked miserable when you told me you were moving out."

"It's been rough."

"Is Marlene softening at all?

Charlie sighed. "If she is, I can't see it."

Charlie led Pastor Thomas into the living room. "Please sit down. Would you like something to drink—coffee, water, a soft drink?"

"No, thanks. I'm fine. I came by to see if you and Marlene have thought any more about counseling?"

"I have. She seems unwilling to consider it right now."

"Yes, but letting the sun go down on her anger night after night will only make things worse."

Charlie leaned his head back on the couch. "I know, but I can't force her. She has to *want* to make things work."

"Then make her believe it can happen," Bart said.

"How?"

"Ask the Lord to show you. He knows. The only thing I know for sure is that He wants the two of you together."

"So do I. I can't even imagine my life without her. She's been my best friend for fifteen years..." Charlie clasped his hands and paused until his chin stopped quivering. "Sorry. Makes me want to shout to every man I know to keep his thoughts where they belong. I can't believe I'm even in this mess. I love my wife. I don't want to lose her."

Ellen sat on the couch in the family room, her hands knitting almost as fast as her mind was racing.

The doorbell rang and she heard voices and footsteps. She looked up and saw Guy and Jordan walk through the doorway, followed by Hal and Aaron, and Terri and Michelle.

Her heart sank. "What's wrong?"

"Nothing," Guy said. "Jordan just needs to talk with us."

Ellen waited while everyone found a seat. The looks on their faces told her something had happened.

"We believe Merlino's in Baxter," Jordan said. "A George Aldridge staying at the Heron Lake Lodge checked in with Illinois plates registered to a nurse in Chicago who's been missing for two weeks."

Ellen slipped her hand into Guy's.

"We went out to the lodge. Aldridge wasn't in, but the manager let us in his room, and we dusted for prints: Merlino's are all over the place."

"No one recognized him from the artist's sketch?" Guy said.

Jordan lifted his eyebrows. "Maybe he altered his looks. Fingerprints don't lie."

Ellen's heart pounded wildly. "Okay, what happens now?"

"We sit tight and wait for him to come back," Jordan said. "He's been registered at the lodge for over a week and probably feels safe there."

"But he could be calling from anywhere," Guy said.

Jordan shook his head. "He's here. That last call to Ellen was made from the pay phone at Miller's Market."

"If Merlino was staying at the lodge when those people were murdered in Chicago," Ellen said, "how do you know he did it?"

"We don't. But he told you before the media reported it. And it was the same gun that killed the three in Raleigh."

Ellen held tightly to Guy's hand. "Why does he think I can help him? I haven't a clue how to find Risotto."

"Merlino's not thinking rationally," Jordan said, "but that should work in our favor. He's bound to get careless."

"What if he knows you're onto him and doesn't come back here?" Guy said. "How can Ellen possibly feel safe with him on the loose?"

Jordan looked at Guy and then at Ellen. "No matter where he lights, we know he'll call back. Here's what I want Ellen to do..."

25

Charlie Kirby picked up the platter with two grilled hamburgers on it and held it in front of Kevin. "Want another one?"

"Okay." Kevin picked up a patty with his fork. "I'll have some more French fries, too."

"Marlie?"

She shook her head and pushed back from the table. "I need to get the little ones bathed."

Charlie slid the last hamburger onto his plate, feeling more awkward than he had the first time he went to Marlie's parents' house for dinner. Surface talk was not something he enjoyed—and especially not with the person who knew him best.

Marlie walked to the sink and got a warm washcloth and wiped the ketchup off two little faces and two sets of hands. "Come on, Mommy will make lots of bubbles and you can play a while."

As Marlie left the kitchen, the other children asked to be excused, leaving Charlie and Kevin alone at the table.

"Mom's acting weird."

"She's a little uptight. It'll get better."

"What if it doesn't?"

Charlie looked into Kevin's eyes. "It will."

Kevin dropped his fork and reached down to pick it up. Three cigarettes dropped on the floor. He quickly stuffed them into his shirt pocket and sat up as if nothing had happened.

Charlie held out his hand, his palm up.

"What?" Kevin said.

"Give me the cigarettes."

Kevin sighed. He reached in his pocket and put the cigarettes in Charlie's hand.

"Where's the pack?" Charlie said.

"I don't have any more."

"The pack, Kevin. Give it to me."

Kevin got up and left the kitchen. A minute later he came back and gave Charlie a half-empty pack of Lucky Strike cigarettes.

"Sit down," Charlie said. "We need to talk."

"About what?"

"About why you feel this need to rebel, and then make things worse by lying about it."

Kevin slouched in the chair, his arms folded, and exhaled loudly.

"Son, this is not just about cigarettes being unhealthy. It's against the law for a twelve-year-old to smoke. Where did you get these?"

Kevin shrugged. "I don't remember."

"Yes, you do."

"Okay, Ricky's brother bought me some. Big deal."

Charlie shook his head from side to side, then leaned forward, his elbows on the table. "Suppose you tell me what's really bothering you."

"Why? It won't make any difference."

"I want to hear it anyway."

Kevin gave him a steely cold look. "I don't think you do."

"*Yes,* I do." Charlie bowed his head and breathed in slowly, finding it difficult to mask his irritation. "I'm waiting."

"The guys at school are talking."

"About what?"

Kevin looked down and played with his fingers.

"Son, I'm about to lose my patience with—"

"They think what happened with Sheila was cool, all right?"

Charlie sat up straight, his face flushed. "*Nothing* happened. But what I'm accused of doing is anything but cool. Just look at the pain it's caused your mother and me—all of us."

There was a long pause.

"Well, they think Sheila Paxton's hot."

Charlie tried to hide his revulsion at hearing the words come out of his twelve-year-old's mouth.

"They need to be taught to respect women."

"By who—*you?*" Kevin glanced up at him and then looked away. "They see stuff on the Internet, stuff you warned me to stay away from. That's all they talk about now. *I* won't. So everyone's making fun of me because I'm not *cool like my dad*..." Kevin's voice cracked. "What am I supposed to say?"

Ellen lay in bed, reading the latest Grisham novel, and heard Guy come in and close the door. He took his pajamas out of the dresser and went into the bathroom without saying a word. A couple minutes later he came to bed and got under the covers.

"It's a little early to go to sleep," Ellen said.

"It beats watching TV with the FBI."

Ellen sighed. "You still mad at me?"

"What do you think?"

Ellen marked her place and closed the book. "I think I don't blame you."

"Maybe I'm getting old, but I'm ready for a change," Guy said. "I can't go through this again."

"Then you're leaving me?" Ellen said jokingly.

"It crossed my mind." He reached over and touched her arm. "But life would seem pretty shallow without you."

Ellen lay down, then turned on her side, her face in front of his. "I'm truly sorry for getting mixed up in this."

"That's what you said. But here we are—again."

"All I wanted to do was report the news."

"Yet once again, you're *making* it."

Ellen clung to his arm. "Guy, I'm scared."

His face softened and he pulled her close. "Me, too. Jordan's idea sounds feasible. Let's hope it works."

Charlie went into his study and locked the door. He fell on the couch, put his hand over his eyes, and wept.

Lord, I don't even know what to tell Kevin. This thing is so out of hand. I've lost everything: my wife, my son, my reputation, my witness—and everyone's respect. I've asked Your forgiveness. I don't think I can take much more.

Charlie wept as he never had before, stifling his sobs in the couch cushion. Minutes passed. How could he ever dig out of this hole? He couldn't imagine feeling any lower.

There was a knock on the door.

"It's me," Marlie said.

"Just a minute."

He rose to his feet, took the handkerchief from his pocket, and quickly wiped the tears from his face, then blew his nose.

"Charlie, would you open the door, please?"

"I'm coming."

He unlocked the door and opened it, hoping she couldn't tell he'd been crying.

Marlie looked surprised but didn't comment. "Can you handle all of us going to church together tomorrow?"

"I'd like that."

"Nothing's changed in my mind. But the kids need stability."

Charlie nodded. "I agree."

Marlie hesitated a moment, and then reached in the pocket of her bathrobe and handed him the pink rose he had left in her Bible. "I wish you'd stop doing this."

"You used to love it."

"That was before you..." She put her hand to her mouth and choked back the emotion. "I'm willing to pretend things are working for the children's sake. But nothing will ever be the same between us."

Giorgio Merlino drove his rental car down the main highway toward Ellison. There wasn't any point in calling Ellen Jones again till she'd had time to dig. And he had no intention of hanging out in boring Baxter till then. Why not go somewhere and have a few drinks, maybe meet someone?

He wondered what kind of woman Mary Angelina had turned out to be. He'd had a crush on her in high school, but the rivalry between their two families made it impossible to do anything about it.

He'd never had much use for her brother. He thought back on his recent trip to Raleigh and his brief encounter with Vincent...

Giorgio had wasted the two feds and hauled Vincent to Haverly Park, where they took a little walk in the dark. "You've been away a long time, *Richard*. Where's your old man?"

"I...I don't know."

Giorgio pressed the gun barrel to Vincent's head. "Don't lie to me, you lousy—"

"The feds separated us!"

"You expect me to believe you haven't seen Spike in all this time?"

Vincent nodded, his body trembling, perspiration soaking his shirt.

"How is it you just happened to set up house with Mary Angelina—huh?" Giorgio pushed Vincent to his knees.

"The feds fixed it so the two of us could stay in contact. All we had was each other."

"That's touching, Vince. *I* want your old man."

Vincent's voice was shaking. "Please don't kill me! I don't know anything!"

Giorgio pushed the gun barrel against the back of Vincent's head. "Think he's worth dying for? Stop messing with me. You know where he is."

"No, I don't! I swear it!" Vincent began to sob.

"Well, then. Let this be a message to Spike that I'm gonna find him if it's the last thing I ever do."

Giorgio fired, the silencer allowing him to walk away with no one the wiser...

Giorgio spotted the Ellison turnoff up ahead and got into the right lane. He might as well have some fun while he figured out his next move.

26

Charlie Kirby stood looking out the kitchen window, glad the forecast called for a warming trend. He looked up at the clock, then turned his head toward the hallway and raised his voice. "Okay, gang. The bus is leaving."

One by one, the kids started coming, followed by Marlie, who looked lovely in spite of her frown.

"Where's Kevin?" Charlie said. "Never mind; I'll get him."

Charlie walked to Kevin's room and saw it was empty. There was a note on his bed. Charlie read it and let out a sigh of frustration, then walked back to the kitchen.

"Is he coming?" Marlie said.

Charlie shook his head. "I'll deal with him later. Let's not be late because of him."

"The idea was to go as a family," Marlie said.

Charlie picked up his youngest daughter and then grabbed his Bible. "I'm not letting Kevin spoil it for the others. Let's go."

Kevin laid his bicycle on the ground and climbed up on the same boulder as last time. He took the red foil wrapper off a cereal bar and took a bite. He looked out over Heron Lake and wondered what he was he going to do out here all day. He stuffed the rest of the bar in his mouth, then licked his fingers and wiped them on his jeans.

Kevin took off his stocking cap and unbuttoned his jacket, then stretched out on his back and let the morning sun melt over him. He slipped off his jacket, rolled it up, and put it under his head. The breeze felt warm. He looked up at the cloudless sky, his eyes following a flock of cormorants until they dropped down behind a bluff. He closed his eyes and felt himself drifting off to sleep.

"Hey, lazy bones, you gonna sleep all day?"

Kevin squinted and let his eyes adjust to the light. Where was he? He lay there a second and then remembered. He smiled and sat up. "Josiah! When did you get here?"

"I'm never far away, boy. Been fishin' for nigh onto three hours while you were up on that rock, just snorin' away."

"I don't snore," Kevin said, a grin taking over his face.

"How do you know?" Josiah laughed. "Come down here and take this other pole for me, would you?"

Kevin hopped off the rock and walked to the water's edge.

Josiah handed him a rod and pointed to a red-and-white bobber floating on the water several yards out. "That thing goes down, you start reelin' like nuts."

"Yeah, I remember." Kevin sat on the ground next to Josiah's chair.

"What brings you out here, boy?"

"Didn't feel like going to church, that's all."

"Your folks know where you are?"

Kevin looked up at Josiah's kind face shaded under a big straw hat. "Not exactly. I left them a note that I didn't want to go to church today."

"I see." Josiah pursed his lips and nodded his head.

"It's no big deal."

Josiah kept his eyes on the bobber and seemed to be thinking. "Been prayin' like we talked about, have you?"

Kevin shrugged. "Sometimes. It's not doing any good."

"How do you know?"

"Because my dad came home, and my mom seems more miserable than ever."

"Your folks fightin', are they?"

"Not really. They just look sad and Mom sighs a lot."

The old man kept his eyes on the two bobbers at the end of the lines. Several minutes went by without either of them saying anything.

"So, how're you handlin' all this?" Josiah finally said.

Kevin looked at the ground between his knees. "It's really hard. Everyone's saying awful things about my dad. Embarrassing stuff."

"I've heard it."

Kevin looked up at Josiah's dark, round eyes. "Then you know who my dad is?"

Josiah nodded. "Do you?"

"What do you mean?"

"He might've fallen, but that ain't no reason for folks to keep steppin' on him. Best I can tell he's a fine man."

"Tell that to my mom," Kevin said.

"The Lord's gotta change her heart, boy. Give it time. The wound's still fresh."

"How much time does it take?"

"No tellin'. But the Lord's got it timed just right."

Kevin sighed. "Well, I'm sick of waiting."

Several minutes passed in silence.

"My dad leaves her a rose every single day, and all she does is throw it in the trash. She doesn't love him anymore."

Josiah reached under his straw hat and wiped his forehead with a red kerchief. "Hurt don't leave room for a person to *feel* much else. But that don't mean those feelin's ain't still there."

Charlie hung his sport coat in the closet, then picked up his Bible off the bed. He started to leave when Marlie came in and shut the door.

"All right, the kids are eating lunch. Let's go talk to Kevin. He'd better have a good excuse for not going to church today."

"You won't find him in his room." Charlie took a piece of paper out of his pocket and handed it to Marlene.

She read it aloud, "'I don't feel like going to church today. Please don't be mad. I'll see you later. Love, Kevin.' He left?"

Charlie nodded. "That's why I didn't say anything before church."

"I would've thought he'd be happy we were all going to church together."

"Kevin and I had words last night," Charlie said. "He had cigarettes on him again. I think he's under as much pressure as we are."

"It can't be easy for him, but running isn't the answer. We need to look for him."

"My guess is he's at the lake with Josiah."

The lines on Marlie's forehead deepened. "I struggle with the idea that Kevin should be rewarded for bad behavior."

"Well, considering all the bad things our son could be doing, I prefer to think of his being with Josiah as an answer to prayer."

Ellen Jones walked into the kitchen from the garage, Terri Farber and Michelle Taft behind her.

Guy looked up, the Sunday paper spread in front of him on the table. "So, how was church?"

"Good," Ellen said. "Marlene and Charlie were there."

"That's good, I guess." Guy raised his eyebrows. "Well, how'd you two enjoy the church *experience?*"

"I'm not big on religion," Terri said. "But the people were nice."

Guy smiled. "A girl after my own heart."

"Well, I loved it," Michelle said. "I don't often get the chance to attend church when I'm working an assignment."

Guy looked over his glasses. "You're one of *them?* Just kidding. Religion seems to work for Ellen. I'm fine with it, as long as she doesn't drag me into it. So, who did you tell people you were?"

"Friends of Ellen's, visiting from Knoxville," Michelle said.

Guy took a sip of coffee. "Well, all's quiet on the home front."

"That's good news," Ellen said. "Anybody ready for lunch? I'm thinking of making fajitas."

Guy smiled. "Count me in."

Michelle nodded. "Mmm...let me help you. I was raised in Texas and we had Mexican food once a week, whether we needed it or not."

"What're fajitas?" Terri said.

"You've never had them?" Ellen said.

"No, I grew up in Rhode Island. I never developed a taste for Mexican food."

"Actually, it's Tex-Mex. A bit more Americanized."

Guy got up and pulled out a chair. "Well, sit down, Ms. Farber, and let us tantalize your taste buds with a dining experience in a class by itself."

"Of course, we'll need to have some of that chocolate dream pie I took out of the freezer," Ellen said. "You do know that the word stressed is desserts spelled backwards, don't you?"

Guy chuckled. "You would know that."

Ellen's cell phone rang and everyone froze.

"Okay, people, let's stay calm," Terri said. "Ellen, do you remember what Jordan told you to say?"

She nodded, her heart racing. "It's probably just Margie. Okay, here goes." She picked up the phone and hit the talk button. "Hello, this is Ellen."

"This is your ol' pal, Lucky Day." The voice sounded slurred. "I'm just callin' to remind you that—"

"I've been waiting for you to call. I've got something for you."

"You do?"

Ellen put her hand over the receiver. "I think he's drunk," she whispered.

Terri motioned her to go on.

"I haven't had time to check it out, but I have a pretty reliable lead on Risotto," Ellen said.

"That was fast."

"I know someone working the Paxton case. But I had to step *way* over the line to get this for you."

"Stop whining and let's hear it."

Ellen glanced up at Guy and saw the angst in his eyes. "About eighteen years ago, a couple by the name of Lawrence and Priscilla Carver moved into the town of Micklenburg in southwest Oregon, and set up a bakery called the Bread Basket. They still run it today. My source claims their real names are Antonio and Rita Risotto."

"Would your *source* just happen to be a fed?"

"Look, my life and my career are in serious jeopardy. If anyone in law enforcement finds out I divulged this information, I'll be facing charges. Do whatever you want with the information, but you didn't hear it from me."

"You'd better be on the level," Merlino said. "I know how to get to you."

"Please, I did exactly what you asked. Now leave me alone."

"If this pans out, lady, you'll never hear from me again—unless of course, you lied. In that case, I'd have to kill you." *Click.*

Ellen hung up the phone, her hand shaking.

"Great performance!" Terri said.

"I'm sure he was drunk. I hope he can keep the details straight. I want this over with."

Guy leaned forward and took Ellen's hands in his. "Did it sound like he believed you?"

"Hard to say. But I doubt he'll be able to resist the carrot."

Terri got up from the table. "I need to call Jordan and fill him in."

Charlie heard a car door slam and went to the front door. Kevin got out of Josiah's truck, and the two of them lowered his bicycle from the bed of the old pickup. Josiah put his arms around Kevin and held him for a moment. Charlie went outside and walked toward them.

"Evenin', Mr. Mayor," Josiah said. "Thought I'd best get your boy home before it turned dark on us."

"Thank you." Charlie shook his hand. "Kevin, go inside and let your mother know you're home."

"All right. Bye, Josiah. Thanks for everything."

"Take care, boy."

Charlie waited until Kevin went inside and then looked into Josiah's kind brown eyes. "I was hoping he was with you. Did he tell you he skipped church this time?"

"Yes, sir. He told me all about it. Hope you don't mind, but I was thinkin' he'd be safer fishin' with an old man than wanderin' around the lake by hisself, tryin' to clear out all the cobwebs."

"No, I'm grateful. His mother, on the other hand, is having a hard time with Kevin enjoying himself every time he skips out. She has a point."

"There's a lot more healin' goin' on than fun."

Charlie nodded. "I'm really worried about him. Is there anything I should know?"

Josiah looked deep into his eyes and held his gaze. "The boy believes you."

Charlie felt an unexpected surge of emotion and quickly blinked the moisture from his eyes. "Kevin talked to you about me?"

"Your boy's heard more than any kid should have to. But he knows what his daddy's made of. And he believes you ain't lyin' to him. Thought it might help to know that."

Charlie bobbed his head up and down, unable to find the right words.

"I best be goin' now. You and yours'll be in my prayers."

Charlie put his hands in his pockets, his feet rocking from heel to toe. "Josiah?"

"Yes, sir?"

"Did you catch anything?

Josiah smiled, his eyes squinted. "Yessir. We got us a bucketful!"

Giorgio dropped two Alka-Seltzer tablets in a glass of water. He waited a minute, then chugged them down. His head felt huge. But even nursing a hangover was better than twiddling his thumbs in Baxter.

He looked at the information he had written on the motel stationery. Was Ellen Jones telling the truth, or was she setting him up?

Whoever she talked to had to be a fed. Who else would've known Risotto went into hiding eighteen years ago? Then again, there was no love lost between the FBI and the Risottos. Maybe her source was implying that they'd turn their backs if someone happened to take Spike Risotto out.

Didn't matter. Giorgio was way past the point of no return. This was as close as he'd ever been to finding the man who gunned down his father. Risotto was getting old. And the thought that he might get lucky and die of natural causes was reason enough to check out Jones's tip.

27

Mark Steele cut the twine on Monday's newspapers and stacked them by the front door of Monty's Diner. He looked at his watch and turned to Rosie Harris. "It's 6:03. What do you suppose is keeping Mort?"

The door to the diner opened.

"Hey, everybody," Reggie Mason said. "Looks like we're gonna have another warm day. Mmm...what smells so good?"

"Leo baked a batch of cinnamon rolls—fresh out of the oven," Mark said. "Since you're the first customer, you get the freebie."

"Where's Mort?" Reggie said.

"I don't know." Rosie poured him a cup of coffee. "Say something smart-alecky, will you? I can't handle the quiet."

The door opened again and George and Hattie Gentry walked inside, followed by Liv Spooner.

"Sorry we're late," Hattie said. "There's a glorious sunrise. We just had to stop and admire it."

George looked around the diner, his eyebrows arched. "Why is it so dead in here? Where's Mort?"

"Nobody seems to know," Rosie said, a grin on her face. "You don't suppose he ran away?"

Reggie laid the newspaper in front of him on the counter. "Looks like Thompson Tire is breakin' ground on the new plant this Friday. I wonder if Avery Stedman and his cronies'll be out at the site throwin' eggs at the mayor?"

Hattie sighed. "Surely the police chief will secure the area, especially if the mayor is going to be there. I'd hate to see any more trouble."

"I wonder what's going on with him and his family," Mark said. "I heard their oldest son skipped school the other day."

"Sheesh, I'd skip the country." Reggie rolled his eyes. "Can't imagine what the pressure must be like for a kid whose dad's involved in a sex scandal."

Liv nodded. "The diary didn't help matters."

The front door opened, and Mort walked in and hung his hat on the hook. "Mornin' all." He picked up a newspaper, put a quarter in the jar, and took a seat at the counter.

Rosie arched her eyebrows, her hand on her hip. "That's all you've got to say: Mornin' all? You're twenty-one minutes late. What gives?"

"Overslept," Mort said.

"Since when?"

"Since I've been workin' on somethin'."

Rosie poured a cup of coffee and set it in front of him. "What kind of *somethin'*?"

Mort blew on his coffee, stealing a glance to the left, and then to the right. "Can't a guy keep anything to hisself 'round here?"

Mark half smiled. "If you'd wanted to keep it to yourself, you wouldn't have mentioned it."

There was a long pause.

"Well?" Reggie said. "What's the big mystery?"

"Ain't no mystery," Mort said. "I just got a hankerin' to find my kids. Been makin' some calls. Writin' some letters."

"After forty years?" Liv said.

"Yep. It ain't gonna happen unless I git after it."

"I think it's wonderful," Hattie said. "I wish you every success."

George nodded. "Really, Mort. Hope it works out."

Mark put a hand on Mort's shoulder. "By the way, since you seem to be tuned in to the Kirbys' situation, do you know if the mayor moved home?"

Mort nodded. "That's what I hear. Harvey down at the florist's told me the mayor's been buyin' roses for the missus, so maybe things is lookin' up. I sure hope so."

"Yeah, me too," Mark said.

Mort wrapped his fingers around his cup, his face somber. "I ain't loved nobody since my wife and kids up and left. Hard to say which done more damage: the affair—or not fightin' ta keep my family together."

Charlie Kirby walked into the closet to get a different pair of shoes and noticed a pink rose in the trash can next to the vanity table. *Oh, well.*

Marlie's voice startled him. "I thought you already left. I'm running late. Would you take Kevin to school? That would save me a few minutes."

"Sure."

"He seems cheerful since his day at the lake," Marlie said. "I hope that doesn't mean he's going to skip school again."

Charlie sat on the side of the bed and slipped a pair of Loafers on his feet. "I know at some point there have to be consequences, but truthfully, Josiah seems to be a good influence on Kevin."

"I can't argue, though I haven't figured out what it is."

"The two of them seem to have a special bond."

"And that doesn't concern you at all?" Marlie said. "We know nothing about this man."

Charlie stood and tucked in his shirt. "I think Josiah's like a grandfather. Kevin's eating it up. Do you realize I don't have a clue how to bait a hook?"

Marlie laughed in spite of herself. "Do you even know what a hook is?"

Charlie realized they were both smiling. He stroked her cheek without thinking, and Marlie's lips resumed a rigid position.

"I've got to go," she said. "Dinner's at six."

"Yeah, okay. I'd better get Kevin to school."

Ellen Jones sat in a folding chair in Jordan Ellis's office, holding Guy's hand and feeling the minutes drag by. Why had they gotten there so early?

Jordan stood with his palms on the windowsill and seemed to be watching the leaves in City Park float down from the trees like confetti.

"South wind's warmed things up," Sheriff Hal Barker said.

Chief Aaron Cameron nodded. "Doubt we'll get much more of this weather before Old Man Winter sets up shop."

Several FBI agents Ellen didn't know were talking softly in the back of the room. She heard footsteps and then the door opening.

"Coffee's here," Agent Terri Farber said. "And sausage biscuits if anyone's interested."

Jordan turned around. "Great. Make sure everyone gets what they want. Then, if you and Agent Taft would take your seats, we can get started."

"Isn't Charlie coming?" Ellen asked.

"Not this time." Jordan moved to his desk, his arms folded, and faced those sitting in folding chairs. "Merlino's through with the mayor. We know what he wants. Let's see if we can nail him."

Ellen noticed the dark circles under Jordan's eyes and wondered if he had found it as hard to sleep as she had.

"I'm going to cut to the chase," he said to everyone in the room. "Our focus now is to get Merlino off the street so the Joneses can get back to their lives. Ellen, I understand you gave an award-winning performance on the phone. Let's hope Merlino bought it.

"Experience tells me he's going to check out the bait. Whether or not he bites is another story. You're probably wondering how we're going to pull this off. We were successful with this sting once before, so we're not going into it blind.

That couple in Micklenburg—Lawrence and Priscilla Carver? They're former FBI agents. They live in that town and have owned the bakery for eighteen years. So when Merlino starts digging, he'll hear all the right answers. We already have our people planted at the bakery, at their home, and in key sites around the town. When Merlino shows up, we'll get him."

"But how will you recognize him?" Ellen said. "So far, nobody has."

Jordan's eyes narrowed. "A rat smells like a rat."

"I'm serious," Ellen said.

"So am I. When you've been doing this for a while, it's not hard to zero in on what just came out of the sewer."

"But what if Merlino figures out what your people are doing before they spot him?"

"Trust me, he won't."

"Let's be realistic," Guy said. "On the slight chance that the operation does fail, what then? Is Merlino likely to come after Ellen?"

Jordan rubbed the back of his neck. "We're not going to fail."

"Look—" Guy paused and lowered his voice. "We're dealing with a gangster here. I want a straight answer."

Jordan glanced at Ellen, and then looked at the floor. "Nothing's foolproof. But if we don't get him in Micklenburg and he's onto us, he might be ticked off enough to retaliate. We'll be ready for that."

Ellen's heart raced, and she couldn't find her voice.

Guy stood up and looked Jordan in the eyes. "Well, I'm *not* ready for that. Get this guy, you hear me?"

Jordan paused for a moment, then his face softened. "We've been through a few things before. Have I ever let you down?"

Guy sat and took Ellen's hand. "No."

"All right, then. Let us do our job. In the meantime, do what you normally do. We've got you covered."

Marlene removed the last cookie from the cookie sheet and placed it in a Tupperware container. The doorbell rang. Hershey jumped to his feet and started barking. She put down the spatula and headed for the front door, determined to get rid of whoever it was as quickly as possible. She looked through the peephole and debated, then opened the door.

"Rhonda...Mary Beth...what a surprise."

"We missed you at Bible study last week," Rhonda Wilson said. "We thought maybe you'd like to ride with us this morning."

"Well, I—I hadn't planned to go."

"Marlene, we've been friends too long for this," Mary Beth Kennsington said. "You haven't returned any of our phone calls. We didn't come over here to tell you what to do, we just want to love and support you. Please talk to us."

Marlene didn't know how she could refuse without hurting their feelings. "All right." She held open the door and let them squeeze by.

"Hello, Hershey, you pretty thing." Rhonda bent down and rubbed the dog's chin.

"Mmm...something smells good," Mary Beth said.

Marlene smiled. "Honestly. You could smell chocolate within a fifty-mile radius. Come in the kitchen and have a cookie."

"Smells like Toll House," Mary Beth said.

Rhonda rolled her eyes. "The word chocoholic comes to mind."

Marlene followed them into the kitchen. She put some cookies on a plate and got out napkins and coffee mugs. "Help yourselves."

"Mmm...these are wonderful," Mary Beth said.

Rhonda poured a cup of coffee and brought it to the table. "All of us were glad to see you and Charlie at church yesterday."

"Frankly, I wasn't sure how warm a reception we'd get, under the circumstances."

Mary Beth's eyebrows scrunched. "Why?"

"The whole diary thing is so...humiliating...."

Rhonda put her hand on Marlene's. "We're church family. When you hurt, we hurt."

Marlene wiped a tear from her face. "I'd like to find a hole and crawl in."

"Are you counseling with anyone?" Mary Beth said.

Marlene shook her head. "Pastor Thomas has asked us to, but I'm not comfortable talking to him about this."

"What about a professional counselor?" Rhonda said. "There are a number of Christian ones in Ellison."

"I don't know if it's worth it."

Mary Beth stopped chewing. "How can you say that?"

Marlene hesitated, then decided she might as well say it. "Biblically, I have grounds *not* to work it out. He's the one who cheated."

Mary Beth looked at Rhonda, and then at Marlene. "Charlie denies having had an affair."

"I know. I don't believe him."

There was a long pause.

"But you do love him, don't you?" Mary Beth asked.

"I don't know how I feel. Charlie and I can never get back what we had."

Rhonda fiddled with the edge of her napkin. "But the Lord can heal the hurt and give you back more than you had before. Just look at what he did with Jed and me."

"And with me," Mary Beth said. "I never thought I could forgive G. R. Logan and Wayne Purdy for Sherry's death. But God changed my heart toward both of them. This isn't too big for Him."

Marlene folded her arms and sat back in her chair. "Well, I'm sure glad you two didn't come over here to tell me what to do." She saw the hurt looks on their faces. "I didn't mean that the way it sounded. But just because you were able to work through your pain doesn't make mine hurt less."

"You're right," Mary Beth said. "And you have every right to feel angry, especially at how public your private business has become. KJNX stooped to an all-time low when they aired what Sheila wrote in that diary. But at some point, you have to let it go and move on."

"I've barely had time to let it sink in," Marlene said. "How am I supposed to let it go?"

Mary Beth arched her eyebrows. "Do you want to let it go?"

"Of course...at least I think I do."

"A good start would be forgiving Charlie."

"How can I do that?"

"Say the words and mean them because it's the right thing to do—and the Lord will eventually help you to feel it."

"I can't imagine."

Mary Beth nodded. "I couldn't either."

"Me either," Rhonda said. "But the healing started when I chose to forgive Jed."

"I'm under no obligation to take Charlie back."

Mary Beth took a sip of coffee. "But you do need to forgive him."

"He cheated on me!"

"I can't speak to that," Mary Beth said. "But I do know he loves you. Would you throw that away just to get back at him?"

"You have no idea what it's like to feel betrayed!"

Mary Beth nodded. "I know, but that's not the point."

"What would *you* do if Joe cheated on you?"

"Cry. Scream. Rant. Rave. I'd probably want to turn the knife every chance I got. I'd want him to hurt as much as he'd hurt me. But none of that would lead to healing and reconciliation."

Marlene wiped a tear from her face. "Nothing can ever be the same."

"But it doesn't have to be *over*," Rhonda said. "You've got seven kids to think about. Don't be too hasty."

"Hasty?" Marlene said. "I'm lucky to function. I hardly have energy to make it through the day. Every morning I wake up thinking it's all a bad dream. But it isn't."

Mary Beth leaned forward, her eyes searching Marlene's. "I know you still love Charlie."

"So what? Every time I close my eyes, I see him with *her*..." Marlene's voice cracked. "I could never give myself to him again."

Mary Beth nodded, her eyes brimming with tears. "Understandably, my friend. But never say never. God is still in the miracle business. I'm a living testimony to that. I remember back when every time I closed my eyes, all I could see were Wayne's hands around Sherry's throat. If God can fill my mind and heart with forgiveness for my daughter's murderer *and* the man who drove him to it, He can fill yours with forgiveness and a renewed love for a husband who adores you."

Marlene put her hand to her mouth. "I'm so afraid of being hurt again."

"Of course you are," Mary Beth said. "But if you don't give it a chance, I think you'll regret it the rest of your life."

28

Ellen Jones sat at her computer, aware of Agent Terri Farber standing over by the window, reading through recent issues of the *Baxter Daily News*.

"You're awfully quiet over there," Ellen said.

"How come you didn't do more reporting on Paxton's diary?" Terri asked.

"We ran a story on it once, and that's once more than it deserved. At least *I* didn't put my own spin on it."

"You lost me."

"There's a TV station about seventy-five miles from here that's notorious for sensationalizing. Of course, they aired the story the minute they got their hands on the diary."

"Can you blame them?" Terri said. "A sex scandal is big-time news these days. People pretend to hate it, but they thrive on it. And the networks love it."

Ellen sighed. "They should stop and think that there are real people behind the allegations. They kill someone's reputation and leave them for dead, then move on to another story. All in a day's work. Sometimes, they act as irresponsibly as the tabloids."

"Do I detect a touch of disdain from the editor's desk?"

"More than a touch, I'd say."

"Okay, off the record. Is the mayor guilty?"

"Why does anyone besides his wife need to know that?" Ellen said. "What I do know is that Charlie Kirby is a good and decent man."

"Then why did he cheat on his wife? Isn't the guy some big shot at your church?"

Ellen paused, thinking Terri's sarcasm sounded much like Guy's. "There's too much good about Charlie to just write him off, guilty or not."

"I hear he maintains his innocence, in spite of what the diary revealed," Terri said. "Isn't that just like a man?"

Ellen leaned back in her chair, her eyes fixed on Terri. "You sound like a woman who's lived it."

Terri's cheeks turned red. She laid the newspaper she was holding on top of the stack. "Sorry. My ex was a real jerk."

"Well, I assure you, Charlie is no jerk."

Ellen heard the receptionist's voice on the intercom. "Ellen, the mayor's on line one."

"Thanks." Ellen picked up the receiver. "Hello, Charlie." Ellen looked at Terri and smiled.

"Hi. I had a minute and was just checking to see how you're doing. Marlie and I have both been concerned about you since our meeting the other day."

"Uh, I'm relatively all right. Things are a bit tentative."

"Did the FBI decide what they're going to do to beef up their efforts to get Merlino?"

"I'm sure they have. I'm just letting them do their job."

"Did Merlino call you back?"

Ellen hesitated. "I'm not allowed to say anything about an open investigation."

"That sounded like a yes."

"We can't have this conversation, Charlie. I'm sorry."

"Sure, I understand."

Ellen picked up a pencil and started to doodle. "Are things better with Marlene? The whole church is praying for you two."

"Not really. The kids are glad I'm home."

"Are *you* glad?"

"Yes, about spending time with them. I feel like an outcast anytime Marlie's around. It's going to take time."

"Of course."

"I talked to Pastor Thomas today," Charlie said. "And Jed

Wilson. And Joe Kennsington. Oh, and Dennis Lawton. All very supportive. I think Rhonda and Mary Beth were going to drop by the house and talk to Marlie. She won't talk to any of the elders, I already know that."

"Things are going to work out; I just know it."

"Thanks, Ellen. I need all the encouragement I can get. Listen, I'm due in a meeting. I just wanted to touch bases with you. Anything specific I can be praying for?"

Ellen glanced over at Terri. "Uh, I can't really say. The Lord knows. Just keep us in your prayers."

"I'm already doing that. Give my best to Guy."

"I will. Thanks for calling, Charlie."

Ellen hung up the phone and noticed Terri looking at her questioningly.

"What did I say wrong?"

"Nothing," Terri said. "I've just never been around people who're into prayer as much as you guys."

Ellen smiled. "Maybe you're not around people in as much trouble as Charlie and I."

Jordan Ellis sat in his office with his feet on his desk, talking to Special Agent Harlan Smith in Micklenburg, Oregon.

"Harlan, you old goat. When's the last time we talked—the McConnell case?"

"Yeah, I believe it was," Harlan said. "It's a whole lot more serious this go-around."

"So's everyone in place?"

"Yeah, the Carvers agreed to carry on as usual. All the bakers and waitresses are our people."

Jordan chuckled. "Guess you don't have to go far for coffee and doughnuts on this stakeout. How do things look?"

"Pretty authentic. A few customers asked about the change in personnel, but most seem oblivious. I think it's going to work."

"Did you see the rap sheet on Merlino?" Jordan said.

"Yeah, I studied the mug shot and the artist's sketch, too. We'll pick him out. Can you believe this guy would take as many chances as he has to get to Risotto?"

"Obsession does weird things, Harlan. Let's hope it delivers him right to your door. He's waited eighteen years to get Risotto. I doubt he'll wait eighteen hours to follow up on Mrs. Jones's tip."

"I'm pretty confident he won't smell a setup."

"Good." Jordan switched the phone to his other ear. "I'm counting on you to make sure the bakery and everyone in it looks like the real enchilada."

"I wonder what Risotto would think if he knew the bureau was tying up all this manpower just to protect a rodent like him?"

"Assuming there *is* a Risotto anymore," Jordan said.

There was a long pause. He could almost hear the wheels turning.

Harlan laughed. "Wouldn't it be funny if Merlino got this far only to find out he'd been tracking down a dead man?"

"I can think of six corpses who aren't laughing," Jordan said.

"Yeah, sorry."

"Look, Harlan. The brass wants Merlino out of the game. The ball's in your court. Don't blow it."

Marlene Kirby drove down Baxter Avenue and almost missed the entrance to the preschool parking lot. She pulled in and shut off the motor, wondering if she could cope with a houseful of energetic children.

Her conversation with Mary Beth and Rhonda had gone better than she would have anticipated. But talking about her pain had brought it to the surface and she felt as though she could bawl at any second. How could she expect anyone to understand how deeply hurt she had been—or how betrayed?

And didn't she have a right to the anger? Surely this betrayal gave her some emotional entitlements.

Lord, I've been avoiding You. I wish I could say I forgive Charlie, but I don't. And this awful depression is only getting worse. Mary Beth and

Rhonda say that if I choose to forgive him, You'll change my heart. But what if You don't? What if I feel this horrible the rest of my life—stuck in a marriage that makes me miserable?

Marlene tried to imagine herself in Charlie's arms. I'll never be able to give myself to him again. Never!

Her mind flashed back to their fifteenth anniversary, to the corner table at the Lakeside Inn...

"This is such a romantic spot," Marlene had said, enjoying the warm glow of the candlelight. "I love it here."

"Hope you don't mind that I reserve the same table every year," Charlie said.

"No, I always look so forward to it." How handsome he looked in his new suit! Trim. Great haircut. She wondered if he'd ever looked better.

Charlie took her hand and kissed it, then took his thumb and moved it across the tiny diamonds on her wedding band. "I really wanted to get you a solitaire. Fifteen years is a milestone."

"But I love this one. I don't want a solitaire."

"You deserve something special."

She pulled his hand to her cheek and held it there. "I already have something special..."

Marlene was aware of a car pulling in next to her. She blinked the moisture from her eyes and saw it was Jennifer Lawton. She breathed in slowly and then exhaled, opened the car door, and got out.

"Hi, Jen."

"Hi, Marlene. Did Mom get a hold of you? She'd been trying to call. Said your answering machine was messed up."

"Uh, yes. Yes, she did. In fact, she and Mary Beth came over this morning."

Jennifer seemed to study her expression. "How about if I take the kids home with me for a couple of hours?"

"I can't ask you to do that again. I know they're a handful."

Jennifer shook her head. "Not for a few hours. And the twins love having other kids to play with."

Marlene saw the sincerity in Jennifer's eyes. "All right. If you're sure."

"I'm sure."

"Thanks. I could use some time to think, although I keep wrestling with the same questions over and over again. I don't feel any closer to an answer."

Kevin Kirby laid his bicycle on the ground and took off his backpack. He climbed up on the boulder and looked for Josiah, but didn't see him. His mother was going to be furious when she found out he had skipped school, even if he hadn't snuck away until lunchtime.

"I see somebody up there who oughta get a whippin'."

Kevin turned his head. "Josiah, you *are* here!"

"What're you doin', boy? This is a school day, and I know you ain't got permission for fishin'."

Kevin jumped down off the rock. "Why go to school if I can't keep my mind on anything?"

"Your mind must be on somethin'. You're here, ain't you?"

"I don't feel like studying, that's all."

"People gotta do lots of things they don't feel like doin'."

"Not you," Kevin said. "You get to fish any time you want."

"Is that so?" Josiah's dark eyes peered out from under his straw hat. "You don't see a fishin' pole, do you?"

Kevin shook his head. "Uh-uh. How come?"

"You don't know much about me, boy."

"Yes, I do."

"Like what?"

"Well, like you're kind. And smart. You talk to God a lot. You listen to me. And don't tear people down. You're even a good cook."

Josiah smiled. "Now that's a mouthful, it sure is. But sweet-talkin' ain't gonna get you on my good side today. You gotta stop hurtin' your mama by takin' off this way."

"She'll get over it."

"Let's climb up on your rock. We need to have us a little talk."

Kevin climbed up on the boulder and held his hand out for Josiah and pulled him up.

Josiah sat next to him, looking out over the lake. "Nice up here."

"I like it," Kevin said. "So, what're we going to talk about?"

Josiah took off his hat and wiped his forehead. "I think we should be talkin' *about* Who you should be talkin' *to*."

Kevin scrunched his face. "Not again."

"You still worried about your folks, are you?"

"Sure I am."

"Are you talkin' to the Lord about it?"

Kevin drew circles on the rock. He couldn't bring himself to lie.

"That's what I thought. See, you ain't usin' what you've been given."

"Did you used to be a Sunday school teacher or something?"

Josiah smiled. "Boy, you're a believer, a child of the King. He's interested in everythin' that's important to you. Why ain't you askin' Him to help your folks? And to help you? That's what He wants to do."

"Doesn't seem like it," Kevin said. "My mom and dad have hardly said anything to each other in over two weeks."

"How much have you said to the Lord in those two weeks?"

Kevin kept drawing circles with his finger.

"People in a relationship got to talk. And just because you're a kid don't mean your Father in heaven ain't listenin'. He treats all his children the same. Don't matter what age they are."

Kevin looked up and met Josiah's gaze. "You really think he listens to me the same as He does you?"

"Yep. But you gotta speak up, boy."

"Why? He already knows what I'm thinking."

"I suspect the Lord likes the closeness, same as we do. Things get lonely when people stop talkin' to each other."

Ellen brought a tray into the living room and set it on the coffee table.

"Jordan, remind me how you like your coffee," she said.

"Black is fine, thanks."

Guy sighed. "Could we just cut to the chase? Obviously, you don't have Merlino or you'd have said so."

"My guess is he's in Micklenburg, but he hasn't showed yet. All our people are positioned and ready. He's not going to miss a chance to get Risotto. He'll make a move."

"I wish I felt as comfortable about this as you do," Guy said. "I have visions of him taking out the Carvers and everyone in the bakery, then disappearing. It's not as though he hasn't done it before."

"We were never waiting for him before."

Guy raised his eyebrows. "Heron Lake Lodge?" He got up and stood by the fireplace, his fingers tapping the mantel. "I have a feeling he knows Ellen involved the FBI. *That* scares me."

Jordan took a sip of coffee and put his cup and saucer down. "Look, I understand this is tough. I hate it almost as much as you do. But I've been doing this a long time, and there's no way Merlino won't show up in Micklenburg. We're going to get him."

"And what if you *don't,*" Guy said. "What then? This guy's into vendettas. He got even with Charlie. He's threatened Ellen. Is there any reason why we should believe he won't follow through?"

Jordan leaned forward, his elbows on his knees. "I can't tell you what to believe, Counselor. But we're taking Merlino out—one way or the other."

There was a loud crash. Ellen turned toward the kitchen, her heart pounding, her hand over her heart.

Jordan jumped to his feet, his gun drawn.

"Nothing's broken," shouted Agent Terri Farber. "I dropped the silverware tray."

29

Ellen Jones tiptoed over to the bed, slipped out of her bathrobe, and turned off the lamp. She pulled the covers up over her, then turned on her side and nestled in Guy's arms, wondering if things would ever be the same between them.

After all that had happened, would she ever know whether or not Merlino had baited her with a lie? What if Sheila really was alive? What if she had been only wounded in the freeway shooting, and the FBI staged her funeral? Then again, why would they have let Richard attend, knowing that anyone who made the connection might show up and recognize him?

"I hear your wheels turning," Guy said. "You need to get some sleep."

Ellen cuddled closer. "Easier said than done."

She was aware of the cuckoo clock ticking and a neighbor's dog barking, the wind blowing outside—and the shower running in the other bathroom.

"I hate this," Guy said. "With a passion."

There was a long, uncomfortable silence before he spoke again.

"I got a call today from Brent McAllister. Of McAllister, Norton, Bateman and Riley. Renee Bateman is leaving the firm...they've asked me to consider taking her place."

Ellen turned over, her head on the pillow, her face in front of his. "That would mean moving to Tallahassee."

"They'd like me to start in ninety days. I realize it means you'd have to give up your position at the newspaper, but you've toyed with the idea of writing novels. Maybe this is a good time to get serious about it... Ellen, say something."

"I'm completely dumbfounded. I don't know that I want to give up my position. And I don't know how well I'd make the transition to a big city."

"I know that. Brent gave me some websites to check out—smaller towns within driving distance. There's one in particular I think you'd really like."

"Well, sounds as though you've got my future all mapped out for me." She turned over on her other side and yanked the covers up to her ears.

"Honey, before you decide it's a bad idea, I want you to look at what I printed out on a town called Seaport—on the coast."

"The coast is too far from Tallahassee."

"But I wouldn't have to drive in every day. I could do a lot of work at home."

"Guy, this is overwhelming. I can't think right now. In case you forgot, there's a gangster on the loose with my cell phone number, my address—and a very bad temper."

"How could I *forget?* I can't take two steps without bumping into an FBI agent!"

Ellen turned over again. "Keep your voice down, Counselor. They're here to protect us."

"I'm not just thinking of myself. I'm genuinely excited about this opportunity, but I think your taking a sabbatical might be a good break for you."

"Well, by all means, thanks for thinking of *me.*"

Marlene Kirby turned on the gas fireplace in her bedroom, then sat in her rocking chair and absorbed the quiet. She held the stem of a pink rose and twirled it slowly between her thumb and forefinger. She didn't need Charlie's guilt offerings. If he thought she was so special, how could he have cheated on her?

Lord, I know divorce is destructive. But what happens when staying married destroys people?

Hershey got up and laid his chin in her lap. She gently stroked his head, and then grabbed a pillow and the afghan and lay down in front the fire. She hated what her life had become. More and more she felt the pressures of a single mom. It was becoming harder to keep Kevin in line. And she hardly had energy left to cope with the other six.

Charlie was willing to do anything she asked, but she didn't want his help. She didn't want anything from him!

Mary Beth's words wouldn't leave her alone. *If God can fill my heart with forgiveness for my daughter's murderer and the man who drove him to it, surely He can fill yours with love and forgiveness for a husband who adores you.*

Marlene felt a tear roll down the side of her face and drop onto the pillow. Charlie had loved her once. Was it possible for a man to love his wife and want someone else at the same time? She didn't see how. It simply didn't compute.

She wiped her tears with the corner of the pillowcase. The mantel clock struck eleven. Only six more hours before the nightmare would begin again.

Charlie Kirby yawned and rubbed his eyes. He put his Bible down and picked up his pen, then began writing in his journal:

> Lord, I can accept that Bart changed his mind about letting me preach the final session at the men's retreat. I can handle not being an elder anymore, if that's what the board finally decides. I can even deal with people whispering and judging me behind my back. What I can't handle is losing Marlie.
>
> There's nothing I can say to make her believe I've told the truth. I can't explain the diary. But I know I was wrong to entertain lustful thoughts. I let my guard down, and the consequences are no different than if I had done it. I can accept that. What's hard to accept is never being vindicated.
>
> Lord, I guess I shouldn't complain about being falsely

accused. You stood condemned, even though You were completely innocent. I'm not innocent. But I didn't do this. I know You have forgiven me. I only wish Marlie could. I can't remember anything ever hurting this much.

Charlie closed his journal and set it on the end table. He got up and walked down the hall, opening and closing bedroom doors, checking on his children.

He walked through the kitchen and looked down the hall toward the master bedroom. He noticed the door was cracked and could tell the fireplace was on. He walked softly and stood at the door, then peeked in and saw a rose petal on the carpet next to the rocking chair. He slowly pushed open the door and saw Marlie on the floor in front of the fireplace, curled up next to Hershey. She looked so lost. It took all his willpower not to lie down beside her and hold her in his arms.

Hershey raised his head, his tail wagging, and Charlie pulled the door shut. He blinked the moisture from his eyes and walked back to his study, wondering how much longer he could hold up under so great a sorrow.

Kevin Kirby lay in the dark watching eerie shadows sway back and forth across the walls of his room. The wind howled and tree branches scraped the window. He reached down and pulled the comforter up to his neck and wondered if his parents had trouble sleeping on opposite sides of the house.

Kevin felt guilty that his mom had cried when she found out he skipped school. She didn't even punish him. She just shook her head and bit her lip, and then went in the kitchen to fix dinner.

His dad grounded him for another week. So what? Kevin didn't feel like doing anything anyway. Nothing in his life felt normal. He felt tired all the time—except when he was supposed to go to sleep.

He was bothered by something Josiah had said. *Boy, you're a believer, a child of the King. He's interested in everythin' that's important to you.*

Kevin thought about that for a few minutes, then got out of bed and knelt by the side of his bed.

Lord, Josiah's right. I'm sorry I haven't been talking to You. I've been pretty confused. And mad. But I think I'm more scared than anything. You know the gross things they're saying about my dad.

Would you please help Mom to forgive him? If she doesn't, they're never going to get back together. And I don't know what will happen to us kids.

I believe You care about what happens to me—and to them. So, would you please change their hearts—make them love each other again? In Jesus' Name. Amen. Oh, and if there's something I can do, please show me.

Kevin got back in bed and looked out at the moon, then closed his eyes and drifted off to sleep...

Jordan Ellis was awakened by a ringing sound and realized it was his cell phone. He groped on the nightstand until he found it. He cleared his throat.

"Hello, this is Jordan."

"It's Harlan."

Jordan yawned. "It's late."

"Sorry, I forgot. It's only nine here."

"Cut to the chase. I was actually asleep for a change."

"We struck out. Spent the day checking the flights out of Atlanta, Charlottesville, and Raleigh—and incoming flights to Eugene. No George Aldridge booked on any of the major airlines. Either Merlino's using another alias, or he's on wheels. We have an APB out on the blue Impala, but no sightings."

"Did you check motels in the area?" Jordan asked.

"We've covered all bases from here to Eugene."

"Yeah, well don't snooze, Harlan. He's coming."

"Okay. You're almost never wrong."

Jordan smiled. "And I'm working on the *almost*."

30

Mark Steele glanced up at the clock at Monty's Diner and took a last look around. "Leo, is the grill hot?"

"Blueberry pancakes comin' up, boss."

Mark turned to Rosie Harris. "You ready?"

She picked up a fresh pot of coffee and gave a nod. "Gentlemen, start your engines."

Mark turned on the Open sign and unlocked the front door.

Mort Clary walked in, hung up his hat, picked up a newspaper, and dropped a quarter in the jar. "Mornin' to ya, Mark."

Rosie looked at Mark, her eyebrows raised. He shrugged.

"Your coffee's on the counter, Mort," Rosie said. "Pancakes coming right up."

Mort smiled. "Thank ya kindly."

Rosie covered her grin with the palm of her hand. "My, aren't we polite today?"

"Thank you for noticin'."

"Noticing what?" George Gentry sat next to Mort, his wife Hattie on his other side.

"Mort's acting like a gentlemen today," Rosie said. "I rather like it."

"Aw, ya don't hafta make over it," Mort said. "Can't a guy be civil without everybody gittin' weird on him?"

"Who's gettin' weird?" Reggie Mason said. "What'd I miss?"

"Our buddy Mort seems unusually cheerful." Mark came and stood at the counter, his arms folded. "You going to tell us why?"

"Why don't we wait fer Liv," Mort said. "Don't wanna say this twice."

The door to the diner opened, and Liv Spooner walked in and hung up her coat. "Hi all."

"Hurry up," Reggie said. "Mort's got somethin' to tell us."

Liv took her place at the counter. All eyes were on Mort, and his face was beaming.

"I found my daughter. She wants ta see me."

"That's great news!" George slapped Mort on the back.

Rosie poured Mort a warmer. "Details...we want details."

"Ain't much ta tell."

Rosie rolled her eyes. "Men! What's her name? How old is she? Where does she live? Is she married? Do you have grandchildren? How and when are you meeting?"

"Oh," Mort said. "Well, her name's Rennie Hopson. She's forty-six now, married to a fella named Bob. Lives over in Greenville. Has two kids, a girl and a boy—both growed up."

"Where does she want to meet you?" Hattie asked, sounding almost giddy.

"Says she'd like to come here to Baxter. Ain't been back since her mama left me."

"When?" Liv said. "This is exciting!"

"Ain't got nothin' in concrete. But I think it'll be right soon."

"What about your other two children?" Hattie said.

Mort shook his head. "Rennie says my boys don't want nothin' to do with me."

George patted Mort on the back. "One step at a time. This calls for a celebration. Breakfast is on me and Hattie—all the way around."

Mort almost looked as though he were blushing "Y'er good friends, all o' ya. I'm glad I have ya to share this with. It's big. Mighty big."

Mark watched everyone rally around Mort, thinking that was bigger than Mort finding his daughter.

Rosie worked her way down the counter, pouring coffee refills. "Anyone notice how boring the newspaper's been lately?"

"No news is good news," Hattie said. "I'm ready for boring."

Reggie blew on his coffee. "I heard there're FBI agents out at the lake."

"Where'd you hear that?" Mark said.

"I stopped in the tackle shop to buy some plastic worms. I heard a couple of good ol' boys talkin' about it. Don't know if there's any truth to it."

"Can't imagine," Rosie said. "Ellen would've put something in the newspaper about it."

Ellen Jones sat at her desk, unable to concentrate even on today's front page. She had never seriously considered leaving Baxter. Except for her time away at college, she had lived here all her life. She had her hand on the pulse of this community. How could Guy expect her to walk away from the *Daily News*, just like that?

"You seem restless today," Agent Terri Farber said.

"I suppose I am." Ellen sighed. "I wish this whole thing with Merlino would end. I feel trapped."

"Jordan thinks he's in Micklenburg—or at least nearby, waiting to make a move."

Ellen shook her head. "I do hope no one gets hurt."

"They're professionals. They know what to do."

"Don't tell that to the two agents killed in Richard Boatman's office building."

Terri raised her eyebrows. "They got surprised. That's not the case this time."

"It's nerve-racking," Ellen said.

"Don't worry. We'll get him. It won't be long till you have your old life back."

Ellen mused. *Not if Guy can help it.*

Charlie Kirby was working through his in box when Regina knocked on the door and stuck her head in. "Mr. Mayor, Dennis Lawton is here to see you."

"Thanks. Show him in."

Charlie walked to the door and got there the same time Dennis did.

Charlie hugged him with one arm, then shook his hand. "It's nice to see a friendly face. Come in and have a seat at the corner table. How about a *good* cup of coffee?"

Dennis smiled. "What've you got over there? Smells great."

"A special Costa Rican blend I share only with discriminating coffee connoisseurs."

"You flatter me," Dennis said. "I'd love a cup. Black."

Charlie brought two mugs of coffee to the table and sat across from Dennis. "I'm glad you called. I hated that we didn't get to play last Friday."

"Charlie, you've been heavy on my heart the past couple of days. How're things going?"

"Not too well." Charlie took a sip of coffee. "If I thought it was all up to me, I'd crater. But I know the Lord wants to heal Marlie's heart and set us back on course. It's up to Him. I don't know what else I can do."

"Is Marlene talking?"

"Sarcasm mostly. I really don't blame her. What is she supposed to believe? I'd love to get my hands on the diary. It's hard for me to believe that Sheila actually wrote that we'd had an affair."

Dennis traced the rim of his cup with his index finger. "You told Marlene the whole story?"

"Absolutely. But frankly, I'm not expecting her to believe me. I'd settle for her forgiveness."

"Think it'll happen?" Dennis said.

"I've got to believe it or I'll go nuts. She's my life..."

Dennis leaned forward, his elbows on the table. "And that's exactly why it's going to work. You two are committed to each other. Deep down, she knows you love her."

"I'm not so sure. Women tend to think that if a husband cheats on his wife, he doesn't love her anymore—or doesn't find her attractive. Both perceptions are the kiss of death to a relationship."

Dennis nodded. "Yeah, I was having a similar conversation

with Jen the other day. I wonder if they realize how many times we turn our backs on temptation without giving it the time of day?"

Charlie stared at the black pool in his cup. "But why should they be impressed with the ten times we walked away when they're devastated by the one time we didn't—or in this case, almost didn't."

"Yeah, you're right."

Charlie lifted his eyebrows. "*Almost* becomes irrelevant when you're talking about measuring faithfulness."

A few moments passed in comfortable silence.

Dennis took a sip of coffee. "Mmm...this is great."

"I'm glad you like it. I'll give you some to take home."

"By the way," Dennis said, "I talked with Lenny Stedman on Saturday. He's pretty upset over Avery's accusation and all the trouble it's caused you. I got the impression it's put a kink in their relationship."

"Well, Avery's probably gloating," Charlie said. "But the diary is the mother of all accusations. The damage done by Avery's big mouth pales in comparison."

"I wonder how the Lord's going to redeem this situation?"

Charlie got up and walked to the window, his hands in his pockets. "The only redemption I want is for Marlie to forgive me. The sad part is, she might find it easier if I admitted my guilt— only I'd be lying if I said I did it."

Jordan Ellis paced in his office and stopped at the window. He placed his palms on the sill and looked out across City Park. The trees were starting to lose their leaves, and there was almost as much color on the ground as on the branches.

He snatched his ringing cell phone from his pocket and hit the talk button. "This is Jordan."

"It's Harlan. Merlino's still a no-show. I'm thinking maybe he's onto us."

"You better not have blown it!"

There was a long pause.

"I don't need this—especially from you," Harlan said.

Jordan turned around and leaned against the window. "Sorry. You know how I get. I want Ellen Jones out of danger—and Merlino off the street. And I'd like to get home to my wife and kids. Being holed up in a dinky office on the second story of Baxter's courthouse isn't my idea of a productive work week."

"Maybe you'd like to try beautiful downtown Micklenburg. Ever try staging a staff change at a local joint without raising suspicion? So how about if you stop whining and support the troops?"

"Touché, pal. I had that one coming."

"There is something we hadn't planned on," Harlan said. "The town is celebrating Oktoberfest starting tomorrow. Goes through the weekend. It'll draw a couple hundred new faces each night. We're bringing in more manpower."

Jordan sighed. "Let the good times roll."

"Hey, it'll give me a chance to give the old accordion a workout. Viva la bratwurst!"

"I don't know how you stay so cool," Jordan said.

"You should see what I'm looking at. Agent O'Brien just brought a fresh tray of chocolate éclairs from the back. You know, he looks real cute with an apron on."

Jordan smiled involuntarily. "I'm glad it's you in charge up there. Sorry for the cheap shot. Keep me posted."

"Will do. Try and give your blood pressure a rest."

Jordan hung up and turned around. He looked out at the water tower in the distance and remembered that grueling week nearly three years ago when he'd worked the Logan-Kennsington kidnapping. This case was a piece of cake compared to that one. And yet Merlino was far more lethal than Wayne Purdy.

Marlene Kirby walked into the kitchen and noticed a wilted pink rose in a vase on her work island. She'd thrown it out once today. She plucked it out of the vase and pitched it in the trash.

"Mom?"

She looked up and saw Kevin standing there.

"Could I ride out to the lake and see Josiah? I promise I'll be home before dark." His eyes were on the empty vase.

"Uh, I don't know—"

"Please? I didn't skip school. I like being with him, and I don't have many friends right now."

Marlene softened at the sight of his pleading eyes. "All right. Why don't you take some cookies to share with him? I baked a fresh batch of chocolate chip. I'll put them in a baggie for you."

Kevin smiled. He walked over to her and put his arms around her. "I love you, Mom."

Marlene waited for a surprisingly long time before Kevin let go. She blinked to clear her eyes, trying to remember how long it had been since he'd hugged her that way.

"You should put a flower in that vase," he said.

"I don't need a flower."

"Maybe you do," he said, his eyes twinkling.

"I thought you were going to the lake." She handed him a bag of cookies.

"Thanks. I'll see you before dark."

"Kevin, take my cell phone. I want you to call and check in so I won't worry."

"You were going to get me my own."

"I know. We'll talk about it again. But for today, use mine, okay?"

"Sure, Mom. See you later."

Kevin left the kitchen, seeming to her more settled than in recent days.

Marlene waited until she heard the front door close, then picked up the empty vase and turned it upside down. She let the water pour down the drain, feeling a twinge of regret that she had emptied her heart of any mercy.

Ellen added half a teaspoon of salt and stirred the pot of beef stew slowly as it simmered on the stove. The oven timer went off. She started to put on her oven mitts when Agent Michelle Taft came into the kitchen and snatched them from her hand.

"Here, let me get the cornbread," Michelle said. "Mmm...everything smells great."

Ellen's cell phone rang and she froze. "I hate this." She breathed in and exhaled slowly. Terri and Guy were already in the doorway. Ellen picked up the phone and hit the talk button.

"Hello."

"Well, I'm glad you picked up," Merlino said. "I thought maybe the feds would run interference."

"What feds?" Ellen said, trying not to let her voice shake.

"The ones listening in on this call."

He's testing you, Terri whispered. *Stand your ground.*

"Do you think I'm crazy?" Ellen said. "Why would I tell the FBI about this? You think *I* want to go to jail? Please tell me you found Risotto."

"What's it to you?"

"Look, I just want you to stop calling. So?..."

"Maybe I did. Maybe I didn't. Could be I'm in Baxter, just around the corner. You never know. So don't cross me." *Click.*

Ellen hung up. She dropped back in her chair, her arms limp.

"You did great," Terri said.

"I'm glad *you* think so." Ellen dabbed the perspiration from her face and neck. "Frankly, I'm fed up with the whole thing."

"That was just a fishing expedition," Terri said. "He doesn't know we're involved. He just wants to be sure you're still available in case the tip turns out to be a bust."

Guy pulled up a chair and sat next to Ellen. "McAllister, Norton, Riley, and *Jones* is sounding better all the time."

Terri's cell phone rang. "This is Agent Farber...uh-huh... okay, sir, thanks. I'll tell them." She put the phone back in her pocket. "Darn!"

"What?" Ellen said.

"The call from Merlino? Made from a disposable cell phone. We still don't know where he is."

31

Ellen Jones sat on the side of the bed and slipped into her heels. She was aware of Guy standing in the doorway and deliberately ignored him.

"It's already Wednesday," he said. "When are we going to talk about my job offer?"

Ellen avoided looking at him. "I was under the impression we already had."

"You know what I mean. The offer is on the table. I have to at least respond to Brent and let him know whether or not I'm seriously considering it."

"Do whatever you want," Ellen said. "Seems to me your mind's made up."

Guy sat on the bed beside her. "That's not how we do things."

"Apparently it is."

"Honey, I know the timing's lousy. But will you at least think about it?"

"That's what I've been doing," Ellen said. "I went to the website you wrote down and clicked on Seaport."

"Pretty impressive, eh?"

"It looks...interesting."

"Oh, come on, Ellen. It's everything we want."

"No, it's everything *you* want, Counselor. I'm happy here."

Guy threw his hands in the air. "Well, I'm not! I'm fed up with living in fear!" He got up and spun around, his face red, his eyes wide and animated. "This is the third time in three years you've been in harm's way because of your position. I can't live this way anymore! *I won't!*"

"All right, Guy. Calm down. Give me a chance to think some more about it." She stood and slipped into his arms. "I'm sorry. I know this is my fault."

"Honey, I don't want to change who you are, but we've got to change something. I can't go through this again."

"I know," she whispered, her heart pounding. "I need time to adjust to the idea. It's a bit all-consuming."

Jordan Ellis took the last bite of a sausage biscuit and downed it with a swallow of lukewarm coffee. His cell phone rang and he took it out of his pocket.

"Hello, this is Jordan."

"It's Harlan."

Jordan glanced at his watch. "It's five-fifteen there. What's wrong?"

"It's too quiet."

"Bad feeling?"

"I guess," Harlan said. "You're the patron saint of hunches. But something feels wrong. Merlino got the tip on Saturday. Where the heck is he?"

"Maybe he's waiting for Oktoberfest. Tonight's the night."

"I wish he'd make his move and get it over with."

Jordan doodled on the back of an old phone message. "Is everyone up on his game?"

"A hundred percent."

"Well, at least you've got all the coffee and doughnuts you want."

Harlan chuckled. "Yeah, we're a bunch of *well-rounded* agents. Look, what's your spin on this?"

Jordan put his pencil down and sat back in his chair. He thought for a few moments. "I think Merlino's watching."

"Think he knows we're here?"

"Not necessarily. Depends on how camouflaged your people are."

"Looks good from my perspective," Harlan said. "But the

wait is giving me a headache."

Jordan laughed. "Welcome to my world."

"Any advice for this old-timer?"

"Don't trust anyone until this thing's over. Keep your eyes peeled."

"Yeah, okay. Thanks."

"And Harlan? Be sure to get a picture of O'Brien in an apron. This I gotta see."

Jordan hung up the phone. The only thing more intense than a stakeout was a stakeout he couldn't control. Merlino was there. He knew it. No way could he pass up a chance to get Risotto.

Charlie Kirby looked over his speech for Friday's groundbreaking ceremony, vaguely aware of Regina's voice on the intercom.

"Mr. Mayor, there's a Mr. Slade on line one. He says it's personal."

Charlie looked at the blinking light on the phone. Did he know a Slade? "Okay, Regina. Thanks." He picked up the phone. "Hello, this is Mayor Kirby."

"Yes, my name's Christopher Slade. I'm a marketing exec for Thompson Tire. Could I have a few minutes of your time?"

"Sure. What's on your mind?"

"I probably shouldn't be telling you this, but some guy named Tony English came to see me a couple of weeks ago."

Charlie switched the phone to his other ear and grabbed a pencil.

"Apparently, Sheila Paxton wrote about me in her diary. Said we'd had this steamy affair, which is a joke. She did come on to me, but I ran the other way. I hate being manipulated. Besides, I knew better than to get involved with someone who works here, especially someone that high profile."

"Why are you telling me this?" Charlie said.

"I heard through the grapevine about what's going on down there and thought you might like to know you're not the only one she lied about."

Charlie's mind was racing. "Did you actually see the diary?"

"Yeah, the guy showed me a couple of entries. My name was in there, all right. But the woman must've been high on something. The closest I ever got to her was a handshake. Of course, English had no reason to believe me. He kept pressing me to tell him anything I knew about her background, where her parents were, stuff like that. He about drove me nuts, but I couldn't help him. And this probably won't help you now, but you deserve to know."

"Have you told this to the FBI?"

"Actually, I did. Right after that TV station got their hands on the diary. A couple of agents took my statement, but that's the last I heard from them. I'm not supposed to talk to anyone about this, but it makes me mad you're getting the shaft. I probably should've called sooner."

"I'm grateful you called at all," Charlie said.

"I gave your secretary my phone number. Feel free to get back with me if you think of anything you want to ask."

"Thanks, Mr. Slade. I really appreciate knowing this."

Charlie hung up the phone. He flipped through his Rolodex, then picked up the receiver and dialed. *Come on...answer the phone.*

"Hello, this is Jordan."

"This is Charlie Kirby. Why didn't you tell me I wasn't the only man named in Sheila's diary?"

There was a long pause.

"This is an ongoing investigation," Jordan said. "I told you what was relevant to your circumstances."

"Oh, and you don't think that was?"

"Charlie, I read the entire diary. Paxton wrote about a half dozen different men. The woman came across as cheap, conniving, and shameless. What good would it do for you or your wife to know that?"

"Because at least one other man says what she wrote was a lie. Did you know *that?*"

Jordan sighed. "Look, I'm sorry for what you're going through, I really am. But that's not what the FBI's concerned with."

"Wish I could say the same for everyone else."

"Trust me, nothing in the diary is going to help you. If anything, it'll add fuel to the fire."

"But it isn't true."

"It's not my job to make those kinds of judgment calls. For me, the diary serves one purpose: potential evidence in a murder investigation. That's it."

Charlie sat back in his chair, his mind on fast-forward. "You asked me not to discuss the case as long as it's open. I've complied, and I'm not going to sneak around now. But my wife believes I've been involved in this sordid affair for which I have no defense. And it's tearing us apart. I'd like a green light to find out more from the man who called me."

"Do anything you want—*after* we get Merlino."

"Are you even close?"

"I'll let you know when we've got him."

Charlie sighed. "All right, Jordan. I appreciate your candor."

Charlie hung up the phone. He sat for a few minutes, then got up and stood at the window. He looked over at the steeple of Cornerstone Bible Church and felt the emotion tighten his throat. *Thank you, Lord.* It wasn't solid proof, but it might be his one chance for vindication.

Marlene Kirby let Hershey out in the backyard, then poured herself a cup of coffee. She saw a sickly rose in the crystal vase she had emptied yesterday. She let out a sigh of disgust, and plucked the rose from the vase and threw it in the trash. She stood leaning on the sink, her lip quivering, feeling uncomfortable with the coldness in her heart.

Marlene took her coffee over to the breakfast nook and sat at the table, letting the morning sun warm the side of her face. She missed Charlie. At least the Charlie she used to know. Maybe pride was the one thing standing in the way of her forgiving him, but who could blame her? She felt justified in her anger and had derived satisfaction from shutting Charlie out. But she felt drained of joy. And strength. And hope.

She stared at the flowers on the side of her mug until she started to nod off. She glanced at the clock, then got up and turned on the radio to this week's session of "The Word Works," disgusted that she had spaced out and it was already half over.

"Yes, we're new creatures, but let's not forget our carnal nature has the propensity to sin. Each of us is capable of anything, given the right circumstances and the right frame of mind. Turn to Proverbs 4:23. I'm reading from the NIV: 'Above all else, guard your heart, for it is the wellspring of life.'

"Such good advice, if only we would take it seriously. It's so important to be aware of our weaknesses and keep our spiritual defenses in place because we're all vulnerable on some level—and the enemy knows where. He's like a lion with his eye on a herd of wildebeests, waiting to attack the weakest. But there's safety in numbers—all the more reason why we need to stay close to the body of believers.

"I'm reminded of an evangelist I greatly admired who had an extramarital affair that resulted in a toppled ministry. This was a good man who had won more souls to Christ than anyone I know. But he let down his guard and was deceived into thinking that a sexual relationship outside his marriage would be a harmless diversion. It ended up costing him his witness, his ministry—and nearly his marriage.

"His wife lamented that she had never considered her husband to be vulnerable to adultery and had never thought to pray for his protection. What a mistake! Satan is out to destroy Christian marriages."

Marlene sighed and sat back in her chair. She had never thought to pray for Charlie's protection. It had never even occurred to her that he was battling this kind of temptation.

"Men seem vulnerable to sexual temptation, but we women tend to fall for a more subtle kind of seduction—the misleading notion that our husbands are responsible for our happiness. And for wives who are continually disgruntled by their husband's imperfections, or deeply disappointed in their circumstances, that lie and the self-pity it generates can destroy a marriage as easily as adultery.

"Satan is a master of disguise and will choose a deceptive approach that works with each of us. The worst thing we can do is separate ourselves from the very people who can pray for us and hold us accountable. *Anything* that weakens our own prayer life leaves us wide open for the enemy's lies—"

Marlene got up and turned off the radio, then folded her arms on the table and laid down her head.

32

K evin Kirby climbed up on a familiar boulder, a ball cap shading his eyes. He cupped his hands around his mouth and called out, "Josiah...where are you?"

"Over here," said a faraway voice.

Kevin spotted a straw hat sticking up over a tattered lawn chair about a hundred yards away. He jumped off the rock and ran along the bank to where Josiah was fishing. "Mom said I could come again today."

Josiah reached up and gently squeezed Kevin's arm. "Good to see you, boy."

"Did you catch anything?"

"Fish don't like this cold front. Here, take the other pole. See if you can get 'em to bite."

Kevin took the pole and sat on the ground, his knees bent. He reached in his jacket pocket, took out a baggie filled with cookies, and handed it to Josiah. "Mom made these for us. You hungry?"

"Must be, the way my stomach's carryin' on."

Kevin closed his eyes and tilted his face upward. "Sun feels good."

"You're lookin' more peaceful. Anything change at home?"

"Not yet. But I keep putting the roses back in the vase like you told me."

Josiah chuckled. "Is she onto you?"

"I don't know, but it's kind of fun."

"Listen..." Josiah said. "Hear that honkin'? Those are geese."

Kevin opened his eyes and watched the V formation move

slowly across the afternoon sky. "What're you going to do when it's too cold to fish?"

"I'll think of somethin'."

"Don't you get bored by yourself?"

"I ain't never by myself, boy. The Lord's with me all the time."

"How do you know?" Kevin said. "I can't tell."

Josiah raised an eyebrow. "He's in your heart, ain't He?"

Kevin nodded. "Yeah, but I'm not sure what I'm supposed to feel."

"That's where the relationship comes in. The Lord wants to spend time with you. He loves you even more than your folks do and is willin' to listen to everything you got to say anytime you wanna say it. Why, he knows you so well He's counted every hair on your head." Josiah lifted his hat and laughed. "Mine, too. Just didn't take Him as long."

Kevin smiled. "I wish I knew Jesus the way you do. You make Him seem so real."

Josiah put his hand on his heart. "Oh, He's real, all right. If you only knew how much He's changed ol' Josiah. Ain't nothin' else I can do but love Him."

"Why, what happened?"

"Aw, you don't wanna hear an ol' man's ramblin'."

"Yes, I do," Kevin said.

Josiah sat quietly for a minute and looked out at the lake, his dark eyes watering. "Ain't easy to talk about what I used to be like."

Jordan Ellis stuffed the last of the Pringles in his mouth and threw the container in the trash. He heard a gentle knock on the door and noticed Hal Barker standing there.

"Come in, Sheriff. You're just in time to save the carpet. If I get up, I'm going to wear a hole in it."

"A little tense, are you?" Hal said.

Jordan nodded. "Yeah, same old."

"What's the latest?"

"We found Merlino's Impala parked in his mother's garage. She says she hasn't seen him since he left the car there last week. We think she's telling the truth. And we don't know what he's driving now. But with Oktoberfest starting tonight, the team in Oregon's on high alert."

"What if he doesn't take the bait, Jordan?"

"He will."

"How long are you willing to wait?"

"Till I get him, Sheriff. Anything *else?*"

There was a long pause.

Hal patted him on the shoulder. "I think I'll go downstairs and get a snack. Can I bring you something?"

Jordan gestured toward the trashcan. "No, thanks. I've already exceeded my junk limit for the day." He inhaled and let it out. "Sorry I bit your head off. You know how I get."

Hal nodded knowingly. "No problem. We'll all be glad when it's over."

Ellen Jones glanced over at Agent Terri Farber, who was entering something into a PalmPilot, and wondered how stunned the community would be when the *Baxter Daily News* was finally able to report the whole story.

"Terri, how are we going to handle things on Friday when Thompson Tire breaks ground on the new plant?"

"You're not going."

"Of course I am. It's a turning point for this town—and also a subject of considerable controversy. I want to be there."

"Jordan's not going to like it."

"Oh, come on. Merlino will be in custody by then."

Terri lifted her eyebrows. "We hope."

"He couldn't get past you and Michelle anyhow—the way you two smother me."

"Oh, then you want us to pack up and go home?" Terri said.

"Over my dead body." Ellen looked at her sheepishly. "Sorry, I didn't mean it that way."

"I really think you should skip the groundbreaking."

"That's not an option. You'd have to live here to understand what an impact this plant may have on our way of life. Which reminds me, I need to call Charlie."

Ellen picked up the receiver and dialed, then leaned back in her chair.

"Mayor Kirby's office, this is Regina."

"Hi, Regina. Ellen Jones. May I speak with Charlie, please?"

"Yes, ma'am, one moment."

Ellen looked up at the framed portrait of Reginald T. Baxter on her wall. What would the town's founding father think of the city council's decision?

"Hello."

"Charlie, it's Ellen. How are things going with you and Marlene?"

"Oh, mostly cloudy, with a chance of showers."

"I'm sorry. I was hoping you had a glimmer of sunshine."

"How are things with you?"

"So-so. Anxious to get Merlino out of my life."

"I'll bet."

Ellen twirled her pencil. "I was just thinking about the groundbreaking on Friday—hoping Aaron and Hal are going to pool their departments to help with crowd control."

"That's the plan. I'm not looking for trouble."

"Don't you think Avery Stedman and company will show up?"

"I don't know," Charlie said. "Maybe. But I can't worry about a few rogues. The plant will be a big boost to our town's economy, and that's what I'll be conveying to everyone present."

"Well, I'll be there."

"But you still think it's the wrong decision?"

Ellen drew stars and arrows on the back of a spiral notebook. "I trust your motives, Charlie. I'm just not convinced that the tire plant is the be-all and end-all to our economic woes."

"Speaking of woes, is the FBI still at the helm?"

Ellen smiled. "Full speed ahead."

"Do they have any idea where this Merlino is?"

"Nice try. You know I can't say anything."

"Isn't it driving you crazy, just sitting on this story?"

Ellen glanced over at Terri. "It's driving me crazier being *in* this story."

Kevin thought he had a bite and started to reel, then stopped and waited for the bobber to come to the surface. He turned to Josiah, studying his expression. "Why don't you want to tell me what you used to be like?"

The old man's face seemed to shrivel up. "Ain't real proud of it, that's all."

"Come on," Kevin said. "How bad could it be?"

"Plenty bad." Josiah pursed his lips and rubbed the white stubble on his chin. "I had a wild streak in those days."

"You did?"

Josiah nodded slightly. "Spent most nights in the bars, blowin' my trumpet in a jazz band, and boozin' and laughin' and flirtin' with the ladies. Then I set my eyes on this woman—the kind a decent man ain't got no business bein' with. Before long, I lost all sense of shame." Josiah paused, his eyes downcast. "Wasn't long before I up and left my wife and kids and run off with her."

Kevin sat quietly for a moment and tried to imagine the sweet man next to him behaving that way. "Didn't you care about your family anymore?"

"Course I did. I wasn't thinkin' straight—too busy bein' caught up in what made me feel good instead of how bad they was hurtin'."

"What happened?"

"My wife got down on her knees and prayed to the Lord to change my heart—make me wanna come home again."

"Did you?"

Josiah shook his head. "Not for a while. And then I was too

ashamed. But eventually I went back. And you know what? My Hannah treated me like somebody special. My young'uns couldn't get enough of me. And those people at the church wrapped their arms around me like I was one of 'em." Josiah wiped a tear from his cheek. "I'll tell you, boy, it was somethin'."

"They weren't mad?"

"If they were, I never could tell. And it was the way they took me back that opened up my heart so's I could make room for Jesus to live in it." Josiah closed his eyes and shook his head from side to side. "I didn't deserve all that. I surely didn't."

"Were you happy after that?"

Josiah turned to Kevin, a smile stretching his cheeks. "That I was, boy. I never did go wild again. And I've been walkin' with the Lord ever since."

"Where are your wife and kids?"

"Oh, my kids are all growed up. I got me nine grandkids now. But my Hannah, she went to be with Jesus almost six years ago. I still talk to her every day. Since she's with the Lord, and He's in my heart, I guess in a way we're still together."

Kevin looked out at the red bobber at the end of his line. "I've been praying that my mom'll forgive my dad."

"That's so good, boy. I've been prayin' it, too. And since the Lord's always listenin', we know He's workin' on her."

Dennis Lawton got up from his computer and turned out the light in his office. He walked to the kitchen and took out the package of coffee beans Charlie had given him yesterday. He measured out beans for four cups, put them in the grinder, and turned it on.

"Ah, you've emerged," Jennifer said.

"Yeah, just another hard day at the office." Dennis smiled. "I love running Grandpa's foundation. I think I've found a good place for twenty thousand dollars."

"Where?"

"There's this amazing high school principal in New York who's got her inner city students pumped for college. The programs she's created are making a huge difference in their grades, self-esteem— even their moral values. She's looking for more program funding. I think Grandpa would give me a thumbs-up."

"Sounds great," Jennifer said. "By the way, what are you grinding?"

"A Costa Rican blend that Charlie gave me yesterday. Why don't you have a cup with me?"

Dennis measured the water and poured it in the coffeemaker, then picked up two coffee mugs and sat next to Jennifer at the breakfast bar.

"Why is it so quiet?" he said. "Are the twins asleep?"

Jennifer nodded. "And as long as I've got your attention, finish telling me what happened with Charlie yesterday."

"Oh, guy talk mostly."

"Is he making any headway with Marlene?"

"No, not really." Dennis picked up a napkin and folded it over and over. "He's really stuck, in a way. Marlene would probably find it easier to forgive him if he admitted he did it—only he didn't. What's your spin on Marlene? You've probably been with her more than anyone else."

"She's devastated, angry, and depressed," Jennifer said. "She hasn't really opened up to me about it. But as a woman, I think I know how betrayed she feels."

Dennis sighed. "It's sad that Marlene won't agree to go for counseling. She refuses to talk with any of the elders, even Pastor Thomas."

"I doubt if she'll ever feel comfortable talking to a man about this. I know she talked to Mom and Mary Beth. Mom won't break a confidence, but I got the impression Marlene was receptive to their visit."

"Well, that's good." Dennis let the aroma of the coffee fill his senses. "I wish there was something we could do to help them."

"I've offered to watch the kids."

"I know." Dennis put his hand on hers. "They have so much

worth salvaging, I can hardly stand to watch this great marriage go down the tubes. No matter what happened or didn't happen, it's so obvious they love each other."

"But what can *we* do?"

"I don't know yet," Dennis said. "I'm working on it."

33

Mark Steele popped a crisp piece of bacon in his mouth and walked toward the Open sign at Monty's. "I'm unlocking the door now."

"Coffee's ready," Rosie Harris said.

Leo turned around. "Blueberry pancakes on the griddle."

Mark turned on the sign, unlocked the door, then bent down and cut the twine on Thursday's newspapers.

Mort Clary came in and hung up his hat. "Why, good mornin' all."

"Hey, Mort," Mark said. "Stay tuned. Your coffee and pancakes will be with you shortly."

"Thank you, kindly." Mort put a quarter in the jar, picked up a newspaper, and walked to the counter. "Mornin' to ya, Rosie."

Rosie smiled and looked over at Mark. "I never quite know what to do with this stranger that keeps gracing the counter."

"Guess ya better see to it he gits fed real good so he don't go back ta rabble-rousin'." Mort winked.

Rosie shook her head. "You're something else. So, what's the latest on Rennie?"

"Wait," Reggie Mason said, hanging up his coat. "I wanna hear."

"Hear what?" George Gentry came in behind Reggie and held the door for his wife Hattie and Liv Spooner.

"Mort's going to give us an update on Rennie," Mark said.

The early crowd took their places at the counter, all eyes on Mort.

"Ain't nothin' new to tell. Rennie's gonna take a little vacation time and come see me," Mort said. "She'll let me know real soon just when."

"Where does she work?" Rosie asked.

"She's a waitress down at Red Lobster. The two of you have somethin' in common."

"How'd she sound on the phone?" Rosie said.

Mort smiled, his eyes twinkling. "Real sweet."

"Order up!" Leo shouted.

Rosie went and got a plate of blueberry pancakes and placed it in front of Mort. "If any of you wants something besides the usual, speak up now. Leo's cranking them out."

Reggie sat with his elbows on the counter, his chin resting on his hands, looking down at the newspaper. "Tomorrow's the big groundbreaking. I wonder if there'll be trouble."

"Can't imagine Avery's going to clam up now," Rosie said. "He's like this self-appointed guru for all disgruntled merchants."

"He's wasting his breath," Hattie said. "The deal's in concrete."

George chuckled. "Maybe we should put some of that concrete between his lips."

Mort shook his head. "Georgie, the man's sittin' on a principle."

Mark laughed. "Think it's going to hatch?"

"Go ahead and make light of it," Mort said. "But guys like Avery git tired of bowin' to people with more money and a different way of doin' things."

"Well, aren't we the Bill O'Reilly?" Rosie said, pouring Mort a refill.

Mort blew on his coffee. "Ya know, this here diner could struggle if businesses go sour on the square."

There was a long pause. Mark looked at Rosie who looked at George.

"I doubt it," Mark said. "Monty's is a destination place. People go out of their way to come here."

"Power to ya. But if the square starts lookin' run-down, folks ain't gonna like the feel of it."

Charlie Kirby pulled the Navigator into the garage and turned off the motor. He reached for his cell phone and dialed. He heard the kitchen phone ring.

"Hello?" Marlene said.

"Honey, it's me. I really need to talk to you. I'm in the garage and didn't want to scare you by just coming in, but—"

"It's okay, Charlie. Come on inside."

Charlie hung up his cell phone. *Come on inside?* She didn't even sound annoyed.

He got out of the car and went in the kitchen. He saw Marlie sitting in the breakfast nook. "Mind if I have some coffee?"

"No, help yourself."

Charlie grabbed a mug and poured himself a cup of coffee. He noticed a pink rose in the crystal vase next to the sink. He walked over to the table and sat across from Marlie.

"I'm not sure what you want to talk to me about," Marlie said, "but I have some things to say. If you don't mind, I'd like to go first."

He nodded, surprised and grateful she was willing to talk.

Marlie sat with her fingers wrapped around her coffee cup. She lifted her eyes and looked into his. "I—I haven't been able to talk about this until now...the pain is so deep. You hurt me, Charlie. But I hurt you, too. And there's a big difference: I *meant* to."

"Marlie, you don't—"

She put her palm out to silence him. "Please, let me finish... I wanted to punish you. I wanted you to suffer as much as I was. That was so wrong, so against everything I believe. Not only did it hurt you and me, it hurt the children. I hope you'll forgive me."

Charlie nodded. "Of course I will."

"As far as my pain goes, I don't know how long it's going to take to get past it. I can't think straight. I don't even know who I am right now. Nothing will ever be the same. But when you asked me to forgive you, I turned my back, even though I knew you were truly sorry. That wasn't right. So, I accept your apology," she said, her chin quivering, "and I forgive you."

Marlie paused and wiped the tears from her cheeks. "It's totally a choice, Charlie. I don't feel any different. But I sincerely forgive you, and I'm trusting the Lord to change my heart."

Charlie's eyes were clouded with tears. He found her hand, surprised that she didn't pull away. "Thank you," he whispered, unable to say anything else.

Minutes passed in silence.

Finally, Charlie got up and brought back a box of Kleenex.

"Marlie, I need to tell you about something that happened yesterday. I got a call from a man named Christopher Slade. He's a marketing executive at Thompson Tire, and he told me that Tony English came to see him a couple of weeks ago."

Marlie looked up.

"English showed him a couple of entries in Sheila's diary, places where she had written about her affair with him. He says it never happened, that Sheila made it up. And that's what he told English. But English didn't believe him and tried to get Slade to reveal everything he knew about Sheila's background—which was zilch. He said the closest they ever got was a handshake."

"What made Mr. Slade call *you?*" Marlie asked.

"He said he heard about what was going on down here and it made him mad that I was getting the shaft. He thought I should know I wasn't the only one she'd lied about."

Marlie put her hand to her mouth and closed her eyes. "Oh, Charlie..."

"He and I can't prove anything," Charlie said. "I called Jordan and asked him why he didn't tell me I wasn't the only man named in the diary. He said he told me what was relevant. Apparently, Sheila wrote about a half dozen different men, and he couldn't see why you and I needed to know that, especially when it seemed so incriminating. He also said I can't call Mr. Slade back and discuss this until they get Merlino."

Marlie shook her head. "I can't believe this. She made up the whole thing?"

"At least about Slade and me, she did."

Jordan Ellis was standing at the window in his office, a cup of coffee in his hand, when his cell phone rang. He put the cup down and took his phone out of his pocket.

"This is Jordan."

"I think we've got something. Is your computer on?"

"Yeah, Harlan. Why?"

"I just sent you an e-mail. Look at the attachment."

"Hang on." Jordan sat in front of the computer and opened the e-mail, then the attachment. "What is this?"

"A picture taken at Oktoberfest last night. Recognize the face on the far right?"

"The guy's a dead ringer for Merlino! Who took the picture?"

"One of our guys is posing as a photographer for the *Micklenburg Messenger.* He took a series of crowd shots, hoping to spot him. If your hunch is right, he'll be back. He's feeling us out."

"The guy strikes like lightning. You can't miss a beat, Harlan."

"I know. I wish he'd hurry up and make his move. It's hard to keep the bakery operation looking normal. And I think the Carvers are wearing out with it."

"He's about to do something," Jordan said. "Don't blink."

"Don't worry, we won't."

"I can hardly believe what just happened here," Charlie said. "Are we back together?"

Marlie blew her nose. "It might be a long time before things are normal between us. But you can sleep on your own side of the bed, if you want to. I'm not over the fact that you considered getting involved with Sheila."

"I know."

"Do you? I'm not sure you understand how much it hurts. You say you love me, that I'm special to you. How can that mean anything if you're attracted to someone else?"

"Honey, it was a physical attraction, nothing more. I didn't have any feelings for Sheila."

"I don't understand how you can separate the two."

"It's hard to explain. Men and women are just different, that's all." Charlie tilted her chin up and looked into her eyes. "But I have a passion for you—physical, emotional, spiritual. I could never have that with another woman. Never." Charlie sighed. "If only I had kept my thoughts where they belonged, this would never have amounted to anything."

Marlie lifted her eyebrows. "If only."

Charlie looked at his watch. "I've got to get to work. I'm writing the speech for tomorrow's groundbreaking." He paused. "Any chance you'll go with me?"

"I suppose it would be politically correct."

"I'm way past caring what people think," he said. "The most important thing on my mind is you—and getting *us* back."

"It won't be the same, Charlie."

"No. Our God is so faithful, it might be even better."

Ellen Jones sat at the kitchen table thumbing through the brochures and chamber of commerce information on the town of Seaport. She took a bite of a Twix bar and let the chocolate coating melt in her mouth, then chewed the cookie part, feeling self-conscious about the crunching noise.

"That's your second candy bar," Guy said.

Ellen looked up, a smile on her face. "Find me a more pleasant way of handling stress."

Guy pulled his chair next to hers. "Well, what's your impression of Seaport?"

"It's pretty."

"And?"

"I suppose I could get used to it."

"Oh, come on, Ellen, it's quaint. It's upscale. It's perfect."

She opened the brochure and looked again at the stately old houses...huge shade trees...palm trees...flowering trees. "This is right on the gulf?"

"A few blocks away. We'd have the best of both—the shady older neighborhoods and the water. Plus, your dad only lives thirty miles from Seaport."

"I've thought about that," she said. "Now that he and I aren't at odds, I wouldn't mind being closer. Of course, it would tickle him to death if I quit working."

"Who says you won't be working? Novels don't write themselves."

Ellen thumbed again through the pictures of quaint neighborhoods. "What about churches?"

"Blue brochure, page six. Take your pick."

Ellen turned the page and read through the listing of churches. How could Guy understand that leaving her church family would be harder than leaving the community?

"What's wrong? There are all kinds of churches there."

"Yes, I see that."

Guy reached over and brushed the curls away from her face. "Honey, I really want to accept this offer. But I need us both to be on board."

She looked deep into his eyes and saw a glimmer of the ambitious law student she had fallen in love with. How could she deny him a partnership? "All right. Call Brent."

"You sure?"

She nodded. "Go on. Call him."

Guy kissed her cheek, then got up and left the kitchen just as Agent Michelle Taft came in.

"How are you holding up?" Michelle asked.

Ellen sighed. "I've got too much on my mind to worry about Merlino."

"I've noticed you looking at brochures. Are you taking a trip?"

"Looks like we're going to be moving."

"Really, where?"

"Guy's been offered a partnership in a law firm in Tallahassee. We've been looking into neighboring communities, just to get a feel for what we like."

"What a nice opportunity for him," Michelle said. "How do you feel about leaving your position here?"

Ellen looked down at the brochures and thought for a moment about what she'd be giving up. "I have mixed feelings."

"How long have you been editor here, Ellen?"

"Going on ten years. It's hard to imagine doing anything else."

"Can't you find a job working for the Tallahassee newspaper?"

Ellen picked up the Twix wrappers and rose to her feet. "I suppose I could. But we're going to live too far from the city to commute every day. Besides, maybe it's time for a change. Guy thinks I should write novels."

"That could be fun. I'll bet you have all sorts of ideas for a story."

Ellen threw the wrappers in the trash compactor, then turned around and looked at Michelle. "We're about to find out."

"Well, I wish you all the best."

Terri breezed into the kitchen. "Okay, if you're determined to go to tomorrow's groundbreaking, there are some things we need to discuss."

Giorgio Merlino leaned on the trunk of a cedar tree and looked at his watch for the umpteenth time. "Come on, Joey, you're thirty minutes late."

He reached in his jacket pocket and took out a pint of peach brandy and took a sip. It would be dark soon. The nip in the air told him that if Cousin Joey had messed up on the directions, Giorgio was in for a miserable hike back to Eugene.

He thought he heard something and listened intently. He stepped away from the tree and looked to the south. A small red-

and-white Cessna was approaching. Giorgio walked to the edge of the airstrip, took off his jacket, and waved it in the air. The plane did a flyby and then circled back around and came in for a landing.

Giorgio picked up a small bag and ran to the passenger side. The door opened and Joey pulled him inside.

"Well, Cuz, long time no see," Joey said. "Had a little trouble finding it, but here I am."

"Let's get this thing in the air," Giorgio said. "I don't think the feds spotted me, but you never know."

Joey hit a few switches and the plane started to vibrate and rattle.

Giorgio fastened his seat belt, and the small craft charged down the runway, bouncing and rocking over the uneven, ridged surface, then lunged into the air, leaving the Oregon forest far below.

Joey turned to Giorgio, a smirk on his face. *"Blue* eyes?"

Giorgio laughed and punched him on the arm. "Nice touch for an Italian boy, eh? Kinda nice losin' the beard, too."

"Actually, you look terrible. Where'd you sleep last night?"

Giorgio rubbed the stubble on his chin. "Salvation Army. I didn't figure they'd look for me there. Hey, thanks for picking me up. Did you bring my plastics?"

"Yeah," Joey said. "With digital timers. Does this mean we're even?"

"Ask me when we're on the ground in Ellison."

"I can't believe you picked up Risotto's trail. What went south?"

Giorgio told Joey everything that had happened from the time he recognized Mary Angelina's face in the freeway shooting until he left Micklenburg last night.

"I was so close." Giorgio slammed his fist into the palm of his hand. "But that Jones woman betrayed me. She told the feds, and they were waiting for me."

"Then why didn't they arrest you?"

"Probably didn't spot me in the crowd."

"How do you even know they *were* feds?"

"You don't have to see the Dumpster to smell it, Joey. The place reeked. I just know."

"What's it to this two-bit newspaper lady if you want to find Risotto?"

"I don't know, all right? What's with the twenty questions?"

Joey reached in his pocket and handed Giorgio a peppermint. "Chill out, Cuz. It's a long way to Ellison."

"Yeah, sorry. I'm just ticked. I told the broad not to mess with me."

"Maybe the feds figured it out on their own."

Giorgio snickered. "Yeah, sure, Joey. After eighteen years, they're still crawling all over the town where Risotto lives? They knew I was coming. Probably moved him again."

"So, it was a long shot. Go back to Chicago. Forget it."

Giorgio looked out at the sea of gray, billowy clouds below. "Not yet. Nobody crosses Giorgio Merlino. I owe Papa that much."

34

Charlie Kirby lay in bed watching Marlie sleep and wondering what their relationship would be like when the Lord healed all the wounds.

The alarm screamed in the quiet. He turned over and hit the Off button. Six o'clock already? He hadn't slept a wink, but the time had gone fast. He could hardly believe he was back in his own bedroom, and Marlie was willing to work things out.

He turned on his back, his hands behind his head, his mind racing.

Today was going to be significant—and controversial. He wondered if Avery Stedman would be at the groundbreaking, trying to stir up trouble.

He also wondered how it would feel, making his first public appearance since the scandal. He needed to let the elders know that he and Marlie had reconciled. He also needed to call Dennis and tell him. And Guy and Ellen.

There was a knock on the door. "Mom?"

Kevin stuck his head in the door, a look of surprise on his face. "I didn't know you were in here."

Charlie put his finger to his lips. He got up, put on his bathrobe, and went out in the hallway. "Your mother and I are finally starting to work things out."

Kevin hugged him. "That's great. Me and Josiah have been praying."

"You have?"

Kevin nodded. "Josiah said God listens to all His children, that it doesn't matter how young they are."

Charlie put his arm around Kevin. "He's been a good friend, hasn't he?"

"Yeah, he's great. Did Mom tell you he's taking me to the groundbreaking?"

"Uh-huh. She said she signed a permission slip so they'd let you out of school early."

Kevin smiled. "Josiah's proud of me for not smoking any-more—or skipping school."

"Well, that's two of us, son. As long as you're choosing to act more grown up, how about if the two of us guys fix breakfast and let your mom sleep a little longer?"

Ellen Jones sat in bed, sipping a cup of coffee and reading Friday's issue of the *Baxter Daily News*.

"You don't look pleased," Guy said, emerging from the bath-room wrapped in a towel, his hair still wet. "Are you unhappy with the paper?"

"No, it's fine." Ellen inhaled the warm steamy air and smelled the fresh scent of soap. "It's just hard to get excited about what's written here when I know what's really going on in town."

"What about the groundbreaking story?" Guy said. "That's big news."

She nodded. "It'll be bigger afterwards. Heaven knows what Avery Stedman might be up to. Rumor has it he's planning some-thing disruptive. He acts like a high school kid."

"Don't worry. Hal and Aaron won't let him cause any trouble."

"He's not the only one in town who's unhappy about the tire plant."

"I know that, Ellen. But I think most are reconciled to the fact that it's coming. I'm hoping the mood is positive and that Charlie can make even the skeptics feel good about it. My concern is that you're going at all."

"I'm not skipping it," she said. "The groundbreaking is a milestone for this community. And whether or not I think it's the best economic move, it's going to affect our future." She felt an unexpected twinge of sadness. "Well, *their* future."

Guy sat on the side of the bed. "Honey, the hardest part of moving will be the good-byes, but after that, we have so much to look forward to. I wish the FBI would hurry up and get Merlino so we can make a trip to Seaport and see if it's as good as it looks. Would you like that?"

Ellen nodded. "Anything to get back to real life."

Guy patted her knee and stood. "I wish you'd forget about going today. Why don't you send Margie in your place?"

"Jordan told us they spotted Merlino in Oregon. I see no reason to miss this event. Besides, I think Charlie could use a show of support."

Guy raised his eyebrows. "Can't argue with that."

"Really?" Ellen said, unable to suppress a grin. "I do believe that's a first, Counselor."

Mark Steele glanced up at the clock at Monty's Diner, then walked to the counter where the early crowd was finishing up breakfast.

"It's seven o'clock," Mark said. "Think something's happened to Mort?"

"Somebody should probably call and check on him," George Gentry said. "I'll do it."

Reggie Mason looked up from his newspaper. "Has he ever been this late?"

"Not since I've worked here." Rosie Harris started working her way down the counter, pouring refills. "He's always here at 6:00 A.M. sharp."

"Or waiting outside at 5:55," Mark added.

The front door opened and all heads turned. Mort walked into the diner and held open the door for an attractive middle-aged woman in a black pantsuit.

Mort hung up his hat, then took the lady's arm and walked to the counter, his eyes twinkling. "Mornin' all. I'd like ya to meet someone real special, my daughter..." Mort's voice cracked, and he coughed to cover up the emotion. "Rennie Hopson."

Each person at the counter got up and introductions were made, then Liv Spooner moved over so Mort and Rennie could sit together.

There was an uncomfortable, almost tangible silence. Mark wished someone would say something.

"Guess ya'll don't have the right words," Mort said. "Me neither. Seems too good to be true, havin' my baby girl come see me." Mort blushed. "She was only six when I laid eyes on her last. But I didn't have no trouble recognizin' that pretty face and them big brown eyes."

"Rennie, we're so glad you joined us this morning," Rosie said. "We have a lot of fun here at Monty's. I'm sure your father has told you all about it."

"To hear him talk about all of you, I feel as if I already know you. He considers you family."

Mark felt a little sheepish, but had to admit that he'd seen a likable side of Mort in the past week.

"Well, I've never seen Mort so excited," George said. "We're all very happy you two have found each other."

"I imagine you have a lot of catching up to do," Hattie Gentry said.

Rennie smiled. "Mama never said much about Daddy, but I always knew I was missin' something." She touched Mort's hand and looked at him adoringly. "I just never knew he would be so kind, and such a people person."

There was a long pause.

Rosie looked over at George who looked at Reggie who looked at Liv who looked at Mark.

"Uh, well," Mark said, "that's our Mort. Always interested in what makes everyone tick. Isn't that right?" he said, his voice prodding.

Rosie stared at Mark like she thought he had a screw loose, then turned to Rennie. "Uh, right! Your father's insights always challenge the rest of us to think off the charts—way off."

Reggie nodded. "Keeps us thinkin' out of the box."

"Yes, off the wall," Liv said.

George took his wife's hand, a smile on his face. "Yessiree. The one thing Hattie and I have always said, that Mort Clary sure knows it all."

"Ya'll are too nice," Mort said. "Rennie's gonna think yer puttin' her on."

"Rennie, since you're the guest today," Mark said, "breakfast is on the house. Rosie, why don't you get her order? Party hearty everyone. I've got to get to work. With the groundbreaking this afternoon at two o'clock, this place is going to be packed out at lunchtime."

Charlie hung his suit jacket on the bedpost, and then walked to the mirror and began tying his tie. *Lord, thank You for a second chance with Marlie.*

"The dark suit looks nice," Marlie said, coming up behind him.

Charlie smiled. "You like this red tie—or that striped one?"

"Definitely the red."

"Guess I'm a little nervous." Charlie sighed. "I can't get this thing tied right."

"Here, I'll do it." Marlie turned him around and began to retie the knot. "Since when are you nervous? You love public speaking."

"I know."

"You worried about Avery?"

Charlie looked down just as she looked up. "No, I'm excited about having you go with me—like we're on a first date or something."

Marlie finished tying his tie. "There, how's that?"

Charlie turned and looked in the mirror. He smiled. "Perfect. Thanks. So, what are you wearing today?" He instantly sensed her annoyance.

"Does it matter?"

"Not really, honey. I was just curious."

"Well, I'm not going to the groundbreaking with you to be an ornament, if that's what you think."

Charlie's heart sank. He turned to her. "That's *not* what I think at all. I'm so grateful to have another chance that I'm beside myself..." His voice cracked unexpectedly. "You'll look beautiful in anything you've got hanging in that closet. I just wanted to picture how we'd look together, that's all."

Marlie's face turned red. "Oh."

"Honey, what is it? What's wrong?"

"Nothing."

"Just say it."

Marlie lifted her eyes and looked into his. "I'll never look as good as Sheila Paxton. I'm ten years older than she was and—"

Charlie put his fingers gently to her lips. "Will you stop? I love the way you look."

"Do you?"

There were a few moments of awkward silence.

"Marlie, please don't."

"Don't what?"

"Compare yourself to Sheila—or worse yet, think that I am."

"Well, you *did.*"

Charlie shook his head. "I never stopped being attracted to you."

"Then how could you even think of getting involved with her? It doesn't make sense to me."

"Me either. I thought I was immune to that sort of thing. But I promise you, it will *never* happen again. And I'm going to spend the rest of my life proving how much I love you. You mean everything to me."

Marlie searched his face as uncertainty welled up in her eyes. He drew closer, his lips almost touching hers.

"I need to get some errands run if I'm going with you," she said. "When and where do you want me to meet you?"

"It would be nice if you could come to the office around twelve-thirty. The Thompson Tire people are coming for a buffet luncheon. Regina has it all arranged. We can all head for the site together around one-forty-five."

"All right. I've got the preschoolers farmed out until the groundbreaking's over."

"Good."

Marlie looked over at her closet and then at him. "I think I'll wear my pink wool suit. It's not too tailored, and it looks nice with pearls. What?"

"Nothing," Charlie said. "Seems very appropriate." *And you know it's my favorite!*

Jordan Ellis sat in his office, his feet on his desk, having his first cup of coffee with Sheriff Hal Barker and Police Chief Aaron Cameron.

"Sure wish Ellen would back off the groundbreaking," Jordan said. "That is one stubborn woman."

Hal smiled. "Yep."

"Are you two clear on where your people are going to be positioned?" Jordan said. "I know you're concentrating on crowd control, but I need to know where everyone is at all times."

Aaron nodded. "I drew my officers a diagram. We're good to go."

"Same here," Hal said. "Last I heard, they're expecting a thousand people to show up."

"Tell me about this Avery Stedman," Jordan said. "The loudmouth who got things stirred up about the mayor and Sheila Paxton."

Hal put his fingers to his chin. "Avery, Charlie, and I are about the same age. We grew up together, went to the same schools. I can't remember a time when Avery wasn't jealous of Charlie. Not that he's a bad guy, just has an inferiority complex the size of Texas."

"Is he capable of causing trouble out there today?"

Hal shrugged. "Hard to say. He's really steamed about the tire plant, but as far as I know, he's never been in trouble. He's mostly mouth." Hal turned to Aaron. "You ever run him in?"

"I got close right after the city council signed the permit for the tire plant. Stedman and some other men were throwing eggs at the mayor's window, shouting some pretty ugly things. But we got them to take their grievances and their picket signs and go home."

Jordan took his feet off the desk and stood. "All right. Ellen and Guy will be here in thirty minutes. Let me go over this diagram with the two of you and make sure we're all on the same page."

"By the way, anything new on Merlino?" Hal said.

"Hasn't been spotted since the Oktoberfest night before last. I have a feeling he's poised and ready to make a move."

35

Giorgio Merlino paid cash for his room at the Starlight Motel in Ellison, then got in his rental car and drove toward Baxter.

He hit the steering wheel with his palms. Why couldn't Ellen Jones have kept her mouth shut? Any hope he'd had of getting Risotto was history. Eighteen years down the toilet! Giorgio felt a twinge of grief. How he missed his father.

Suddenly, his mind exploded with the sound of gunfire. Giorgio ducked—painful memories of screaming and blood-spattered walls and Papa's faceless body racing through his mind. He heard a horn blaring and quickly turned the car back into his own lane, narrowly escaping a head-on collision.

He gripped the wheel with both hands, his heart pounding, his head soaked with sweat, and wondered how many times those flashbacks had haunted him, pulled him out of the present into the past.

But the past was all that mattered. Since the day Papa was gunned down, he'd been a killing machine for the Mob. All his good feelings had died—except what he had for Papa and Mary Angelina.

He reached in his shirt pocket and pulled out the photograph of the Risottos. Giorgio's anger had kept him going all these years. But he'd often wondered what his life might've been like had the feds not given Papa the ultimatum to testify against Spike Risotto, and Giorgio had been free to fall in love with Mary Angelina. The way she died bothered him, and he wondered if she'd suffered.

Giorgio rubbed his eyes, then opened them wide and blinked several times. He reached in the glove box, pulled out a baggie filled with speed, popped two capsules in his mouth and washed them down with half a bottle of water. He could catch up on his sleep later. He had a brief window of time to make a statement—and he planned to do it up big.

Jordan Ellis turned off his cell phone, walked over to the window in his office, and let out a string of swear words. There was a knock on the door.

"Jordan?" Hal Barker said. "I'm getting ready to head out to the site. I'll see you out there, okay?"

Jordan turned around. "Come in, Hal. Sit down for a minute."

"What's up?"

Jordan leaned against his desk, his arms folded. "Merlino must've made us. The sting didn't work."

"How do you know?"

"We can't know for sure, but our profiler thinks he should've hit like a bolt of lightning by now. I have a bad feeling. How much you wanna bet he's not in Oregon?"

"You don't think he'd risk his neck to come after Ellen?"

Jordan arched his eyebrows. "Merlino sees himself as his old man's legacy in the world of organized crime. He'll do anything it takes to bring honor to the Merlino family name, including making good on all his threats."

"Yeah, just ask Charlie." Hal sighed and glanced at his watch. "I need to get out to the site. What should I tell my deputies?"

"Tell them to remember what we talked about: Watch the crowd like a hawk. Concentrate on outsiders. Everyone's got a copy of the picture Harlan e-mailed me."

"Are you going to tell Aaron, or should I?"

"Go ahead and tell him. I'll touch bases when I get out there. I need to talk to the Joneses first."

"Maybe Ellen won't go," Hal said.

Jordan got up and paced. "In a way, I hope she does. I'd like to force Merlino's hand. He wasted two of our agents." Jordan's hands turned to fists. "I'm not going to lose that piece of garbage. I want him out of circulation."

Ellen Jones leaned her head against the back of the couch and heaved a sigh. "I don't need this today."

"Sorry," Jordan said. "There's no way we can know where Merlino is. I thought you should know."

"You really think he'll come after me?"

"At some point."

"That's a bit vague, don't you think?"

"Sorry. I can't tell you what I don't know."

Ellen felt her face get hot. "Well, I'll tell you what I know: I'm tired of being intimidated by this—this—"

"Gangster?" Guy said.

Ellen inhaled and exhaled loudly. "I refuse to hide anymore! I'm going to the groundbreaking! I can't live this way! Period! I've had it!"

"Welcome to *my* world," Guy said. "But you're not going to put yourself in jeopardy."

"It's a little late for that, Counselor. But I'm tired of feeling like a prisoner."

Guy looked at Jordan, his eyes full of desperation. "Are you sure Merlino's not in Oregon?"

"There's no way to be sure. Like I told you, he was spotted night before last. But our profiler says he would've struck swiftly. He thinks Merlino smelled a sting and left."

"What do you think?" Ellen said.

"I'm inclined to agree. You fed him the tip last Sunday. What's he waiting for?"

"Maybe he's waiting until your people get tired and call it off," Guy said. "He doesn't strike me as a quitter."

Ellen turned to Guy, her eyes pleading. "What are the odds

he'd show up at the groundbreaking, even *if* he's coming?" She looked over at Jordan. "His every move has been surreptitious."

Jordan arched his eyebrows. "True."

"And this may be the last significant community event to happen while I'm editor of the *Daily News*. Please don't deny me this."

Guy took her hand and looked into her eyes. "The idea of you being in a crowd right now gives me chills. But I know when your mind is made up. I'm going with you."

Ellen squeezed his arm. "Just think—ninety days from now, we'll be in Seaport."

"It can't come soon enough for me."

Charlie Kirby stood near the elegant buffet table the caterers had set up in a meeting room down the hall from his office. He held a plate in his hand and sampled a variety of finger foods while he mingled with the executives from Thompson Tire Corporation.

Marlie approached him, her voice a whisper. "Jordan Ellis is waiting for you in the reception area. Regina says it's important."

"Okay, honey, thanks. Would you mind taking over for a few minutes? I'll be right back." He smiled at her. "You look positively stunning in that pink suit."

Charlie excused himself and went out to the reception area.

Jordan stood and extended his hand. "Sorry to barge in unannounced, but I need to fill you in about something. Is there someplace we could talk privately?"

"Let's use my office," Charlie said.

He led Jordan down the hall past the meeting room, then went into his office and closed the door.

"Sorry," Jordan said. "I see you're in the middle of something."

"That's all right. What's this about?"

Jordan filled Charlie in on Ellen's feeding false information to Merlino, the setup in Micklenberg, and their current concern over Merlino's whereabouts.

"*If* he spotted feds in Micklenburg," Jordan said, "then he thinks Ellen double-crossed him. He's threatened her life if she involves us."

Charlie sighed. "What can I do?"

"Nothing really. I just want you to be aware that agents will be posted in strategic locations around the groundbreaking site. Hal and Aaron are working with us. We've got the place covered. If Merlino shows up, we'll get him."

"You really think he will?"

"Hard to say. But he's not going to get by us."

Charlie thought for a moment. "Are Marlie and I in danger?"

"Our profiler doesn't think so. Merlino already made sure you got yours."

Charlie looked at Jordan squarely. "And when this is over, I want to talk to you about the diary."

"Fair enough. Well, I think that brings you up to speed. I need to get out to the site."

"Ellen certainly doesn't have to be there," Charlie said. "Couldn't you talk her out of it?"

Jordan smirked. "Yeah, right."

Charlie nodded knowingly. "Aaron told me this morning that the police have their eye on Avery Stedman. I think they're ready for a skirmish or two."

"Well, cries of protest and a few fists thrown would make me real happy, considering what could happen."

Dennis Lawton walked into the house from the garage. "Jen, you ready? The groundbreaking starts in forty-five minutes, and we still have to pick up your folks."

"I'm in the bedroom."

He hurried down the hall to the master bedroom and stopped in the doorway. "Don't you look smart?"

She smiled. "You like it?"

"Turn around. Wow! You look great in olive green. Is that silk?"

She nodded. "Did you get the twins situated at Flo's?"

"Oh, yeah. They're in seventh heaven. By the way, did you hear Charlie and Marlene are working things out?"

"No! How'd you find out?"

"I talked to Charlie this morning. He sounded great. Said he and Marlene had an emotional breakthrough yesterday, and that she was going with him today."

"That's almost too good to be true," Jennifer said.

Dennis came in and sat on the side of the bed. "Did you know he's been giving her a pink rose every day?"

"Marlene never mentioned it. That's really sweet."

"I thought so. Charlie did that the first year they were married. So after they started having problems, he went back to leaving her a rose, hoping it would soften her heart. She threw each one in the trash—until yesterday, that is. I'm not sure what made the difference, but they were able to do some serious talking."

"Oh, I'm so glad."

Dennis got up and stood behind Jennifer, his arms around her. "Do I make you happy?"

"Very."

Dennis turned her around in his arms. "Nothing's ever going to come between us, right?"

"Dennis, why are you acting so weird?"

He kissed her forehead. "Just a reality check. If a couple like Charlie and Marlene can be driven to the edge of a cliff, it can happen to any of us."

"Maybe as long as we're aware it can, we won't let it."

Dennis took her right hand and ran his thumb along the platinum band. "I love you so much. In some ways, this ring symbolizes more to me than your wedding ring."

"Why?"

"Because my understanding of commitment was even deeper when I gave you this one."

Jennifer smiled. "Good answer."

Dennis glanced at his watch. "We'd better go get your folks. I want us to be close enough for the Kirbys to spot us. I think they'd appreciate looking out at friendly faces."

Jordan walked slowly along the perimeter of the crowd and picked up his walkie-talkie. "Hal, can you hear me?"

"Affirmative. Where are you?"

"About fifty yards to your left. Next to the lady in the red coat."

"Yeah, I see you."

"Are your deputies in place?"

"That's a yes."

"Okay, out." Jordan turned his head the other way and saw Aaron Cameron looking in his direction. "Aaron, how are you situated?"

"All my officers are at their posts. Heard anything new?"

"Negative. Just keep your eyes and ears open. I'll keep you posted. Out."

Jordan let his eyes move from left to right across the field where the crowd was gathering. Charlie Kirby and the entourage from Thompson Tire Corporation had just arrived and were being photographed.

Jordan put his walkie-talkie to his ear. "Agent Farber, give me your location."

"A few yards in front of the platform, sir. Agents Taft, Wenger, Milton and I have the Joneses surrounded. Can you see us?"

"Affirmative. What's the mood?"

"Cautious. And cooperative."

"Sounds good. Out."

Jordan checked in with the rest of his team and felt confident that every player was in place. He could feel the adrenaline rush, but knew better than to get overzealous. He couldn't afford to make a mistake.

He looked beyond the colored treetops and spotted the clock tower on the county courthouse. He thought back on the various situations that had brought him to Baxter in recent years: the

McConnell murder investigation, the Logan-Kennsington kidnapping, then the firebombings by the Citizens' Watch Dogs, and now a death threat by Giorgio Antonio Merlino, one of the most ruthless mobsters still at large.

Jordan noticed the time: 1:40. He moved his eyes slowly across the crowd. Merlino might have outsmarted Harlan, but he was not getting away on Jordan's watch.

36

Kevin Kirby sat in the front seat of Josiah's old pickup, beaming with the hope that his parents were working things out.

"You warm enough with the windows down?" Josiah said.

Kevin smiled. "Yeah, the air feels great with the sun coming in."

"I sure am glad your folks are doin' better."

"Me, too," Kevin said. "Are we almost there?"

"Be another couple minutes. It was nice of your mama to let me bring you out here, boy."

Kevin looked over at Josiah and thought how different his old friend looked in slacks and a bomber jacket—and without the straw hat. His dark head looked polished except for a few runaway strands of white, curly hair. "Think maybe we can do some more fishing before it gets too cold?"

Josiah's ivory smile stretched across his face. "Just a little hooked, are you?"

"Kinda."

"Well, we'll see what we can do. Fish don't like cold too much. But we can sure try to get after 'em."

"Good, I was hoping."

"You ain't afraid old Josiah's gonna forget about you once the fishin' ain't good, are you?"

Kevin shrugged. "I guess not."

"Don't worry, boy. You can come down to my place, and I'll make us some chili and light a fire. Maybe get out the Chinese checkers. You'd like that, would you?"

Kevin smiled. "Sure."

Josiah turned the truck down a gravel road and rolled up his window. "Best you roll yours up so we ain't covered in dust when we get there." He looked over at Kevin and patted his knee. "If I didn't say it, I'm proud of you for supportin' your daddy."

"I'm not listening to what Mr. Stedman or anyone else says anymore."

"That's the spirit, boy."

Kevin looked up and saw rows of cars parked in the grass up ahead, then his eye fell on the cross dangling from the rearview mirror. "Josiah, do you ever feel bad about the time you left your family?"

The old man mused. "If I think about it the wrong way. But most of the time, I'm content believin' the Lord's grace was big enough to erase it all. And I'm grateful my sweet Hannah and my young'uns didn't hold it against me neither. There's somethin' mighty powerful about bein' forgiven when you don't deserve it."

"Look, there're the Lawtons. And Mr. and Mrs. Wilson. They go to my church. Hurry up and park. I want them to meet you."

Ellen Jones stood near a wooden platform on which the podium had been set, and a blue and white banner with Thompson Tire's corporate logo had been draped across the front.

She held tightly to Guy's hand, aware of the wall of bodies surrounding her.

"The Kirbys look great," she whispered to Guy.

"Did you know Marlene was coming?" he asked.

"Heavens, no. I'm shocked. And tickled."

"I suppose you're going to tell me it's another answer to prayer?" Ellen smiled. "I plead the Fifth."

Guy didn't say anything for a few moments, then whispered in her ear. "Well, I'll say one thing: The people from your church sure came out in droves."

Ellen waved at Pastor Thomas and Joe and Mary Beth Kennsington.

"Ellen, who's the black gentleman standing with Kevin Kirby?"

She looked down the row. "I don't know. Must be a friend of the family."

Ellen felt a tap on the shoulder. "How're you doing?" Agent Terri Farber asked.

"I think we're fine." Ellen looked up at Guy and then at Terri. "Really."

"Things ought to be underway in a minute," Terri said. "Nice crowd. I couldn't have imagined all these people coming out on a Friday afternoon."

"The tire plant's a big deal," Ellen said. "Whether one is in favor of it or opposed, it's going to have a major impact on this town."

Guy put his lips to her ear. "Is that G. R. Logan over there, *praying* with Charlie?"

Ellen shaded her eyes from the sun and spotted G. R.'s snow-white hair. "Uh-huh. Charlie insisted he be here for this. Few people realize how influential G. R.'s been on the economic development committee or how generous he's been with his money. He's truly a changed man."

"I know," Guy said sarcastically. "Ever since he joined the ranks of the born-again brigade."

"Is that so shocking?"

"I can't understand why a wealthy, powerful dynamo like G. R. would need all that Jesus hype."

"Maybe you should question him, Counselor. He might make a key witness."

Guy half smiled. "Shhh...looks like they're ready to start."

Charlie Kirby went up the steps to the platform where Marlene, members of the city council, and representatives from Thompson Tire were already seated.

He stood at the podium and looked out across the sea of faces, amazed at how many people had shown up for the groundbreaking. *Lord, let my words bring unity, not division.*

"Distinguished guests, respected colleagues, friends and neighbors, what a beautiful afternoon for us to come together on this site, to break ground for a new plant that will spark a revival of prosperity in this community. When Logan Textile Industries shut its Baxter operation nearly eight years ago, almost three hundred jobs were lost, and the citizens of Baxter suffered a recession at a time when most of the country prospered.

"All that is about to change. Through the efforts of the economic development committee under the direction of G. R. Logan, we are about to enter a whole new era. The Thompson Tire plant will create more than six hundred jobs, most of them to be filled by Baxterites. Not only will the added revenue stimulate the local economy, but it will enable us to grow in ways that will make us attractive to other nonpolluting industries. And that, dear friends, cannot help but advance the quality of life here—across the board."

Charlie stopped, relieved to hear applause. He noticed Avery Stedman and a few other men carrying picket signs. Two police officers were following alongside.

"I realize there are some who do not share our belief that Thompson Tire will be an asset to this community. There has been skepticism...and opposition...and sadly, even bitter division. Merchants operating on the town square have openly aired concern that their businesses will not survive if Baxter's hometown ambiance is lost in the name of progress. Let me just say, I completely agree. And that's not going to happen."

Charlie paused, only vaguely aware of the applause, his mind reeling with a radical new thought. Was it prompted by the Lord—or his own desire to look good to a community he had disappointed?

Jordan Ellis let his eyes wander over the crowd, stopping every few seconds to study the faces. He put his walkie-talkie to his ear. "Agent Farber, how does it look from your vantage point?"

"Nothing out of the ordinary, sir. The birds are in the nest. Out."

"Hal, you out there?"

"Yeah, Jordan. I'm straight across from the picket signs. Kinda hard to miss. Look for the Stetson."

Jordan chuckled. "How tall are you anyway?"

"Six four. Looks good from up here. Out."

"Aaron, is that you next to Stedman?"

"No, that's one of my officers. I'm holding up the rear. See the bright yellow Hummer parked behind me?"

"Yeah, copy that. How's it look back there?"

"Wonderfully boring. I'd like to keep it that way. Out."

"Okay, everybody, keep your eyes and ears open. The mayor's got everyone's attention. Watch for anyone moving slowly through or around the crowd. Out."

The applause died down, and Charlie was held captive in a long pause, a thousand pairs of eyes on him. *Lord, this must be coming from You. Talk about a step of faith!*

"I love this town as much as any person here and want to pre-serve our rich heritage. And being an investor myself, I understand that every business decision involves a degree of risk. I have always relied on the Lord to give me good decision-making capabilities, and He has blessed me with more money than I'll ever spend.

"And so, fellow Baxterites, to stand behind my belief that bringing Thompson Tire to this community will boost our economy, I'm making this promise to each merchant operating on the town square: If your business hasn't maintained a growth of at least 5 percent during the twelve months after Thompson opens its doors, I will offer to buy it from you."

Charlie looked directly at Avery Stedman. Avery returned his gaze, a look of disbelief on his face, then lowered his picket sign and walked over and stood next to his father. The other picketers followed suit. The crowd was wild with applause.

"Bravo!" Ellen smiled at Guy, clapping until her hands tingled. "Charlie did it again. That man has a gift for bringing us together. I'm so glad I didn't miss—"

BOOOOM! The sound shook the ground, evoking gasps from the crowd.

"What was that?" Ellen clutched Guy's arm, her heart pounding.

"You two stay behind me," Terri said, taking her gun out of the holster.

"Look," Ellen said, pointing toward town. "There's a stream of smoke."

Guy nodded. "Yeah, I see it. Something must've blown."

"Friends, please stay calm," Charlie said from the podium. "Let's find out what—"

BOOOOM!

BOOOOM!

BOOOOM!

Three deafening explosions rocked the ground. Ellen ducked, her hands over her ears. She waited a few second, then looked up and saw flames shooting from clouds of smoke across the back row of the parking area. People started screaming and running in all directions.

"Come on," Terri said. "We're getting you out of here."

Ellen felt herself being pulled along in a wave of bodies.

Jordan put his walkie-talkie to his ear. "Farber, are the birds in the nest? Repeat, are the birds in the nest? Over."

"Affirmative. We moved them behind the platform. Any idea what's going on, sir?"

"Not yet. Stay put. Out."

"Sheriff, can you hear me?"

There was a long pause.

"Sheriff?"

"Yeah, Jordan. I just spoke to my deputy in town. There's been an explosion in a residential area. That's all I know."

"All right. Keep us posted. Out."

"Okay, everyone, listen up. This is too sophisticated for a few folks mad about the tire plant. My guess is Merlino just sent us a message. Those explosives were probably timed so he could be out there in the crowd, ready to make a move. This guy's quick, and he's lethal. Agent Farber, keep your people planted right where they are, and listen to your instincts. All other agents...let's get out there and find him. Out."

Jordan moved his eyes across the crowd. People were huddled in groups, their faces anxious, their demeanor confused.

Jordan put his walkie-talkie to his ear. "Aaron, give me your location. Over."

"I'm out in the parking area. It's a real mess—cars burning, debris everywhere. My officers aren't letting anyone leave, but we can't hold off a crowd this size indefinitely. I've called Parker and Hannon for reinforcements."

"Good move. Out."

Jordan's eyes stopped on a stocky man in a sport coat and dark glasses who seemed to be nonchalantly inching his way to the platform. The guy seemed much too cool, considering what had just happened.

"Farber, do you read me? Over."

"Yes, sir."

"I may have spotted Merlino moving toward the front of the platform. I'm on my way. Out."

Jordan pulled his gun out of the holster and moved swiftly through the crowd, trying not to create a scene and desperately wanting to avoid crossfire.

Ellen huddled next to Guy, her heart racing, her imagination on tilt. "Terri, what did Jordan say?" Ellen whispered.

"To stay where we are."

Ellen read the anxiety on Terri's face and knew she wasn't telling everything she knew. "Did Merlino do this?"

Terri avoided eye contact. "It's way too soon to know that. We're just being extra cautious."

"Cautious, nothing. Your hands are shaking."

Terri glanced at Michelle and then at Ellen. "Would you keep your voice down, please?"

Ellen started to comment and Guy put his finger to her lips. "Shh. Let the woman do her job," he said.

"Don't you care about what's going on out there?" Ellen said.

Guy pulled her closer. "Not enough to risk getting shot. Let's do as we're told. I want them to get this guy."

Jordan moved stealthily along the edge of the crowd and made eye contact with two of his agents. He motioned toward the man in dark glasses, then quickly came up behind him and put his gun to the man's head. "FBI, freeze!"

The man stiffened. "Don't shoot. What did I do?"

"Put your hands in the air and don't move," Jordan said, holding the gun while the other two agents patted him down.

"He's clean, sir."

Jordan spun him around. His heart sank. It wasn't Merlino—not even close.

Giorgio Merlino drove his car out of the Baxter city limits toward Ellison, trying to picture the chaos his explosives had created. He knew Ellen Jones would be shaking in her boots. But she wasn't worth dying for.

The FBI presence was more than he was equipped to contend with. He'd have to deal with her another day, another time.

37

Ellen Jones sat at one end of a couch in the parlor at Morganstern's, her finger tracing the white flower pattern on the blue fabric. Guy came and sat next to her, a cup of soup in his hand.

"Sure you don't want some?" he said. "Mrs. Morganstern's specialty—broccoli cheese."

Ellen shook her head. "Thanks anyway."

"You can't give in to this, honey. We'll be back in our own house before you know it."

Ellen closed her eyes, the warmth of the fire making her drowsy.

"What are you thinking?" he said.

"I don't know what I'm thinking. I've never felt this numb before."

Agent Terri Farber came and sat in the chair next to Ellen. "It's okay to feel whatever you're feeling. You had a terrifying day."

Ellen sighed. "What would've happened if Guy or I had been at home instead of at the groundbreaking?"

Terri patted her arm. "Well, you weren't."

Ellen stared at the crackling fire, unable to shake the image of twisted, smoldering metal in her driveway. "Merlino thought the Lexus was mine, you know. He probably started following me when I was in Raleigh."

"Ellen, we'll get him," Terri said.

"Before he gets *me?*" Ellen's eyes brimmed with tears. "This is all my fault. I got greedy for a story and cared more about..." Her voice failed.

Guy took her hand and brushed the curls away from her face. "The car can be replaced. And the house won't take long to repair since the damage is mostly on the exterior."

"And what about us?" Ellen said. "How do we repair the damage to us?"

There was a long pause.

Terri rose to her feet. "If you'll excuse me, I think I'll have some more of Mrs. Morganstern's soup."

Ellen watched the flames dance in the fireplace.

"Honey, I've loved you for twenty-nine years," Guy said. "It's going to take more than one bad decision to do permanent damage."

"I still can't believe I deceived you," Ellen said.

"Me either. You're usually honest to a fault. Maybe I put too much pressure on you."

She sighed. "No, the tip was just too tempting."

"Well, like you said, the story did get personal after Merlino tried to blackmail Charlie."

Ellen shook her head. "It was more that I wanted to be the one to break this story."

"Is that so bad?"

"It is if I had to compromise my values to do it." Ellen got up and stood facing the fire. "Three people died because of me."

"No, three people died because Merlino pulled the trigger. Honey, let's put it behind us."

"I'm no better than KJNX," she said.

"Oh, give me a break, Ellen. Your integrity is so far above theirs it's not worth discussing."

She dabbed the corner of her eyes. "Thanks for wanting to defend my honor, Counselor, but what I did was no better. The end doesn't justify the means."

Guy got up and slid his arms around her. Ellen rested her back against his chest.

"So, how long are you going to punish yourself?" he said.

"That's not what I'm doing. It just grieves me that I'm capable of stooping that low to get what I want. And now we're both reaping the consequences."

"What ever happened to this Jesus you claim to be sold out to?" Guy said. "I thought if you confessed your sins, He was supposed to wipe the slate clean?"

Suddenly the heat from the fire felt uncomfortable and Ellen wiggled out of Guy's arms.

"Well?" he said. "Do you believe Him or not?"

Ellen was astounded he knew enough to call her on it. She turned around, her eyes searching his. "Of course, I believe Him. My emotions just haven't caught up yet."

"Okay, then," Guy said, stroking her cheek. "That's what we need to work on."

Charlie Kirby sat on the side of the bed and put on his slippers, his mind racing with the day's events.

Marlie came out of the bathroom, sat at her vanity table, and began to brush her hair.

"You all right?" Charlie asked.

"I wouldn't go that far. Did you get a hold of Guy and Ellen?"

"They're staying at Morganstern's until the mess is cleaned up. The Lexus was totaled and the explosion damaged the front of the house, but it looks like they can get back in soon."

"It's a wonder no one was killed. Why can't they catch this man?"

Charlie got up and put his hands on her shoulders. "They will. Why don't you come sit? You haven't stopped since we got home."

Marlie got up and walked over to her rocking chair. "Is it cold in here, or is it just me?"

Charlie turned on the gas logs in the fireplace, then sat in his chair, his feet on the ottoman. He stared at the flames and tried to relax, but the events of the day—good and bad—seemed to compete for his attention. "What a day," he finally said.

"Thank God there were no serious injuries," she said. "When the cars exploded in the parking area, all I could think about was Kevin. I still can't get over how protective Josiah was."

"Too bad his truck was destroyed. I'm sure a vehicle that old wasn't insured. Maybe we can do something to help him."

Charlie slipped back into silence, his mind racing from one image to another until he heard Marlie's voice.

"It's a shame you didn't get to finish your speech."

Charlie looked over at her, glad she finally brought it up. "You're not angry that I put my neck on the chopping block?"

"That part wasn't in your speech, was it?"

"No, I felt the Lord prompting me. And I just stepped out in faith."

"I thought so." Marlie closed her eyes and rested her head on the back of the rocker. "Charlie, do you even realize what He did?"

"What do you mean?"

"He set you on a lamp stand and let you shine. It was amazing."

Charlie smiled without meaning to. "It was, wasn't it? When I wrote the speech, I couldn't think of anything that would help heal the division over the plant or soften the negative effects of the scandal. This did both."

"You couldn't have done it," she said. "This was a gift."

Charlie got up and stood in front of the fire, trying to absorb the magnitude of such mercy. He blinked the stinging from his eyes, then turned around and looked at Marlie. "I know He's a God of second chances, but this is more than I would've ever asked for."

Marlie looked up at him, a tear escaping down one cheek. "That's how I knew it was Him."

Jordan Ellis lay in bed, his hands behind his head, his heart beating hard enough to make his shirt move. He kept asking himself what went wrong.

It was easy enough to put plastic explosives on three cars in different locations in the parking area. But why hadn't the police officers assigned to that area noticed Merlino messing around out there?

Jordan sat up on the side of the bed and rubbed his hands through his hair. Why fault the cops? Merlino was a professional hit man. He stayed alive by staying invisible.

His cell phone rang and he reached over and picked it up. "This is Jordan."

"Sir, I think we just found our perp!"

Jordan's heart raced. "Where?"

"A dump called the Starlight Motel—just this side of Ellison. A George Aldridge checked in just after three-thirty this afternoon. Description fits. And he's driving a rental car. We're standing across the parking lot. The lights are out. We're going in."

"Don't you dare lose him! Call me back the minute you've got him!"

Giorgio Merlino lay half asleep, vaguely aware of deep voices and someone pounding on the door. Suddenly, the door flew open and the lights came on.

"FBI. Freeze!"

He grabbed his gun and pulled the trigger, then felt a sharp pain pierce his right hand, causing him to drop the gun on the floor.

Giorgio saw four men lunge toward him. He fought with everything he had, but someone rolled him over on his stomach, yanked his arms behind his back, and cuffed him.

He winced. "Easy on the hand!"

"Should've frozen when I told you to. Don't worry, you won't need your trigger hand where you're going."

One of the feds pulled him to his feet. "Just for the record," the agent said, his face in front of Giorgio's, "Spike Risotto and his wife died in a plane crash six years ago. Oops."

Giorgio felt as though he would explode. He felt robbed—and duped. He fought wildly to free his hands, then someone shoved him facedown on the bed and held him so he couldn't move.

He closed his eyes and concentrated on the activity in the room. One agent read him his rights. Another called for an ambulance. Someone activated a cell phone.

"Sir? Merlino's in cuffs. It's over."

38

ark Steele heard a thud and hurried to the front door
of Monty's Diner. He opened the door and pulled the
bundle inside, then bent down and cut the twine.

Rosie Harris stood over him, her hand out. "What do the headlines say?"

Mark held up a newspaper and read the bold black print:
"Mayor's Boomtown Speech Rocked by Explosions." He looked up
at her. "That's an understatement."

"What is?" Mort Clary said, hanging up his hat.

"This morning's headlines," Mark said. "Here, take one.
Where's Rennie?"

"She'd had ta git back." Mort dropped a quarter in the jar and
walked to the counter.

"I can't believe this," Rosie said.

"Sounded like half the town was goin' up." Mort laid his paper
on the counter. "Me and Rennie didn't know what ta think."

Rosie arched her eyebrows. "Is that why she left?"

"Who left?" Reggie Mason said, taking his place at the counter.

"Rennie had to go on back," Mort said. "She's got a husband, ya
know."

George and Hattie Gentry walked in the diner, Liv Spooner
behind them.

"Was anyone else at the groundbreaking?" George said.

Rosie put three mugs on the counter and filled them with coffee. "You and Hattie were out there?"

He nodded. "Liv, too. It was something! What does the paper

have to say? Somebody has it in for Ellen Jones. The woman can't seem to get a break."

Reggie scrunched his face. "Doesn't tell any more than I heard on TV."

"Before we came here, we heard some breaking news on KJNX," Hattie said. "The FBI has a suspect in custody. He's been linked to the *Mob*."

"Organized crime—in Baxter?" Mark's eyebrows furrowed. "What's here to draw the Mob? The hottest thing in this town is Friday Night Bingo at Saint Anthony's."

"Why the heck would they go around blowin' up cars?" Reggie said.

"Who knows?" Liv wrapped her fingers around her mug. "Brings back the same fear I had when the CWD attacks were going on."

"Hattie and I went by the Joneses' place to see what the damage looked like," George said. "My word, her car looked like it'd been in one of those car bombings in Ireland." George looked over at Mort. "Why are you so quiet?"

"Just havin' my caffeine."

"Come on, Mort," Mark said. "We've given you enough ammo to shoot off your mouth for an hour. What's wrong?"

"Who says anything's wrong?"

"You're moping," Rosie said. "Was it hard having Rennie go home?"

Mort shrugged. "I guess so. Kinda liked havin' her here."

"When's she comin' back?" Reggie said.

Mort blew on his coffee and took a sip. "Don't know just yet."

"I thought you said you were going to visit her in Greenville," Hattie said.

Mort took another sip of coffee and didn't say anything.

"You change your mind?" Mark asked.

"I'm a little shy about it, all right?"

"Shy?" George said. "About what? She's taken with you."

"What if her husband don't like me? Might spoil what we got

started. Ain't that many folks that take ta me the way Rennie did."

There was a long stretch of silence.

Finally, Rosie put her hand on Mort's shoulder. "Anyone who loves her isn't going to stand in her way. It was obvious she's crazy about you."

Mort's face lit up. "Seemed like it."

"Definitely," George said. "You oughta go. If your truck won't make it to Greenville, you can borrow my Buick."

Mort drew circles around the rim of his mug. "Mighty nice of ya, Georgie, but that ain't it. My truck'll make the trip. Just don't know if my heart can take it. I sure did feel somethin' powerful for that girl. Don't know if I could stand ta lose her again."

Rosie wagged her finger. "You went forty years not seeing her. No way are we letting you talk yourself out of this."

Ellen Jones sat in the parlor at Morganstern's reading Saturday's issue of the *Baxter Daily News*. Guy came away from the buffet table carrying a tray of assorted breads, fruit, juice, and coffee.

"Did you get any sleep after Jordan called?" he said.

"Actually, I crashed for the first time in ages."

He kissed her forehead. "Me, too. How's the paper look?"

"Margie outdid herself. She didn't obsess over the explosions and gave just the right importance to Charlie's speech."

"I take it you're pleased?" Guy said.

"Yes, very." Ellen lowered the paper. "Wait till I fill her in on Merlino. She doesn't know the half of it."

"Guess you're going to spend all day working on it?"

"No, I've recorded the facts on audiotape. I'm going to meet with Margie this morning. She's going to do it."

"But this was *your* big story."

"That was ego talking," Ellen said. "Margie can handle it as well as I can. Why not let her start off big? Once I give notice, the board will probably offer her my position."

Guy stared at her in disbelief. "You didn't have to do that."

Ellen folded the paper and put it aside. "I'm ready for a sabbatical. I can't seem to get excited about leaving Baxter, though."

Guy poured her a glass of orange juice and set it on the coffee table. "How about if we check out of here and go find out if Seaport is as good as it looks?"

Ellen's eyes met his; there was that ambitious law student again. "Okay," she said, trying not to sound negative.

Guy sat next to her on the couch. "I know what a sacrifice this is for you."

Ellen picked up the glass of orange juice, her eyes stinging, and swallowed the emotion with a couple of gulps.

Guy turned her head toward him and lifted her chin. "But did you ever stop to think maybe it was meant to be?"

"What do you mean?"

"Well, you're the one who always says God is in control."

"Guy, why are you suddenly throwing my beliefs in my face? This is about the third time—"

"I finally read the book."

Ellen raised her eyebrows. "*Evidence That Demands a Verdict*?"

"Don't look so shocked."

"Why didn't you tell me?"

"I just did."

Ellen spilled orange juice down the front of her and grabbed a napkin and dabbed her blouse. "When?"

"While you were off in Knoxville and Chicago."

"And?"

Guy's gaze was intense. "It was compelling, I have to admit. It would *almost* take more faith not to believe in God."

"You don't sound convinced."

"At least I'm open. I'd like to read it again. Maybe I'll take your suggestion and talk to G. R. He's a straightforward kind of guy."

Ellen sat staring at him, marveling at how the Holy Spirit had been working. "I don't even know what to say. This is so unexpected! The book does make a powerful argument."

"Yes, but I've also had my eye on you, and Jed and Rhonda,

and Dennis and Jennifer. Whatever you have seems to hold you together."

Ellen felt a twinge of regret. "I haven't exactly been a shining example lately."

"Honey, don't negate everything else. You never waver in your beliefs—even when I give you a hard time. I figure there has to be something powerful at work for you to have stood your ground this long."

"All this time, I thought you were turned off."

"Oh, I was. And I might be again. But for some reason, it won't leave me alone. I have to resolve it." Guy looked at his watch. "Okay, enough of that...are we going to drive to Seaport or not?"

Ellen slipped her hand into his, her heart overflowing with amazement and gratitude. "Give me until noon, Counselor. After that, I'm all yours."

39

Charlie Kirby loaded the last of the lunch dishes in the dishwasher and turned it on. He went out to his car and got a fresh pink rose and put it in the crystal vase by the sink.

"You still doing that?" Kevin asked.

Charlie turned around and shrugged. "I'm sort of enjoying it."

"I think it's pretty cool. Can I talk to you for a minute, Dad? I've got an idea."

"Sure, let's sit at the table."

"Where is everybody?"

"Grocery shopping. I opted for kitchen duty." Charlie smiled wryly. "What's your idea?"

"I want to help Josiah get another truck."

"You're talking about a lot of money, son. What did you have in mind?"

"I thought maybe I could start my own business—like be an errand boy or something. I could put flyers out with my name and phone number. Maybe I could get pledges from people at church who would match whatever I make." Kevin's eyes were pleading. "I really want to help him, Dad. He has to have a way to get around."

"You know, I'd been thinking of helping Josiah out, but I like the sounds of your plan better," Charlie said. "When do you want to start?"

"Right away! Monday after school, if I can."

"All right. Maybe we can work together and make some flyers on the computer. We'll get the whole family to help distribute them."

Kevin smiled. "Cool. I have another idea, too. I talked to Jason Kennsington and we're going to get the youth group from church to do some repair work on Josiah's house next weekend."

"What kind of repair work?"

"Oh, he's got loose boards on the steps and the porch. There's a place on the roof that leaks. It needs paint, stuff like that. I don't know how to do it all, but somebody can show me. Mr. Abernathy's going to donate whatever we need."

Charlie smiled. "If you need an extra hand, I'm available."

Kevin reached across the table and shook his hand. "It's a deal."

Charlie felt an unexpected surge of emotion at how suddenly grownup his twelve-year-old seemed. "Josiah's been good to you, hasn't he?"

"Yeah. I like spending time with him."

"What do you do besides fish?" Charlie asked.

Kevin's eyes lit up. "Oh, we take walks, call the ducks, look through his old pictures, carve things out of wood, play Chinese checkers—and we talk a lot. He tells me all kinds of stuff. Mostly, he gets me to think about how I ought to act."

"What do you think's the most important thing he's taught you?"

Kevin looked at his hands and seemed to be deep in thought. Finally he looked at Charlie. "Two things: One, God wants me to spend time with Him and tell Him what's on my mind—that He listens, even if I'm only twelve. And two, if you love somebody, you need to forgive them even when they mess up. And not make them feel bad about whatever they did because they already feel bad enough."

Charlie blinked quickly to clear his eyes. "Sounds like he's taught you well."

Kevin nodded. "I've never had a friend like him. There're so many things I want to do to make life easier for him. He doesn't have much."

Charlie smiled. "Maybe not, Kevin. But he sounds richer than most."

Charlie drove around the town square and pulled into a parking space. He got out and walked across the street to Stedman's General Store. He went inside, then walked to the back and slipped in the door to the receiving room.

Avery looked up. "Don't expect an apology just because you gave a big-shot speech."

"I didn't come here to ask for an apology. I came here to call a truce—and ask your forgiveness."

Avery's eyebrows gathered. "Yeah, right."

Charlie pulled up a chair in front of Avery and sat. "Look, we both love this town. We're on the same side. It's time to put the boyhood rivalry behind us."

"So what do you want my forgiveness for?" Avery said.

"For anything I've done to hurt you."

"Who said you *did* anything?"

"Something's wrong. I'd sure like to set it right."

Avery got up and stood next to a crate, his hands in his pockets, his eyes looking down. "Well, I don't know what I should forgive you for—except you bein' smarter, richer, better lookin' and well liked. Sounds pretty stupid, huh?"

"Not if it hurts. I'm sorry, Avery. I've just tried to do the best with what I've got. It was never a competition."

"Yeah, I know." Avery came and sat, his eyes searching Charlie's. "Why'd you put your own money on the line?"

"It's not my money," Charlie said. "Every nickel I've made really belongs to the Lord. And I think it pleases Him that we all go forward without hard feelings and without the fear of financial ruin."

"What if we *all* go out? Could ruin you."

"I'm trusting God that it won't. But I could cover it."

There was a long, uncomfortable silence.

Avery wiped the perspiration from his upper lip. "Wasn't any of my business if you slept with that attorney. I should've kept my mouth shut."

Charlie started to agree with him, then didn't. "I forgive you, Avery. Can we let it go?"

Avery looked surprised. "Uh, yeah, sure."

Charlie held out his hand. "Truce?"

Avery put his hand in Charlie's and squeezed. "Truce."

Dennis Lawton walked with Jennifer down Acorn Street, dead leaves swishing under his feet. He looked over at his grandfather's old house and felt a pang of grief. "I still miss him, Jen."

"Me, too. I'm glad Angie's coming for Thanksgiving. I miss her, too."

Dennis looked across the street and saw Lenny Stedman smoking a stogie on his front steps. He waved. "Hey, Lenny!"

"Come on over here," Lenny said.

Dennis took Jennifer's hand and hurried across the street and up the walk to the Stedmans' front porch.

Lenny puffed on his stogie. "Wasn't that something out at the site yesterday?"

"The explosions or Charlie's speech?" Dennis said.

"Both. But that speech is gonna stay with me a whole lot longer. Did you know Charlie came down to the store this afternoon and made peace with Avery?"

Dennis nodded. "Yeah, I ran into him when we were coming out of Monty's. I'm so glad."

"I don't have to tell you it's been rough. Didn't want to bad-mouth my boy, but didn't feel proud of what he was doing, either. Took a big man to do what the mayor did."

"Well, Charlie's like that," Dennis said.

Lenny puffed his cigar. "Still can't believe he put up his own money. Can't tell you what a relief it is to know we don't have to worry about our business because of the tire plant. I heard Avery whistling this afternoon, but I think it had more to do with Charlie's visit than the business. Wonder what he said?"

Dennis shrugged. "But judging from the way Charlie looked, I have a feeling that things between him and Avery are going to be different from now on."

"Who'd have thought it after all this time?" Lenny said. "Well, what else you hear?"

Dennis smiled at Jennifer and then at Lenny. "We heard at Monty's the *Daily News* is going to break a big story in the morning that's going to knock our socks off."

40

On Sunday morning, Mark Steele sold the last of the newspapers, then looked out across a capacity crowd at Monty's Diner, glad that he had anticipated a big turnout and had scheduled extra help.

He waited until patrons were engrossed in the headlines, then walked to the counter and read over George Gentry's shoulder:

PAXTON CASE HITS HOME

The FBI has arrested a suspect in connection with Friday's car bombings in Baxter and the shooting deaths of Sheila Paxton's boyfriend and two FBI agents in Raleigh earlier this month.

Giorgio Antonio Merlino, 36, of Chicago was apprehended late Friday night after agents learned he had registered at a motel in Ellison under the alias George Aldridge, a name FBI agents have been tracking for some time.

Jordan Ellis, the special agent in charge, said, "The bureau has known for years about Merlino's ties to organized crime, but we've never had enough evidence to nail him until now."

Merlino's connection to Sheila Paxton goes back eighteen years to a house on Marquette Road near downtown Chicago...

Mark read every word of the article, completely absorbed in the story, until he heard George Gentry's voice.

"I'm speechless." George took off his glasses and laid them on the counter.

"Sounds like a godfather movie," Reggie Mason said. "Listen to these names: Spike Risotto, Giorgio Merlino, Bennie Stassi. Sheesh!"

Liv Spooner shook her head. "I wonder how many people this Merlino actually killed?"

"I wonder what kind of life Sheila Paxton had as Mary Angelina Risotto?" George said. "Just think, we actually saw someone who was in the witness protection program and didn't even know it."

"I wonder more about Ellen," Hattie Gentry said. "Can you even imagine how traumatic this has been?"

Mort Clary shook his head and folded his newspaper. "Ain't been a picnic fer the mayor neither. KJNX jumped the gun on that diary. Did terrible hurt to him and his family."

Rosie Harris hurried past the counter and put several green slips on the clip. "Order!" She picked up a fresh pot of coffee and started working her way down the counter. "Okay, what'd I miss?"

"Mort was bemoaning the diary," Mark said.

Rosie put her hand on her heart. "Just kills me to think our mayor was being blackmailed by a gangster. And because of something he didn't even do."

Liv took a sip of coffee. "Lucky for him that guy from Thompson Tire said Sheila lied in the diary about him, too."

"Well," Rosie said, "makes me sick that I defended her and said she was a classy lady. She was anything but a lady."

"Told ya that all along," Mort said.

Rosie squeezed his shoulder. "Yes, you did. How come you're so subdued?"

"I ain't subdued. I'm just a little distracted about goin' ta see Rennie."

George looked down the counter. "So when you going?"

"Soon as I leave here. Rennie asked me to come and stay a spell. Says Bob don't seem ta mind."

"That's great!" Rosie said.

Everyone at the counter nodded in agreement.

Mort gathered the toast crumbs on his plate with his finger. "Could be after we're all together, things'll go sour. Old hurts might come spillin' out. Maybe I oughta leave well enough alone."

"No way!" Reggie turned Mort's stool around and pulled him to his feet. "You're gonna have the time of your life and come back here with all kinds of stuff to tell us."

Liv nodded. "That's right. And we'll be right here—waiting."

"Come on," George said. "I'll walk you to your truck." George got up and put his hand on Mort's shoulder, and the two of them started walking toward the coatrack.

Mort put on his hat, then turned around. "I ain't never been good with words, but you folks've been the family I was missin'. And no matter what happens with Rennie, I ain't never gonna change how I feel about ya."

Mark stood watching as the early crowd gathered around Mort and wished him well. He realized for the first time that nothing here would be quite the same until Mort came back. For all his irritating ways, Mort was as much a part of Monty's as Leo's blueberry pancakes.

"Hey, Mort," Mark hollered, a grin on his face. "Don't stay away too long, hear?"

Jordan Ellis packed the last of his things and zipped up his suitcase. He heard a knock at the door and got up and looked through the peephole. He smiled and opened the door.

"Hey, Sheriff. Come to run me out of Dodge?"

Hal chuckled. "I knew you were heading out this morning and hoped I could catch you first. I wanted to say thanks."

"You're welcome. Thanks for not getting possessive of your turf. Made things go a lot smoother."

"Aaron and I are grateful for your hard work on this case," Hal said. "I can't imagine trying to handle this with our limited resources."

"Well, what are feds for?"

Hal smiled and shook his head. "Here, I brought you a newspaper. Ellen did a good job—as usual."

Jordan took the paper and glanced at the headlines. "Thanks. I'm anxious to read it."

"Well, I need to get my family to church," Hal said, extending his hand. "Just wanted you to know how much I appreciate the job you did to protect Ellen and get Merlino off the street. My stress level is back down to tolerable."

Jordan shook his hand and slapped his back. "We're a good team. Try to *keep* the peace, will you?"

Hal smiled. "I'll do my best."

Jordan closed the door and stood for a moment at the window. Beyond the trees, he saw the clock tower on the county courthouse. It seemed to epitomize the proud history of Baxter and its unbreakable community spirit.

He tucked the newspaper under his arm, put his cell phone in his pocket, and picked up his bag. He went outside and pulled the door shut behind him, then skipped down the steps and walked to his car, satisfied with a job well done.

41

SIX MONTHS LATER...

Charlie Kirby straightened his tie and brushed a piece of lint off his black suit. In the mirror, he saw Marlie come up behind him, and he turned around. "Do you ever look stunning!"

"So do you. Would you zip this?" She turned around and pulled her hair out of the way.

Charlie zipped the ivory dress, then slipped his arms around her, his cheek next to hers. "Nervous?"

"Not at all. Why?"

"You seem preoccupied this morning."

"I'm just amazed that I feel this way again."

"And what way is that?" he said playfully.

She turned around in his arms and smiled. "Passionately and madly in love with you."

Charlie leaned down and gave her a soft, lingering kiss that turned into a smile. "I just smeared your lipstick, didn't I?"

She giggled and pushed him away. "We need to stick with the program. Pastor Thomas wants to start right at nine o'clock."

"Tell me again why Dennis and Jennifer picked the kids up early?"

"Because they wanted us there without spots or wrinkles." Marlie chuckled. "This will be a first since Kevin was born."

"Okay, fix your lipstick. I'll get the ring. I wish you'd have let me get you a corsage or something."

Marlie shrugged. "Dennis was adamant that we weren't to do any of that. He and Jennifer are taking care of everything."

Ellen Jones sat with Guy in the third row at Cornerstone Bible Church, her eyes taking in the majesty of this elegant old structure, and her heart overflowing with gratitude for what God had done to restore Charlie and Marlene's relationship. This might be the last time she ever set foot in here, but what a glorious memory to take with her.

Her eyes fell on Dennis and Jennifer's handiwork: A white gazebo covered in pink roses had been set in the center of the sanctuary, and white candle stands covered in fine greenery and pink rosebuds sat on either side.

From the choir loft, a chamber quartet began to play "This Is the Day," and the congregation turned their attention to the center aisle. Ellen watched as the Kirby children filed in one by one, holding white baskets and dropping pink rose petals along the way. She looked at the happiness in each of their faces: Kristen, then Kyle, then Kara, Kathleen, Kelly, Kaitlin—and finally Kevin, who carried a Bible.

The children formed a semicircle in front of the gazebo and faced the congregation. There was a hushed moment of anticipation, and then the organ began to play "Great Is Thy Faithfulness." The congregation stood and turned toward the center aisle.

Marlene and Charlie walked arm in arm down the aisle, looking as radiant as any bride and groom. When they reached the gazebo, the children parted to let them through.

Ellen's eyes brimmed with tears and her heart filled with utter amazement as the Kirbys renewed their wedding vows before God, their children, and their church family. Who else but the Lord could have healed the wounds inflicted on this family? There was no doubt in her mind that she was witnessing a miracle.

The clock tower struck one as Ellen stood in the doorway and watched the moving van drive off.

"You about ready to leave?" Guy said.

"In a minute."

He put his hands on her shoulders. "It's bittersweet, isn't it?"

She nodded and wiped a tear from her cheek.

"We'll come back to visit, Ellen."

"I know."

"There's no way we'll ever not feel at home here."

"Seaport is lovely," she said. "I'll be fine after I get past this part."

She turned around and slipped her arms around his waist. "Charlie and Marlene looked absolutely radiant. I'm so happy for them."

"Which reminds me, Pastor Thomas called when you were outside and asked if we would stop by the church on our way out of town. I think he has something he wants us to see."

"Okay," she said. "I'm ready."

Ellen walked down the front steps and got in the car. She looked up at the beautiful Victorian home and the Sold sign in the yard. For a split second she was thirty again and her boys, barefoot and giggling, were chasing her across the front lawn with a garden hose.

Guy got in the car and put his hands on the wheel. "You need more time?"

"No, I'm fine. Really."

"Okay, one brief stop—then off to Seaport."

When they were almost to the town square, Ellen noticed people lining the streets around the square.

"I wonder what's going on?" she said.

Guy smiled knowingly and slowed the car to a crawl. "Just a few people who wanted to see us off."

"A *few* people?" Ellen rolled down her window and looked out at the faces—scores of people standing with signs and banners and smiles all around the town square. "How'd they know we were leaving?"

Guy laughed. "Isn't it great? Dennis set this up."

Ellen waved to Dennis and Jennifer, then Jed and Rhonda, and Mary Beth and Joe. She blew kisses at Charlie and Marlene, then waved at Margie, and Hal, and Aaron, and Pastor Thomas and neighbors and church family—all the while recording every detail in her heart.

"I'm going to miss you so," she whispered, blinking to clear her eyes. "But you'll always be a part of me. Always."

Guy made a loop around the square, then tooted the horn and drove down Baxter Avenue toward the main highway.

Charlie waved until the taillights of Guy's Mercedes disappeared, then put his arm around Marlie and pulled her close. "You about ready to go, Mrs. Kirby?"

She smiled and kissed his cheek. "I just need to give Jennifer the house keys and the garage door opener. I'll be right back."

Charlie stood with his hands in his pants pockets and felt a tap on his shoulder.

"What a great day," Dennis said. "How come you two are still here?"

Dennis glanced over at Marlie talking to Jennifer. "The girls are taking care of some last-minute details. You and Jennifer have been unbelievably generous on so many levels. I can't tell you how much it's meant to us."

"We've enjoyed doing it. We're so glad you and Marlene are back together."

"I won't forget how you stuck by me, Dennis. I felt your prayers."

Marlie came over and put her arms around Dennis. "Thanks for everything. You and Jennifer are too much."

Dennis looked at his watch. "It's almost one-thirty. Am I going to have to kick you two out of here?"

Charlie winked at Dennis, and then turned to Marlie, the corners of his mouth turning up. "Okay, honey, we might as well have some fun with this. Hang on!"

Charlie lifted her into his arms, then carried her toward the car, the sound of her giggling evoking squeals of delight from the children.

He stopped and turned around, touched by the joy on their faces. "We'll see you tomorrow. Be good for Mr. and Mrs. Lawton. And say your prayers."

As Charlie walked toward the car, Marlie laughing in his arms, his wedding vows still echoing in his mind, he knew to the depth of his being that as long as God gave him breath, he would be faithful to guard that which had been so graciously returned to him.

AFTERWORD

Dear Reader,

How my heart ached for Charlie in this story! He was a good and decent man buried under the rubble caused by one of Satan's fiery darts—a proverbial smart bomb designed to hit its target with frightening precision. Had Charlie's defenses been in place, he could have stopped the lusting before it ever materialized and avoided the devastation that nearly destroyed his relationship with Marlene—and his Christian witness.

And poor Marlene, so crushed by this surprise attack on her marriage that she was unwilling to pray or seek counsel, setting herself up as a target for the enemy's lies. Had she not listened to the prompting of God's Spirit, she might have divorced Charlie without ever considering the fifteen good years they'd had—and never experienced God's faithfulness to restore what had been shattered.

How many good people have to fall before we realize the enemy takes this war seriously? It's true he wants to destroy marriages and families. But he's looking for vulnerable targets of any kind. Let's not take for granted that a sin we've overcome will never again become a point of attack—or be so sure there are things we would *never* do. Ellen never thought she was capable of deceiving her husband, but when the circumstances were tempting enough, she did the very thing she abhorred.

As believers, we should expect to be targeted—but we're not defenseless. In Christ, we have the best defenses known to man, if only we would use them. We must put on the whole armor of God as laid out in Ephesians 6:11–18. And guard our hearts as if the enemy is determined to defeat us, because he is. But take heart: We are more than conquerors in Christ Jesus!

Friends, I have to admit that leaving Baxter is as bittersweet for me as it was for Ellen. I have so enjoyed being the vessel through which these stories have come to life. The characters are a part of me, and I'm going to miss them. But I'm not leaving without a plan! Watch for my next novel, *Poor Mrs. Rigsby,* which will be as exciting and fast paced as any of the Baxter books. And then we will catch up to Ellen and Guy in the Seaport Series, where new characters and new adventures await us.

I'm eager to hear from you. You can write me through my publisher at www.multnomah.net/baxterseries or through my website at www.kathyherman.com. I read each and every comment from my readers, and greatly value your input.

In Him,

Kathy Herman

The publisher and author would love to hear your comments about this book. *Please contact us at:* www.multnomah.net/baxterseries

DISCUSSION GUIDE

1. Do you think a Christian man can willfully entertain sexual temptation and still love his wife? How do you think it might impact his relationship with her? His kids? His church body? His Lord?

2. Why was Charlie's first inclination to lie? Have you ever lied to keep someone from thinking less of you?

3. Could you relate to Marlene's anger? Did you think she was foolish to forgive Charlie before she believed him? Did you think Charlie deserved her forgiveness?

4. Do you think divorce would have been the right solution had Charlie been guilty of adultery, and Marlene then had biblical grounds? Do you believe God can heal broken hearts and put marriages back together? If your answer is yes, explain what you think needs to happen first.

5. Do you think Kevin's "acting out" was realistic? Could a middle school child be affected that deeply by the fear that his parents might split up? Why do you think it wasn't enough for him to know both parents loved him?

6. Do you think a child's feelings should be considered when the actions of his parents are tearing his world apart? Why or why not?

7. Was it wise for Charlie to tell his twelve-year-old son the truth about his lusting? Was it risky? Was it necessary? Would you have handled the matter differently? If so, how?

8. Has God ever put someone like Josiah in your life to help you through a situation that seemed overwhelming? Have you ever been used that way in someone else's life?

9. Do you think Ellen's deception was as wrong as Charlie's? Was she too hard on herself? Not hard enough?

10. What relationships in this story touched you the most? Who was your favorite character? Your least favorite? Who do you think was the most effective character? The least effective? If you could write your own ending, what would you change?

11. What did you take away from this story? Was there a phrase, a truth, a scene, or a character that will stay with you? What kind of a spiritual response did it evoke? Were you persuaded to take a closer look at your own vulnerability to sin?

12. After reading *A Fine Line*, what do you think is the most dangerous attitude a Christian can have toward temptation?

The Baxter Series, Book One
Dead Men Tell No Tales. *Or Do They?*

"A suspenseful story of touching characters that is richly seasoned with God's love."

—BILL MYERS,
author of *Eli* and the
Fire of Heaven trilogy

When a bizarre houseboat explosion rocks the close-knit community of Baxter, firefighters and friends stand by powerless as the blazing hull of their neighbor's home sinks to the bottom of Heron Lake. Have all five McConnells perished in the flames? No one wants the truth more than Jed Wilson, Mike McConnell's best friend. When rescuers recover the remains of all but one family member, suspicion spreads like wildfire. Was it an accident—or murder? Jed finds himself in a race with the FBI to track down the only suspect, and is thrust into a dynamic, life-changing encounter with his own past. Baxter's mystery and Jed's dilemma are ones only God can solve in this suspenseful, surprising story of redemption amidst despair in small-town America.

ISBN 1-57673-956-2

The Baxter Series, Book Two

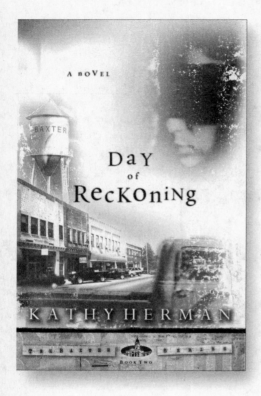

"Kathy Herman's *Day of Reckoning* is a suspenseful story with intriguing twists and turns. Prepare to get hooked!"

—RANDY ALCORN

One man's hatred sets off a community crisis in a chilling page-turning read that is also startlingly inspirational. Textile magnate G. R. Logan lays off a thirty-year employee who dies weeks later, and the man's son means to make Logan pay. In her second novel in the dramatic Baxter series, Kathy Herman unleashes a kidnapper's unresolved anger and explores the honest depths of a believer's anger at God. Sinister messages threaten the lives of two teenage girls while the citizens of Baxter struggle to cope with the evil that plagues this once-peaceful town. How will they react when they learn who's responsible? Can anything break their cycle of bitterness?

ISBN 1-57673-896-5

The Baxter Series, Book Three

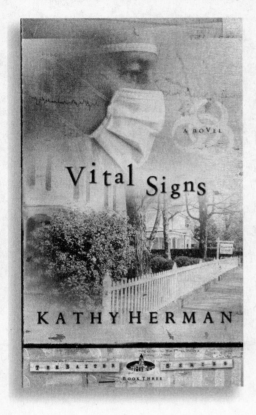

"If you're looking for a gripping story that will keep you turning the pages, *Vital Signs* is for you. Kathy Herman knows how to raise the stakes with every scene..."

—NANCY RUE,
author of *Pascal's Wager*

Furious that his girlfriend chose to bring twin babies to term, Dennis walks out of Jennifer's life. And now the Center for Disease Control has quarantined Jennifer, along with two-hundred others who attended the reception for a missionary couple bearing a deadly virus. Is Jennifer at risk? Does Dennis even care what will happen to the twins, separated from their mother at birth? Fear takes hold in the town as violence erupts, and Baxter experiences an outbreak deadlier than any virus. Still, woven through the tale of violence and victims is another story: one of divine love and purpose.

ISBN 1-59052-040-8

The Baxter Series, Book Four

"Mystery and murder, an offbeat heroine on a secret mission, and changed lives... Herman brings it all vibrantly to life in this winning addition to the Baxter series."

—LORENA MCCOURTNEY, author of *Whirlpool* and *Riptide*

Eighteen-year-old Angie Marks, tattooed and pierced, shows up in the small town of Baxter without a place to stay. Eccentric millionaire Patrick Bailey hires her to be his housekeeper, and when Angie risks her own safety to help Mr. Bailey get his twin great-grandsons out of a rattlesnake's strike zone, she finds herself fully at the center of the town's curiosity. At Monty's Diner they say she might be involved with Billy Joe Sawyer, using rattlers to intimidate the key witnesses in his upcoming trial. Is she? Or does Angie Marks have her own agenda?

ISBN 1-59052-081-5